PRAISE FOR THE
Beeline

"Secrets in the pasts of chara[...]
come to know play a large pa[...]
usual, Reed weaves the diffi[...]
Story's family into her just-intricate-enough plot, keeping her
readers well entertained and satisfied." —*Fresh Fiction*

"Story is a strong character, and her antagonism with the police
chief provides a convincing motive for why the man would so
quickly suspect her of murder." —*RT Book Reviews*

Plan Bee

"An entertaining amateur-sleuth mystery starring a fascinating
protagonist whose amusing asides about family and friends
make for a jocular small-town tale. Fans will enjoy the dynamic
duo [as they] work Plan Bee in the case of the murdered
sibling." —*Genre Go Round Reviews*

"You will not want to put [*Plan Bee*] down until you find out
whodunit. I love, love, love this series. The characters grab you
immediately, and Story follows a wonderful, winding cozy
path. Run, don't walk, to your favorite bookstore and get your
hands on this new title—and if you haven't read the first two,
pick those up as well. Then sit down in a comfy chair with a
warm blanket and cup of tea (with honey) and enjoy."
—*Cozy Corner*

"Story and her comedic sidekick, 'Pity Party' Patti, know how
to delve into clues and uncover the most unlikely suspects using
unconventional methods and flying by the seat of their pants.
This is a very funny and entertaining mystery that will have
readers laughing until the very end."
—*RT Book Reviews* (4 stars)

WITHDRAWN

continued . . .

Mind Your Own Beeswax

"Reed pollinates this novel, like its predecessor, with a smart story, characters who leap off the page, and, of course, interesting material about beekeeping. It will keep you busy."

—*Richmond Times-Dispatch*

"The characters are as colorful as the rainbow . . . With the perfect blend of humor and drama and a gutsy heroine . . . Readers will be thoroughly entertained by this madcap mystery."

—*RT Book Reviews*

"Story Fischer is one of the spunkiest heroines of a cozy mystery that I have had the pleasure of reading! I love the character's strength, her fearlessness, and her smarts . . . A delicious series that is a sweet treat for cozy mystery fans!"   —*Fresh Fiction*

"The prose is witty, charming, and peppered with beautiful imagery, the plot is rich and complex, and the mystery is cleverly constructed and skillfully written, tying past events to the present in a way that adds import and intrigue to both. Story makes for a fabulous heroine and an engaging narrator. Strong, smart, snarky, and positively bullheaded in her independence, she's a character for whom readers can't help but root . . . Run out and buy yourself a copy."   —*The Season*

"The second in Hannah Reed's terrific Queen Bee Mysteries that serves up all kinds of interesting beekeeping information and honey recipes, a wacky and totally likable cast of characters, and a frenzied hive of story activity . . . I loved *Buzz Off*, the first in the series, and this one is even better."   —*Cozy Corner*

Buzz Off

"A great setting, rich characters, and such a genuine protagonist in Story Fischer that you'll be sorry the book is over when you turn the last page. Start reading and you won't want to put it down. Trust me, you'll be saying 'buzz off' to anybody who dares interrupt!"

—Julie Hyzy, *New York Times* bestselling author of *Fonduing Fathers*

"Action, adventure, a touch of romance, and a cast of delightful characters fill Hannah Reed's debut novel. *Buzz Off* is one honey of a tale."
—Lorna Barrett, *New York Times* bestselling author of the Booktown Mysteries

"The death of a beekeeper makes for an absolute honey of a read in this engaging and well-written mystery. Story Fischer is a sharp and resilient amateur sleuth, and Hannah Reed sweeps us into her world with skillful and loving detail."
—Cleo Coyle, *New York Times* bestselling author of the Coffeehouse Mysteries

"Reed's story is first-rate, her characters appealing—Story's imperfections make her particularly authentic—and the beekeeping and small-town angles are refreshingly different."
—*Richmond Times-Dispatch*

"Will appeal to readers who like Joanne Fluke and other cozy writers for recipes, the small-town setting, and a sense of community."
—*Library Journal*

"A rollicking good time. The colorful family members and townspeople provide plenty of relationship drama and entertainment . . . This series promises to keep readers buzzing."
—*RT Book Reviews* (4 stars)

"A charming beginning to what promises to be a fun series! . . . A yummy treat for fans of cozy mysteries."
—*Fresh Fiction*

"[A] honey of a book."
—*Cozy Corner*

"A sparkling debut . . . Delicious."
—*Genre Go Round Reviews*

"You'll get a buzz from this one, guaranteed."
—*Mystery Scene*

Beewitched

Hannah Reed

BERKLEY PRIME CRIME, NEW YORK

THE BERKLEY PUBLISHING GROUP
Published by the Penguin Group
Penguin Group (USA) LLC
375 Hudson Street, New York, New York 10014

USA • Canada • UK • Ireland • Australia • New Zealand • India • South Africa • China

penguin.com

A Penguin Random House Company

BEEWITCHED

A Berkley Prime Crime Book / published by arrangement with the author

Copyright © 2014 by Deb Baker.
Penguin supports copyright. Copyright fuels creativity, encourages diverse voices,
promotes free speech, and creates a vibrant culture. Thank you for buying an authorized
edition of this book and for complying with copyright laws by not reproducing, scanning,
or distributing any part of it in any form without permission. You are supporting writers
and allowing Penguin to continue to publish books for every reader.

Berkley Prime Crime Books are published by The Berkley Publishing Group.
BERKLEY® PRIME CRIME and the PRIME CRIME logo
are trademarks of Penguin Group (USA) LLC.

For information, address: The Berkley Publishing Group,
a division of Penguin Group (USA) LLC,
375 Hudson Street, New York, New York 10014.

ISBN: 978-0-425-26161-3

PUBLISHING HISTORY
Berkley Prime Crime mass-market edition / February 2014

PRINTED IN THE UNITED STATES OF AMERICA

10 9 8 7 6 5 4 3 2 1

Cover illustration by Trish Cramblet; Honeycomb1 © Ihnaxovich Maryia/Shutterstock;
Honeycomb2 © William Park/Shutterstock; Bee © vdLee/Shutterstock.
Cover design by Judith Lagerman.
Interior text design by Kristin del Rosario.

This is a work of fiction. Names, characters, places, and incidents either are the product
of the author's imagination or are used fictitiously, and any resemblance to actual persons,
living or dead, business establishments, events, or locales is entirely coincidental.

PUBLISHER'S NOTE: The recipes contained in this book are to be followed exactly
as written. The publisher is not responsible for your specific health or allergy
needs that may require medical supervision. The publisher is not responsible
for any adverse reactions to the recipes contained in this book.

If you purchased this book without a cover, you should be aware that this book is
stolen property. It was reported as "unsold and destroyed" to the publisher, and neither
the author nor the publisher has received any payment for this "stripped book."

And those who were seen dancing were thought to be insane by those who could not hear the music.

—FRIEDRICH NIETZSCHE

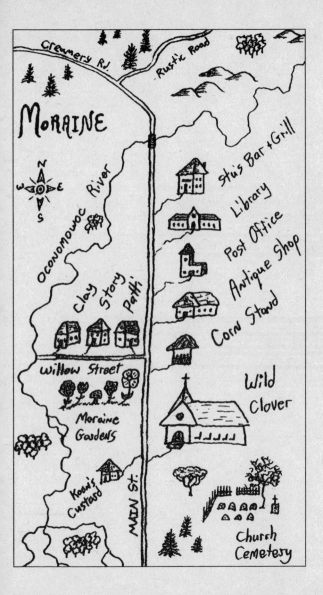

One

It all started on Wednesday morning when the witch moved in next door.

Patti Dwyre, my next-door neighbor on the other side, watched the action with me through my kitchen window, as a male-model-worthy beefcake hauled furniture inside the same house where my ex-husband used to live, which had been lingering on the market for well over a year. Lori Spandle, Moraine's one and only real estate agent—and my longtime nemesis—hadn't even given me a heads-up that the place had been sold. Par for the course.

Since I was focused on the buff guy, Patti noticed our new neighbor's unusual affinity first.

"There goes the neighborhood," she whined in that awful grating tone that has earned her the nickname Pity-Party Patti (aka P. P. Patti). "And my house is already underground."

Underground? What was she talking about? Ah . . . "You mean underwater," I corrected her. "And that statement isn't even close to true." Patti didn't have any financial problems.

"It will be now."

I tried to pry my eyes away from the male in the land-scape but failed. I might be living with my boyfriend, Hunter Wallace, but that doesn't mean I'm blind to other males. In fact, I read in the latest issue of *Cosmo* that ogling keeps certain hormones ultra-active and in prime working order. Which reminds me, I should hide that magazine from Hunter. He doesn't need any more ideas than he already has, ogling wise or ultra-active wise. The man is insatiable. Thank goodness he's also a workaholic, or I'd never get anything done.

"And why is that?" I asked. "Just because we have new neighbors?"

"Nothing will ever be the same with the devil's appren-tice living on the same block."

"I think he's just devilishly handsome."

"Not him. Her. She's a witch!"

"Oh, come on," I said, tearing my eyes away from the hunk and giving the woman next to him a quick once-over. "You decide she's a witch just because she's wearing a gypsy skirt and a shawl?" Although I had to admit it was a little weird. Sure, it was October, and the nights were cooling off, but today Indian summer had arrived, gloriously warm and sunny. Not exactly shawl weather. "Aurora dresses just like that," I added, "and she's not a witch."

Aurora Tyler owns Moraine Gardens, the plant nursery across the street. All her plants are native, and she does extremely well for herself during these autumn months when tourists pass through our little Wisconsin town following the Rustic Road in search of homemade apple cider and spectacular fall colors. Aurora is all into new age happen-ings and vegan eating and whatever else comes along on the fringes of the regular and routine. She might march to a slightly different drummer, but I still can follow her tune.

"The biggest clue that our new neighbor doesn't belong here is the wand," Patti pointed out, her complexion paler than usual, which is saying a lot since Patti's skin is a shade lighter than Elmer's glue. That's what happens when a person gets absolutely no sun year after year. "Yes, an actual wand," she continued, her voice getting squeaky. "That was a big clue, Sherlock, and look! She's casting a spell of some sort, probably a curse!"

Patti sounded on the verge of hysteria. Not like her. Not like her at all.

My eyes bored in on the woman who was destroying Patti's cool confidence.

Sure enough, she was moving around the outside of her house, going from window to window, looking like she was practically wafting through the air a few inches above-ground, all light and breezy. Or was that my imagination? Since I had more than my fair share of flight of fancy (my grandmother's term for make-believe), that was a question I asked my overactive mind pretty often.

With a practiced flick of the wrist, my new neighbor cast the end of her wand toward the driveway that ran between her house and mine. Patti's newfound paranoia traveled my way faster than any magic the wand could muster, and I started to wonder if she *was* conjuring something against me. I tried to see her face, but it was concealed by the shawl she'd drawn up over her head.

"Go over and introduce yourself," I said to Patti, thinking that was a brilliant idea. If Patti didn't go up in smoke, I'd follow shortly after. "Get her story. This could be newspaper worthy. You might get reinstated to your old position."

Patti had been fired from her job as a journalist for the *Reporter*, our local newspaper. I refer to it as the *Distorter*, since it was trashy even before Patti worked there, though her articles had stretched the truth like a rubber band pulled taut along the entire length of Main Street. Accusations of libel followed rapidly by the three-letter word all publications fear the most (S.U.E.), and Patti was thrown out the door on her duff.

Still, nothing in the paper has been interesting since she was canned. Patti has been determined to get her old position back, but apparently she wasn't willing to do absolutely anything to get it back, since this very minute she was saying, "No way am I going anywhere near her! I wouldn't touch this breaking story with a ten-foot pole. Even if the pole was made of pure silver."

"Silver is for protection against vampires," I informed her, which anybody watching current vampire shows would know. I'm certainly not a true believer in the bloodsucking undead, but I've stored a bit of trivia. "Silver doesn't do a thing to guard against witches."

"This is awful. It couldn't be worse. What are we going to do?!"

Patti's whining really was getting to me, so I took a stand. "I'm going over to meet her," I decided, moving toward the door.

"Brass!" Patti almost shouted. "It's brass that protects against witches." She frantically scanned the kitchen, spotted an antique brass canister my grandmother had given to me, and slung it into my arms. "Take this with you."

"What is *wrong* with you?" I returned the canister to its place on the counter.

Speaking of brass, though, Patti Dwyre is the brassiest woman I've ever known. She considers herself some sort of one-woman covert operation, dresses in black stealth-wear, and is always the first to impulsively infiltrate the most dangerous situations where violence could erupt at any moment. Patti has almost been the death of me more than once when she sucked me into one after the other of her operations.

And here she was, scared nearly to death at the thought of a witch with a wand moving in on Willow Street. Willow, witch, wand . . . Well wasn't that a weird coincidence. I wondered if the new neighbor had been drawn to town by the name of our street.

Our block is a short dead end right off Main Street, with

three houses on one side of the street (mine, Patti's, and the until-now-vacant one next door) and Aurora's gardening business and attached home taking up the other side. At the east end of the block, running perpendicular to Willow, is Main Street, and down at the west end is the Oconomowoc River, which winds not only through the rolling hilly countryside but kisses up against my backyard.

It's a sweet deal, a great place to grow up (which I had, in this exact house), and I planned to play nice with the latest additions. Being on the outs with a neighbor is the pits, especially when you have as few as I do. Believe me, this wasn't going to be half as bad as when my bitter ex-husband had spied and plotted from over there.

I strolled through my backyard while Patti remained glued to the action from behind the protection of my windowpane.

"Welcome to the neighborhood," I said to the new neighbor woman, stretching out my hand, thinking I should have put together a welcome basket for them. Maybe I still would. "Story Fischer," I said, introducing myself. "I live next door."

The shawl slid down around her shoulders, revealing a woman about my age—mid-thirties—with nary a single facial wart or any trace of green wicked witch skin. She shifted the wand to her left hand and took my hand in a firm shake. I noticed lots of rings, although her wedding finger was bare. So she wasn't married to the hunk.

"Dyanna Crane," she said. "But my friends call me Dy. You're the beekeeper, then."

She had me pegged, which was pretty much a no-brainer. She couldn't have helped seeing that my backyard is filled with honeybee hives, adjacent to a small honey house where I bottle and distribute Queen Bee Honey. I also own The Wild Clover, a grocery store that specializes in local products. The Queen Bee business and store go together like buttered sourdough bread and pure raw honey.

"You're not bothered by them at all, are you?" I said,

with a big grin plastered on my face when I noted that she hadn't scowled or shown any hostile emotions whatsoever. Whew. According to Lori Spandle, it was my fault she'd had so much trouble selling the house. We'd even tangled in town hall meetings where Lori had made serious attempts to ban my bees from the community. Guess who won every round? Me, that's who. Although I can't let my guard down, since the woman is tenacious, never giving up in her quest to annoy me and destroy my livelihood. We've been at each other's throats since grade school, and it's starting to get really old.

"Bees are fascinating," Dy said. "They're an important part of the natural world, and I'm all about nature."

Any doubts I'd had about her slipped away. I liked this woman already.

"So," I said to my new friend Dy, "I can't help noticing you have a wand."

That might have sounded a bit blunt, but I couldn't think of a subtle way to bring it up. I mean, really? I've never seen a magic wand except in movies. A real honest-to-goodness wand up close? It had never happened, until now.

"I'm casting a protection spell," she told me. "Making sure demons stay outside of my new home. A properly executed spell keeps them at bay." She raised her wand and pointed it at my house, exactly like a musical conductor during a symphony orchestra performance. "Want me to do one on yours?"

I glanced over at my yellow Victorian with its white trim work and realized that Dy was too late. The demon was already inside, staring at us out the window. At least she was more pesky than dangerous. Patti ducked out of sight when we turned our attention her way, and even at a distance and through the sun's reflecting glare on the pane, I had been able to tell how afraid she was.

"I'll take a rain check, but thanks for the offer," I said to my new neighbor, getting ready to pry. "So, where are you from?"

"Milwaukee," she said. "The east side." No surprise there.

That's where most of the alternative lifestyles happen in the southeastern corner of our state. The university located there draws a lot of unique personalities.

"My old stomping ground," I told her, having a pleasant flashback—a bar on almost every corner, ethnic food from around the world, and strange and interesting people. All kinds of diversity, including witches and warlocks.

Moraine might be no more than forty miles from Milwaukee, but the two places are Great Lakes apart. Not physically, but socially. Here in my town, wearing a nose ring is considered over-the-top. Tattoos are only okay if they're associated with veterans of a U.S.-supported war, or Harley Davidson, which Wisconsin is darn proud to call our own, so if a person wants to wear that fact permanently dyed in his or her skin, so be it.

"Hey, Greg," Dy called out to the hot guy. "Why don't you take a break?" Then to me, "I couldn't have done this move without Greg's support."

"Is he your boyfriend?"

"No, he just offered to help me get settled."

"Wow! I wish my friends looked like that!" I blurted out, a trait that runs in my family, one that I'm trying to control. My mother has the same problem, only her blurts come off as mean and insensitive. Mine are dopier. Either way, thoughtless or awkward, blurts aren't usually a wise thing.

Dy laughed at my reaction, though. "Come on, I'll introduce you."

I wanted to ask if he was a warlock but decided to save that for another time. Actually, now that I thought about it, he couldn't be, because he was manually transferring her personal items from the truck to the house with no sorcery involved at all.

Listen to me, acting like I believe in those kinds of things—witches and wizards and magic. Which I don't. Not at all . . . uh . . . okay, I *do* have some doubts, but they're very small ones. Barely ripples in a sea of wonder.

Up close, Greg had dark, lively eyes, bulging muscles, and jeans so tight I could pretty much guess his private measurements. It was all I could do to keep my eyes above his waist.

"Are you from Milwaukee, too?" I asked Greg.

He nodded. "Yup. Brewskis, Brewers, you bet." He smiled. "You don't recognize me, do you?"

I took a good long look. Nothing. "Uh . . ."

"I'm Greg Mason, Al Mason's son. You know, from Country Delight Farm?"

He waited for my reaction.

But the Greg Mason I remembered was gawky, skinny as a skeleton with thick glasses and lots of pimples. When his parents divorced, he left to live with his mother. How far back was that? Maybe when we were thirteen or fourteen. What a difference contacts and access to a fitness club can make for a person!

"It's been a long time," I said, laughing lightly. "You've changed."

"So have you," he said, with the same implied meaning—*For the better.* "Besides offering Dy my brawn, I'm helping my dad finish putting in this year's corn maze."

Dy gave him a warm smile. "When Greg showed me his dad's farm a few months ago, I just fell in love with the area. Then this house came up on my radar, and here I am."

"Touring the farm would convince anyone that this is the place to live," I said, meaning every word of it. Country Delight Farm is just outside the Moraine town limits, but we still consider it one of our own pride and joys.

The farm was fun to visit year-round, but it really shone in the autumn. It consisted of an enormous apple orchard with a variety of apples, a pumpkin patch, a petting zoo, a corn maze redesigned each year, and an open-air market featuring seasonal goodies like apple cider and caramel apples and fall decorations for the home. Smart business-man that Al is, last year he added a stand in the center of town, selling cider and apples and corn on the cob, and it's been a big hit with both visitors and locals.

"I didn't know you'd bought the house," I told Dy, "or I would have put together a welcome basket."

"Thanks for the thought," she said, "but the whole move was rather spur-of-the-moment."

Greg joined in. "Dy is actually just renting with an option to buy," he told me. "You'll have to convince her to exercise that option."

"We'll see." Dy tucked her wand into a hidden deep pocket in her skirt.

While Greg went back to moving things inside, I gave Dy a little info about Moraine, like how Stu's Bar and Grill is the local watering hole, to make sure to stop on Main for frozen custard at Koon's Custard Shop, where to find our cozy library, and of course about The Wild Clover.

"Stop in the store when you want a tour. You can't miss it," I told her. "Just look for a converted church with a blue awning. If you end up walking past the old cemetery, you've gone too far."

Dy grinned. "Main Street is about the equivalent of three city blocks. I doubt I'll have any trouble finding your store."

"That's true," I said. "Well, welcome again. And please let me know if you need anything."

"I will. Thanks."

By the time I returned to the kitchen, Patti was a blubbering mess. "Did you see her try to zap me?" she practically yelled. "Mind control with that stupid wand of hers, that's what she's up to, mark my word. We have to get rid of her before it's too late, before something really bad happens."

I'd had enough of Patti's blather. "Like what could happen? Monsters coming out of the river? Demons knocking on your door? Get real."

"Where there's one, there are more."

"That's in reference to mice, Patti, not witches. Besides,

she's really nice. Her name is Dy, short for Dyanna. The guy helping her move in is Greg, and he used to be a local. His dad owns Country Delight Farm."

"This can't be happening!"

"Keep your voice down. She'll hear you through the screen door." I closed the inner door. "You're way overreacting. Dy was perfectly friendly and normal."

Patti grabbed me by the shoulders and stared into my eyes. "She already got to you, didn't she?"

"Believe what you want. I like her. And Greg is nice and normal, too."

"An entire coven, I bet! Like I said, there's always more than one."

"If that guy is your example of a typical warlock, count me in." I broke free from Patti's grip.

"I'm telling Hunter," she said, threatening to tattle. "He's not going to like this at all."

I gave her an *I don't care what you do* shrug. Hunter wouldn't mind. We've known each other since both of us were in diapers (well, maybe not quite that long) and our current relationship is based on trust. I might tell him a fib here and there to protect someone, or sometimes to protect him or his position as a Waukesha detective, or to save myself unnecessary grief, but that's the extent of it.

Neither of us would ever, ever consider being unfaithful. Never, ever. It's one thing to look, but "hands off" is our shared and most important rule, especially now that we're living together and have committed to a monogamous relationship. Six-packs and quads and all that are nice to view, but give me a capable man with a sense of humor and integrity, like Hunter, and I'm totally turned on. He also has a great smile and sexy feet (a small fetish of mine).

Part of our success as a couple is because of our career choices. Hunter is a detective and a member of the Critical Incident Team. The C.I.T. handles all things in the county beyond the call of the average cop. Hunter is also head of the K-9 division. His partner is Ben, a Belgian Malinois with jaws of steel and a mind as fine as (or finer than) most humans'. I used to be afraid of dogs, but Ben has changed my attitude.

Hunter's law enforcement work keeps him intensely focused and extremely busy, and owning the grocery store and bee business has me jumping through my own hoops, so we have plenty of time to actually miss each other. Therefore, we cherish every minute we can find to be together. Absence making the heart grow fonder really works for us.

"Are you paying attention to what I just said?" Patti asked in her whiny voice, and the big, strong image of Hunter evaporated from my mind as quickly as it had appeared.

"Of course," I lied.

"We have to remove that woman from our block ASAP."

"Don't look at me." She was glaring, actually. "I'm staying neutral."

"You have to help out," Patti said, replacing her glare with a pout. "You're directly in the cross fire between her house and mine, right in the middle, and that's a bad place to be. But if we work as a team, we will eliminate the threat faster and more efficiently."

I crossed my arms over my chest. "I'm not participating in any bullying tactics. And I'm going to make sure you don't, either. You certainly aren't the welcome wagon."

I refrained from mentioning that Dy was renting, and so didn't have her whole financial future wrapped up in staying permanently in Moraine. That would have just encouraged Patti even more. "Until you settle down," I told her with as much authority as I could, "stay away from our new neighbor."

"You're openly declaring war, then!"

What? War? I was pretty sure I was attempting to declare peace. "We can all get along," I insisted.

"She's got you under a spell of some sort, that's what's happened. Incredible. You never should have gone over there without brass. Now look at you." Patti stared at me and I could almost hear the paranoid wheels turning in her head. Then she said, "We'll have to remove you from her influence. Stash you someplace safe until this is over. Or until I can figure out how to remove the curse she's cast on you."

"That's ridiculous." But I did feel a little fuzzy-headed, now that Patti mentioned spells and all. I shook it off and held firm. "I'm not going anyplace."

"Then consider *me* gone until this is over. If you won't cooperate, I have no choice but to leave you behind where you might possibly suffer even more harm. Be warned."

After staring into my eyes and seeing my strong resistance, Patti made sure the coast was clear before opening the inner door. She let the screen door slam behind her.

She had to be kidding, right?

Unfortunately, she wasn't. I've known her long enough. Patti's nuts, but she rarely kids around. I would probably have a hard time coming up with five fingers' worth of times she'd joked around. And come to think of it, she wasn't good at it the few times she'd tried.

Now she was mad. Great—without intending to, I'd managed to tick off a neighbor anyway. Although if anyone was going to snub me, I'd pick P. P. Patti any day. Hunter would be thrilled to find out about our disagreement and parting of the way. He thought she was a rabid rabble-rouser, a menace to society, and a big gossip. All true, I'm afraid.

I had to tell my sister, Holly, about the new neighbor and her hot guy friend. Holly is happily married, but she likes to look, too. I pulled out my cell phone, then remembered that Holly was working at The Wild Clover, and I was due to take over for her.

Before I left, I walked out into the beeyard to check on my honeybees. When a beekeeper is doing her job well, she should be intuitively aware of the smallest changes within the colonies, because any variance from the norm could spell trouble.

And I was witnessing a change, all right. Something was off.

On a routine morning when a honeybee leaves the hive to forage, she flies away at a predetermined angle, gaining whatever altitude her little radar determines. That is her natural flight pattern. Others join her, and they fly off in a line. An honest-to-goodness beeline.

Lori Spandle's last town hall argument against neighborhood hives was based on the false premise that honeybees will fly fast and low, zinging and zapping right into our residents' faces and stinging them to death. Her outrageous claim didn't hold up once I invited the entire town board over for a demonstration. Lori's no-buzz-zone attempt ended up in ruins. Instead the town implemented a honeybee free-flight zone.

Anyway, several of my honeybees' well-established flight patterns were over the house next door.

Today, with the witch moving in, not a single honeybee was flying in the direction of her house. They were all taking alternate routes.

What the heck did that mean?

Two

When I arrived at The Wild Clover, Aurora Tyler, my gardening center neighbor, was at the checkout counter with a small shopping basket filled with her usual—tofu, soy milk, granola, grapes, and lots of dark green leafy vegetables. She wore a loose-fitting forest green sundress and had let her dark hair, which she usually wore in a ponytail, cascade loose for today. She reminded me of a woodland fairy.

"I like your hair that way," I told her.

"Thanks. Something weird is going on in the atmosphere," Aurora said, her voice all whispery and filled with awe. "Whatever it is, it's making me feel breezy and extra feminine. I just had to put on a dress, let my hair down, and then I got a craving for a spinach smoothie with grapes and tofu, and I practically danced down here for the ingredients."

I smiled, thinking about The Wild Clover's customers and how much effort I put into satisfying their every need and want. I'm proud that I've established a business rapport with the local farmers, stocking my shelves with their products as well as other Wisconsin products, like cranberry items from the northern part of the state, wines and cherries from Door County, award-winning cheeses from every corner of our state, and soy products we produce right here in our farm fields where we alternate annually between soy and corn to keep the soil at maximum richness. And of course, the shelves are well stocked with my very own special honey creations—honey in all its glorious forms: combs, creamed, raw, sticks, and now I've been expanding into candles, soaps, and lip balms created in my backyard honey house.

"Wish I felt like dancing," I said to her. "Right now I feel weighed down and stressed out." Conflicts like the one with Patti did that to me. Our confrontation over the neighbor had really messed up my psyche and left me feeling unbalanced.

My sister, Holly, bounced toward me from her station behind the register where she'd been in the middle of checking out Aurora. "Your turn," she said, looking as breezy as Aurora with not a single care in Holly world. "I know I owed you this early morning shift, but never, ever in the future will I agree to work before eleven again."

My sister is the antithesis of a workaholic. The only two reasons she shows up (and, trust me, that's not too often) are because, one: she owns a piece of the store, and two: I manipulate her either by way of guilt trips or else I play the sister-needs-you card like I did yesterday. Or, one more reason: Mom makes her.

What works the best is threatening to make her help out in the apiary. She's deathly afraid of bees, which is almost beyond my mental ability to grasp. Yellow jackets I can understand, but honeybees? Really, they are so industrious they don't even notice people unless we intentionally try to hurt them or their queen. Otherwise, they're perfectly harmless. But just try telling Holly that.

"I've got to take off." She tried to brush past me, and we did a little jostling, which she won as usual, making me wish for the umpteenth time that I'd wrestled in high school like she had. My sister knew all the moves. "Business is slow right now anyway," she said, heading toward the back door, "so you can handle it alone. Mom needs my advice on picking out flowers for the wedding."

"Wait just one minute." I hustled over in time to block her path (like that would actually stop her). "Hold on." Then to Aurora, "Can you wait just one second?"

"Shopping here is always an experience," Aurora said, all dreamy. "I enjoy finding out what the Fischer sisters are up to. Take your time."

Holly turned to face me. My sister and I are both on the tall side, with hazel eyes and light brown hair, or dark blond, depending on who's doing the describing. And I like to think we were both gifted with our father's athletic skills. Holly with her wrestling in high school, back then taking her competition to the mat, and these days occasionally finding a use for her skills off the mat. She's a takedown artist when she needs to be. Shoplifters beware!

Me? I used to participate in track and still can haul if I have to and if I'm not wearing flip-flops, which I love. I have an awesome collection of footwear and I add to it frequently.

However, the similarities between us end there. I'll describe the distinctions my favorite way, in bullet points:

• Holly lives in a McMansion on a lake.

• She drives a Jag.

• She is filthy rich after marrying Max the Money Machine.

While:

- I live in the old family home after our mother cut me a good deal.

- I drive an old pickup truck.

- I have to budget to make ends meet.

Not that the store and honey business aren't doing well. They both are, but I put most of the profits back in, making everything better and better as time goes by.

There's another difference between us, one I try to overlook, but the fact keeps smacking me right in the face. Mostly because my family members work, eat, and breathe the air of the same community, and some facts of life are just impossible to totally ignore. That in-my-face fact that is so true and hurts on a regular basis whether I try to stop it or not is this:

Holly is Mom's favorite.

Always has been, always will be.

Hands down, she's our mother's pet.

That's the main reason, besides the fact that she has too much time on her hands and lots of money to contribute, that she gets to act as wedding consultant for Mom and Tom's wedding, which is coming up in two weeks. After five years of widowhood, Mom is tying the knot again. It's been hard imagining anybody taking Dad's place, even though I like Tom a lot. He makes Mom happy (therefore tolerable), and that's all that should count. So I'm doing my best to adjust.

Right now, however, hearing my sister talk about selecting flowers brought back that old familiar twinge of jealousy. It reared its ugly head and roared inside me. But to be perfectly honest, Mom and I get along best at a distance. We don't work well together. In fact, we've butted heads at the store so many times I've probably lost some of my more important brain cells. Putting our noggins together to come up with wedding ideas could result in one of us losing our head and saying or doing something non-retractable. Or possibly I'd just lose my mind completely and sit around babbling on the bench in front of what used to be my store before I was declared insane and the entire business I'd built from scratch was awarded to Mom.

My hope is that our Wild Clover conflicts are a thing of the past, though, now that Mom is going to be a Mrs. again and won't have time to interfere in my business. Tom owns an antique store in town, and that should keep her plenty busy.

"She didn't ask *me* to help," I said, trying to keep the whine out of my voice, realizing after being around P. P. Patti how truly annoying that childish tone can get.

"You didn't offer," came the reply.

"She would have turned me down."

Holly harrumphed before saying, "You didn't even try." Which was sort of the truth, but hey, there are just so many times a daughter will stick out her neck only to have it chopped off time after time. I might be slow on the initial uptake, but eventually I learn to avoid rejection.

I'd totally forgotten about Aurora until she called out to us, "I hope your family is going to order flowers from my garden center."

"Of course," I replied back, not sure at all what Mom's plan was, but whatever it was really ought to include as many local businesses as possible. Then to Holly, "What kind of flowers were you thinking?"

"Cultivated and fresh ones," my sister said, sliding her eyes to Aurora. I caught her meaning. Mom didn't want purple cone flowers and native asters. She wanted tradition all the way, and that meant cut flowers stored in a cooler until the very last minute.

"Mine couldn't be fresher," the green-thumbed, greensundressed gardener pointed out. "Still potted, in fact. Flowers don't get any fresher than that."

"True," I had to agree.

"Well, since the fall colors are peaking," Holly said to us, "I thought dahlias would be nice, bright yellows and burnt oranges, with ivory roses, and dried grasses."

Holly and I both knew that Aurora's garden carried native plants, so roses were definitely not doable for her. At least not the kind used in weddings. The dahlias I didn't know about until Aurora piped up and confirmed she didn't have them.

"But I can supply the dried grasses," Aurora said, always the businesswoman.

Holly's flower arrangement *did* sound beautiful.

Okay, maybe there was a logical, practical reason I wasn't in charge of flowers. My idea of a bouquet is an eclectic bunch of blooming flowers cut from my garden—mums, hydrangeas, marigolds. Not that my arrangements aren't pretty, they just aren't as orderly and structured as my mother likes things to be.

"The bouquet sounds nice," I muttered, but grudgingly, watching Holly take off. I hadn't even had a chance to tell her about the new resident on my block. Oh well, I had another neighbor right here who would find it fascinating.

As I finished checking out Aurora's groceries, I brought her up to speed. "Right this minute, a real, honest-to-gosh witch is moving in on our street," I told her, watching her perk right up at the new information.

"I saw the moving truck," she said, suddenly more animated than I've ever seen her before. "But how do you know she's a witch?"

I knew this would be right up Aurora's alley. That is, if we had an alley, which we don't.

"Her name is Dy," I said. "And I know because she has a wand and she's waving it around, casting spells to keep out demons."

"Really?"

"Don't tell me you have witch tendencies of your own," I said, opening up my eyes wide in pretend surprise, leading her along. I knew Aurora would jump right into any magic realm standing in her path.

"I believe in pretty much everything," Aurora said, confirming my take on her. "And who really knows? If fairies and elves are real, why not witches?"

Okay then. If you believed in fairies and elves, witches would be a piece of cake.

"I have to go meet this person right this minute. Thank you, Story, you've made my day." With eyes like saucers—the UFO kind—Aurora grabbed her bag and disappeared out the door, traveling at warp speed.

What a positive reaction compared to Patti's dreadful one. Different strokes for different folks, as my tolerant grandmother would say.

I'd barely thought of Grams when the little woman herself bounced into my store as perky as ever. She had her point-and-shoot dangling from her wrist and a fresh spray of tiny blue autumn asters tucked into her gray bun. Grams loves taking photos just as much as she digs gardening.

"A white van filled with women just pulled up outside, so get ready for business," she said, scooting behind the register and giving me a hug. "They're all dressed in black mourning dresses."

"Did somebody die?" I asked her. Grams has lived in this community her entire life and knows everything going on at any given moment, sometimes even before it happens. If anybody was dead, she'd know.

"Not that I'm aware of, sweetie."

The door to the store opened, and in they came.

There were eleven of them (I actually counted as they filed past the register), all females as Grams had said, but only about half of them were really wearing black clothes. Grams shrugged when I pointed that out once they were out of earshot. "Those were the first ones I saw," she said in a whisper. "I just assumed about the rest. What do you suppose is up?"

I had a pretty good idea why they were here and where they were heading, but The Wild Clover (like all of the shops on Main Street) has its share of passersby traveling the Rustic Road, tourists heading to Holy Hill, a national shrine that draws plenty of attention. Still, even with all our traffic, these women stood out.

We watched them from our vantage point behind the register as they walked through the store, picking out items and putting them in the baskets dangling from their arms. I don't know about Grams, but personally I've never seen so many big rings and chunky pendants in one place, other than the time I'd mistakenly entered a Milwaukee head shop thinking it was a thrift store.

My bevy of new customers ranged in age from around thirtyish to mid-sixties, and not a pair of pants in the bunch, all free-flowing skirts, shawls, and lightweight caftans—half of them all black, the others every color of the rainbow.

Grams, being old enough to get away with anything, took pictures of them without anyone complaining or threatening to break her camera. I would have felt uncomfortable, but not Grams.

"You're here to visit our newest resident, aren't you?" I asked one of the women, who looked to be about my mother's age, as she took in my honey display.

"Yes, we are," she said, turning overly rouged cheeks toward me and looking a little surprised at my observation. "Our friend Dy Crane just moved here. Are you psychic?"

I laughed. "Don't I wish. The truth is she's my new neighbor. We met this morning while she moved in. Nice necklace," I said, admiring the woman's accessory—a five-pointed star in a circle with a blue crystal in the center.

"It's a pentacle," she told me, fingering the necklace. "It protects me."

What was with the paranoia? First Dy has to cast spells around her house to keep out bad spirits, now a customer arrives with a protection necklace. Apparently the witch business is fraught with perceived peril.

"Rosina," someone else called out to her, rather demandingly, I thought. Pentacle woman looked annoyed but turned and went over to the woman who'd called her away, and they picked through the garlic basket, bent over in hushed tones.

"Mabel has been using garlic to ward off witches and spirits," Grams said to me, her voice a whisper in my ear as she referred to her best friend.

"Tell Mabel to stop bothering," I suggested to my grandmother as Rosina chose a bulb of garlic and placed it in her basket. "Obviously garlic doesn't work."

Grams went over and asked the one called Rosina to pose holding her garlic and took a picture of her as proof for Mabel. I can't believe how my grandmother can charm people. She even got the witch to smile for the camera.

Just then Stanley Peck came through the door. Stanley is a widower in his sixties, a good friend, who works at the store periodically when I'm in a bind, and he's also an enthusiastic newbie beekeeper. Lately he's been experimenting with a different type of hive, one that will be great for urban beekeepers, building it himself.

Ever since Stanley shot himself during an altercation with a temporary worker at his farm, he's been limping. And packing heat. My friend has a thing about governmental interference in his right to bear arms, and he likes to stick it to 'em even if he has to hide his defiance in a shoulder holster. (Or wherever he hides it. I'm not exactly sure.)

Stanley wasn't on the schedule to work since a run-in with my mother that caused him to quit before he up and shot her. And he'd been in yesterday to stock up on grocery supplies, so that left only one explanation for his timely appearance.

He was as much a busybody as the rest of the town.

Behind Stanley came a few other local customers, then a few more, making up a beeline just like my honeybees. This beeline, among other locals, also included Emily, Moraine's library director, claiming she needed juice boxes for story time; Stu from the bar and grill, who had already picked up his morning paper but went ahead and bought a second one to keep up appearances; and Larry from Koon's Custard Shop, which should be opening about now, but he was taking his time about it. DeeDee Becker, Lori Spandle's klepto sister, decided this was a perfect opportunity to fill her gigantic tote with free products, which sent Stanley hot on her trail as she ducked down aisles. Even Joan Goodaller, Al Mason's main squeeze, had held off opening the farm's corn on the cob and caramel apple stand down the street in favor of mouthwatering gossip.

If I'd told the witch Rosina ahead of time that this was about to happen, that the store would be deluged with business during the brief time they were shopping, she would have been totally convinced of my psychic ability. I don't really have any, but predicting what Moraine's residents will do when a van of strange women pull up in front of the store is so . . . well . . . predictable.

They're gonna hustle right over to the store to snoop.

Mid-afternoon isn't usually very busy, as Holly had pointed out during her escape, so I was alone for the unexpected rush of business. But everyone was patient and friendly in line, and Stanley pitched in as my bagger. What a guy!

Grams hung around the whole time, gathering details and more photos to share with her card-playing senior citizen group.

I had to chuckle to myself, thinking about how once the regular customers figured out we had honest-to-goodness witches in town, one of whom had moved in right under their noses, we were going to have some lively debates going on. I just hoped for less of the Patti-type reactions from them and more of the Aurora kind, although there wasn't really much hope of that.

Lori Spandle, nasty real estate agent and nemesis extraordinaire, came in, all round faced like a tomato and ripe for a fight. Before she whipped out her arsenal of verbal weaponry, she took in the action and said, "Well, my, my, what do we have here?"

The first to figure out the truth about the new customers? Really? Insensitive Lori? It wasn't possible.

"Is a convention in town?" she said to the room in general, focusing in on Rosina, who happened to be closest to her. "Women in Black, right?"

Just as I suspected. Almost as dense as her cuckolded husband, the only person in town who didn't know his wife was a big two-timing slut.

The witches looked from one to the other. I hoped one of them would feel offended and zap Lori with an irreversible hex. One that would make her hair fall out and her big boobs sag down to her knees.

"Want me to take out the *trash*?" Stanley said to me, using our code for throwing Lori out of the building if she looked like she was gunning for me. He was perfectly aware of our history.

"That won't be necessary," I decided, then to clueless Lori I said, "Why don't you guess again?"

Grams giggled, an indication that she found Lori as dopey as I did.

"On the way to a funeral?" Lori guessed again.

"We have a new resident, remember?" I gave her a big clue, since her guesses were going from bad to worse. "In the house next to me. Weren't you responsible for negotiating that? These are her friends who've come to help her settle in."

I sensed that the witches were listening intently. They weren't talking amongst themselves like earlier. The atmosphere went positively eerie, as though they recognized something about Lori and didn't like what they saw. At least that's what I would've suspected.

Lori, who doesn't have typical human sensibilities, didn't pick up on the change in the air. She walked right up to the woman who had called Rosina away from our conversation earlier—the most intimidating, imposing one of the bunch—and put a fake smile on her backstabbing face. She was in real estate sales mode. "And who do I have the pleasure of meeting?"

"Lucinda Lighthouse," the woman said, taking Lori's hand reluctantly without even a tiny smile in return.

Her name is Lucinda? Doesn't that just figure? Where do they come up with these names? Lucinda? Rosina? Dyanna? Although Aurora's real name *is* really Aurora . . . On second thought, was it? I guess I'd just assumed.

Lori handed out business cards to everybody in the store, which I could have thrown her out for (the no soliciting sign was prominently displayed), but I was still hoping the witches would do something fun to her. Unfortunately, her next order of business was to torment me. "I discovered that the town has an old law on the books about cohabiting without benefit of marriage," she told me. "It's illegal, you know."

I snorted, considering the source of this information.

"That trash?" Stanley asked. "Are you *sure* you don't want it taken out?"

"Maybe soon," I said.

Lori glared. "I'm considering going to the police chief and filing a citizen's complaint over you and Hunter. You're a bad influence on our impressionable young people."

Before I could zing her right back, Lori turned on her heels and marched out the door.

I absolutely hate that woman's guts. I know that's not very charitable, and I'm supposed to be a bigger person than she is, but her behavior toward me is out of control. If only she'd stay out of my store and out of my life forever!

It took a few minutes to slow my heart rate back where it belonged and return my mind to the store. By now, Rosina was over in the corner, using her cell phone. After a minute she joined Lucinda. "She still isn't answering her phone."

"Well," Lucinda said, "it's up to you to fix this situation. And you're running out of time."

Next, I overhead Rosina say to one of the others, "We're short and I'm in trouble with Lucinda."

"What are you short of?" I piped up and butted in. "Can I help out?"

Rosina opened her mouth to answer, but Lucinda cleared her throat and shot her a warning glare. Rosina clammed up and gave the stage to her boss.

"We're having a special meeting tonight," Lucinda, obviously the queen bee spokeswoman, explained. "And we need one more person. But you couldn't possibly help. You don't have the right . . . er . . . attitude."

Okay, I could do the math. I'd counted eleven of them. Then there was Dy back at the house to make it twelve. So they needed thirteen for whatever magical event they were planning for tonight. Part of me should have remembered that the number thirteen is supposed to be unlucky. Like Friday the thirteenth.

Unlucky!

But I wasn't paying attention to superstitious beliefs at that particular moment in time, so I made a huge mistake by opening my own big mouth and inserting not my own flip-flopped foot into the equation, but my friend's name.

"I know just the person you need," I said. "Aurora Tyler would love to help out!"

Three

❧

It wasn't quite dark yet when I made the short walk home from The Wild Clover after college students and twins Brent and Trent Craig arrived to take over for me and close up as they did most nights.

Those two had been lifesavers for me, always on time, hard workers, and loyal as can be. I was really going to miss them once they graduated and moved on. Replacing them would be difficult, if not impossible.

After Dy's friends had made their purchases and departed, I'd done some online research in my office in the back supply room and learned all about warding off evil with horseshoes and wind chimes. I also found out that the ideal number of members in a witch coven is thirteen (which I'd guessed) and that covens gather at certain times for special rituals inside magic circles.

Aurora had called to profusely thank me for giving the witches her name as an alternate. Thank goodness, because I'd been feeling a bit guilty about that. But she was ready to rock and roll. Dance, sing, whatever they were planning for the big event, she was willing and able.

As I turned onto Willow Street, fallen leaves crunched underfoot from white birches and other early shedders, but most of the other tree species were still showing their amazing colors. As the day ended, a chill took over the air where earlier sun had warmed the earth. Soon we would be waking up to frost on the ground and a more distant arc of the sun's path. I saw the witchy women's van parked on the street behind the moving truck, and candlelight flickered in Dy's windows. I could hear voices inside, unintelligible from this distance with so many conversations going on at once.

I half expected to see horseshoes nailed all over Patti's house, to ward off the witches, but luckily she'd chosen to add wind chimes to her yard instead, which now sang softly in the breeze. Her house was dark, as was mine, unfortunately. I really love when Hunter beats me home, which isn't often, because he knows how to make the place welcoming: soft, indirect lights; music playing in the background, usually light jazz; and he'll wine and dine me while we share the highlights of our day with each other.

I couldn't wait to tell him about the witch next door.

Hunter called my cell as I let myself inside the dark house. "Hey, sweet thing," he said. "How was your day?"

"Stranger than usual. Things are getting interesting on Willow Street. Wait until you hear this!" I told him all about our new neighbor as I held the refrigerator door open, perusing its meager contents. I was hungry, but nothing inside appealed to me.

He was surprisingly indifferent when it came to Dy and her magic wand, but he liked the part about Patti's phobia. "With any luck, Patti will move someplace far, far away," he said, focusing on our other neighbor.

"Don't you have anything to say about the new neighbor?"

"As for the witch, I have experience getting along with them, as you well know."

"That isn't funny." I closed the refrigerator door and opened the cupboard instead, taking out a jar of peanut butter.

"I didn't mean you," he said. "Uh. I meant your moth . . . um . . ."

I could have let him sputter and try to backtrack, but instead I interrupted. "There are a whole bunch of them over there right now, getting ready for some kind of ceremony. When are you coming home?"

"I'm not sure yet. We're handling a situation. This could go late."

"What's going on?"

"A high-risk prisoner transfer."

"Ah."

I hated Hunter's job right that moment and wished I hadn't even asked for information. And I knew better than to request more details. My man's job with the Critical Incident Team demanded discretion and discipline. Veering from his professional training wasn't in his makeup. Part of me was surprised he even told me as much as he had.

"Remind Ben to watch your back," I said, grateful for Hunter's K-9 partner.

"I'd like to watch yours. Or rather . . ." His voice dropped to a moaning groan, and I didn't have to be Einstein to figure out that this conversation was heading toward the gutter.

"Go fight bad guys," I told him. "Do a good job, and I'll have a reward waiting first thing in the morning."

Which was true. Because I worried nonstop about the danger associated with his job and was thankful every single time he walked through the door with Ben at his side.

"That promise is worth staying alive for," he said.

"Be careful."

"Happy witching," he said, signing off.

I stood at the kitchen counter, eating peanut butter from a soup spoon and wondering what *high-risk* meant. Was the prisoner the dangerous one? Did he have friends out there somewhere, targeting my man?

I shouldn't let Hunter's job worry me so much. The team was comprised of the best of the best. When was the last time anything had happened to any of them? Never, that's when.

I stuffed my worries into a secret compartment in my brain, then quickly slammed the door shut on them.

But what was I going to do with the rest of my evening? For starters, I figured I'd sit outside at my patio table with a hot cup of tea and get ready to watch the show next door. I got myself comfy with herbal tea and a warm fleece for the cooling fall evening. After I'd settled at the table with my tea, I thought of a question, so I called Aurora's cell.

"Are the guests all staying with Dy tonight?" I asked, wondering how eleven women plus Dy, and maybe Greg, would all fit.

"No," she said, her voice dreamy. "They're pitching tents over in Al's apple orchard at Country Delight Farm for a few days while they help Dy prepare her new home properly. They brought camping gear, so they're set."

Witches camp out? Who knew? Although they're all into the natural world, so it made sense. Greg must have arranged it with his dad, but I couldn't see him telling Al, who was a straight-and-narrow type of guy, that a coven of witches would be camping on his land. I bet he left out that detail.

"Thanks for caring about everybody, Story," Aurora gushed. "You're so sweet. And thank you so much for suggesting me for this. I get to be in a real Drawing Down the Moon ritual! I've always wanted to be part of one of those."

Drawing Down the Moon?

"When are they doing their circle thing?" I asked, fascinated with the whole foreign-to-me process.

"As soon as it gets dark, but there's a lot of prep work going on right now, like finishing the crescent cakes and preparing our bodies and building the blaze. Actually, I should go, there's so much to do, but just ignore us! Especially don't pay attention when we go skyclad."

"Okay," I said, planning to do the exact opposite of ignoring them.

Building the blaze? That sounded dangerous in an exciting sort of way. And the smell of baking crescent cakes wafting in my direction on the light breeze was delightful and almondy, my favorite flavor. The witches were putting the supplies they'd purchased at my store to good use.

But what was *skyclad*? That word hadn't popped up in my quick research.

Greg came out of the house and began building a fire in a fire pit he must have dug earlier. He gave me a wave and a friendly grin. The Girl Scout in me (which felt like a zillion years ago) was mindful of how close we were to the river in case the blaze got out of hand, but we'd had rain recently and the pit was a decent distance away from any flammable foliage.

Patti's house remained dark. Either she was avoiding the neighborhood or else she was spying from afar. At least I didn't have to worry about her pulling something foolish. She'd been terrified of one witch. Imagine how she'd handle an entire coven?

I decided I'd work on learning more of the women's names, too, since I figured I'd likely end up seeing them around. In my line of work, with the store and all, it's important for me to be able to put a name with as many faces as possible, and at the beginning I was terrible at remembering. But The Wild Clover is more than just a place to stop for meal fixings on the way home from work. It's part of our community, a place like on *Cheers* where everybody should know your name. So I make a concerted effort to remember my customers no matter how seldom they show up.

So the trick (as I remind my staff constantly) is to:

- make the commitment to remembering in the first place

- then concentrate hard

- totally focus during introductions

- follow by associating an image or a few words that begin with the same letter as the person's name

For example, for Greg's name and an accompanying picture and words beginning with G, I imagined him as *greg*arious with great jeans.

As for Dy, she has a to-die-for friend named Greg. Easy peasy.

Rosina can be shortened to Rosa, which reminds me of a rose and the woman by that name's red-powdered cheeks.

And Lucinda was scarily easy, close enough to Lucifer that I'd never forget it. Or her.

Tomorrow, I'd learn a few more of their names.

From my position in the shadows, I could see everything going on without being too obvious. Women drifted in and out of the house dressed in long, flowing hooded capes. It would be much more reassuring to me if their clothing were lighter, but black seemed more fashionable for their big event. Their dark clothing combined with the cloud-filled sky made it hard to tell who was who. The coven wasn't using modern conveniences like lights, even though I knew Dy's house was equipped with plenty of outdoor lighting. Instead, warm, glowing candles flickered everywhere, casting long, wavering shadows.

Part of me was still enthralled by the aspect of an actual

witch ritual, but another part of me started getting a little anxious.

Uncertainty and doubt circled around me right along with the cinnamon incense they were burning next door. I shook it off. Or tried to. But this concern refused to go quietly into the compartment in my head where I'd stored "Worry About Hunter."

I overheard Rosina and Lucinda exchange a few tense words, recognizing their voices from conversations earlier at the store. Their tones seemed dark and sinister as the night.

"This better work out," Lucinda said, threateningly.

"I told you it would, now leave me alone." I detected traces of doubt tinged with fear.

They moved off toward the house.

Soon after, Dy came outside and joined Greg while he added more wood to the pit from logs he brought from the back of his moving van. The guy had really come prepared.

Dy's voice, even though low, carried my way. "I wish I hadn't agreed to this," my new neighbor said to him.

"All you have to do is get through this evening," Greg replied. "Then she'll leave you alone."

"Rosina's had enough of her, too."

Greg gave Dy a reassuring hug before she went back inside.

My secret surveillance was starting to bother me. Should I be listening in like this? These little snippets of conversation were private, personal, none of my business. But there wasn't anything wrong with a person sitting out in her own backyard, was there? Patti certainly would have agreed. Besides, I was intrigued by what I was overhearing, and it was entertaining to puzzle out interpretations of their meanings with so little information.

My imagination took off to the moon.

The "she" Dy had referred to had to be Lucinda. I'd just assumed that Dy was a willing part of the coven, but what if she wasn't? And what had gone on between Rosina and Lucinda? Why the worry? What was the *it* that had to work "or else"?

Before I could ponder those questions further, Lucinda came back outside. At first I couldn't tell what she had in her hand, but as she walked close to the flame that Greg had built up to a roaring blaze—-OMG! She was carrying a scary-looking double-edged dagger!

That certainly got my undivided attention, and not in a good way. Little hairs stood at attention on the back of my neck, and not because of the dip in air temperature, either. My heart decided all on its own to pick up the pace.

It's one thing to get a bunch of women together around a fire. It's quite another to introduce a dagger that size.

I stopped to consider a serious question regarding these strange people. Were they good witches? Or bad ones? Clearly, Patti thought the latter (she didn't seem to believe in the former), but I'd just assumed they were Wiccans: not exactly mainstream, but harmless. But what if they really thought they were Satan's children and were into human sacrifice? And what if that somebody was Aurora? She was the newbie, filling in for a last-minute vacancy. Or so they'd said. What if they had been pretending, just so that they could lure in an innocent naïf like Aurora to shed her blood? My guilty imagination conjured up a sinister plot. Lucinda would be the one to do the deed. Or maybe that was Greg's job. Looks can really be deceiving. Just because he was drop-dead handsome didn't mean he was a good person.

If not for the chill of the October night, I would be sweating bullets.

Why was I imagining such terrible thoughts? This was Moraine, Wisconsin. Human sacrifices didn't happen here. If someone around here wanted to get rid of a problem person, they ran that person over with a car or shot them while out on their daily walk. Guns are big in my area. Knives the size of this one aren't common at all.

Unfortunately, I'd lost control of my reasoning process and bad stuff just kept popping in uninvited.

Then suddenly I went all calm—which, ironically, worried me even more. Had I been zapped with a spell after all? Had Patti been right? Probably not, or I wouldn't feel so nervous. Did a person under a spell know it, though? Somehow I doubted it. What if . . . ?

Stop that, I said to myself with as much firmness as I had in me.

Where the heck was my man when I really needed him? Come to think of it, he rarely was available when it mattered the most. Like when I discovered a wood tick buried in my leg. Where had he been then? Gone, that's where. And this was way huger than a bloodsucking bug!

What about Patti? Why wasn't she creeping through the darkness, watching for trouble, prepared to insert herself if something wicked raised its ugly head? On second thought, Patti tended to create more trouble than she stomped out. Plus, she was more scared of the witches than I was at the moment, so scratch the possibility of her actually making a heroic appearance.

I tried calling Hunter, as that brief but glorious moment of calm disappeared and my fear for Aurora returned as strong as ever, though I wasn't too hopeful that he'd pick up. He usually silenced his phone when working a case, something we'd discussed numerous times without me getting my way.

He actually thought his cell phone was for his convenience, not mine, using it any old way it suited him. I'd been up to my neck in alligators a few times when the situation wouldn't have happened in the first place if my guy had just answered his stupid phone.

The last remaining relaxed hairs on the back of my neck rose as I went over more options for an intervention to rescue Aurora from what I now considered a potentially dangerous situation.

It would've been nice if we had a decent police chief, one I could call with a serious emergency witch alert, a cop with a professional attitude who wouldn't give me grief and disparage me for being a good citizen. One who could be counted on to make a few drive-bys, look-ins, and check that everything was copacetic. Chief Johnny Jay, current law enforcer and big bully from way back, was absolutely *not* that guy. Johnny Jay is one of this town's few drawbacks, up there at the top of the list with Lori Spandle. Both are petty and vindictive. It's as though they both drank the same bad water from a contaminated well when they were growing up.

I could just imagine our conversation:

"We need police protection over on Willow," I'd say. "Right now, and hurry."

"Fischer," he'd reply, "ever hear the story of the boy who cried wolf?"

"But, but, evil witches might be sacrificing Aurora. I saw a knife."

I could imagine him, kicking back, plopping his Dumbo-sized feet on his desk and smirking into the phone. "Uh-huh. Whatever, Fischer."

But even redirecting my attention to the chief and all his flaws didn't stop my scary thoughts from pushing through, tapping on my brain for attention. So I tried to focus on the positive side. Those crescent cakes smelled heavenly, and I'd spotted several bottles of wine, which was always a big draw with me, and I was lonely without the company of my man. See? All perfectly legit reasons for what I was about to do, the one and only option still available to me (other than running and hiding, which I'd considered but reluctantly rejected as cowardly).

Instead of turning tail, I found myself trotting directly into the radiating heat of the burning fire, and asking the only man in the group if I could join the circle.

Four

I found out pretty quickly how much (or rather how little) input a guy has in a coven's decision-making process. Sure, I'm used to women ruling roosts, given all the matriarchs in my family—and of course my honeybees are girls and don't have much use for their drones—but this group seemed overboard with female dominance and control.

"Sure, if it were up to me . . ." Greg said. But it turned out that he didn't get a vote, and wouldn't be staying for the ceremony like I'd thought, so his support wasn't one bit useful. At least he wasn't a crazed warlock; one less obstacle for me to worry about. His lack of magical influence was a huge relief to my sense of community given that he was originally from here and was Al's son and all.

"No males allowed," one of the witches said, overhearing us.

"It's the girls' thing," Greg told me. "The inner sanctum and all that. I'd vote to let you stay if, uh, I had a vote."

So I asked the next witch who came along, careful to

avoid Lucinda (who was nowhere in sight, thank my lucky stars), hoping for a more positive response.

My request to participate created a lively discussion among the witches. It was a numbers thing. Thirteen and all that. What was the big deal? Twelve, fourteen, I couldn't see the difference. Like, who was counting and who cared?

Aurora's voice came from the background with a rather weakly stated vote in my favor. Since she owed me big-time for getting her this gig, I'd expected more of a positive response from her quarter, but I guess since she was only a fill-in, she didn't much count, either.

Some of the women had big issues with my presence. Some didn't.

A few were on the fence. Like Rosina, who had sort of bonded with me at the store when I'd admired her necklace. Right now the crystal in the center of it was sparkling from the reflection of the fire's flames.

A huge cloud of earthy, exotic patchouli oil hung over us.

"She's uninitiated," one dark purple–caped witch said.

"A mundane!" one with pointy glasses added.

That certainly didn't sound like a compliment.

"A muggle," somebody else said with a snorty little laugh.

The sassy part of me wanted to say, "Just because I sweep with my broom instead of ride it isn't a reason to discriminate against me," but that wouldn't have helped my case. Besides, I hadn't seen a single broom yet to reference.

Eventually Dy came outside with Lucinda, who settled it once and for all. "Absolutely not!" said the ringleader. Hers was apparently the deciding vote, as head honcho, dictator, the high priestess, or whatever they called her, because everybody fell into line, clammed up, and went about their business like I no longer existed.

"You'll have to leave," Lucinda said to me, giving me a big frightening sneer in the yellow light from the flames. But when I blinked, the scary image had vanished, and she was turning away. "This male has to go, too. Dy, what is he still doing here? Out! Now!"

I slunk back to my yard, instantly missing the warmth of their fire, while Rosina walked Greg to the street and stood watching as he drove away. She lingered there as if in deep thought before returning to the backyard.

At least I'd had an opportunity to see everything up close. They'd constructed an altar with witchlike tools on it—an ornate pewter goblet that reminded me of a scene in an Indiana Jones movie, a black kettle (à la the Wicked Witch of the West in *The Wizard of Oz*) and bowls of what was probably water, and a large saltshaker. Then there were bunches of candles, cinnamon incense, and Dy's wand. The dagger had been placed right in the middle of everything like it was the most important piece of the ritual.

I shivered just thinking about that knife. And redialed Hunter.

He still wasn't answering his cell phone.

I sat in the deep dark of my backyard, watching from afar as the women formed a circle and began to fill the space with their moving bodies. Voices rang out. I heard several references to the moon and to goddesses (which I liked a lot), and found myself really wishing I was in their midst. Lots of chanting and dancing ensued. I was shocked when I glanced at my watch and saw it was already midnight. Midnight? It seemed like the evening had just begun. Had I lost track of that much time? Or fallen asleep?

I checked my cell phone and realized I'd unintentionally silenced it. How could that have happened? Of course, it figured, Hunter had left a recent message—he'd been successful with his mission and still had a little paperwork to do but thought he'd check on me. I did my usual "Thank God he's okay" thought, shot him a quick text to let him know I was okay, and swung my attention back in the direction of the ceremony.

Hunter was too far away to come to anybody's rescue if

things got "dicey" soon anyway. It was up to me to make sure Aurora stayed safe.

Magic was in the air, electric energy zipping back and forth in the nighttime. I felt it like a physical presence. The women seemed lost in the freedom of the ritual as flames from the fire flicked skyward.

I stood up, pulled my fleece tighter around my body, and edged closer, careful to stay in the shadows, trying to pick out which one was Aurora. I scanned for her familiar face, but with full capes flapping, the circle seemed filled with way more than thirteen witches. More like thirty.

Suddenly, everybody stopped moving as Lucinda approached the altar and picked up the knife. Gazing into the sky, she began waving the blade in what looked like a figure eight.

Then the witches formed a more perfect circle than their earlier undulating one and passed around the goblet. Then each of them ate a little crescent cake. I couldn't help noticing that the double-edged dagger wasn't on the altar where it had been a moment before. And it wasn't visible in Lucinda's hand, either. With all the loose clothing, it could be anywhere.

Was this really going on right next door?

Dyanna Crane wasn't exactly who I had had in mind regarding a new neighbor. I'd expected to live next door to a young family buying their first starter house, or a downsizing elderly couple who enjoyed gardening and a lot of peace and quiet. Once again, Lori Spandle (the worst real estate agent on the planet) had messed up my cozy little street. Once I got my hands on the woman, I would gladly offer her up as the next sacrifice for one of the coven's rituals.

The circle of witches went back to slithering around the fire.

Since I hadn't stumbled across the definition of *skyclad* during my research, I just wasn't prepared for what happened next, when the entire group, after some hocus-pocus

stuff I didn't catch, dropped their capes to the ground and
stepped out of them. Not a single one was wearing a stitch.
It was all I could do not to gasp out loud in surprise. I really
hadn't seen that coming.

Suddenly in unison as though they'd rehearsed ahead of
time, they left the warmth of the fire and, completely bare
naked, danced their way down toward the river.

I stood up, stunned.

Was that a cackle I heard?

No, really, my imagination was working overtime.

What should I do?

The knife that had vanished concerned me big-time.
Where had it gone? Something as large as that thing would
have been hard to hide on a butt-naked person. Under a
cape, sure, but those were on the ground.

If I followed them to the water and they saw me, would
I look like a Peeping Tom? Or rather a Peeping Tomette?
Did I care about that? Not at all. But what if they fell on me
like a murder of crazed crows and poked my eyes out?
(Maybe I'd read too many tales in the horror genre in my
early formative years.)

Still . . . thirteen was a lot of women. I'd be at their
mercy, if they caught me. So they just wouldn't catch me.

To make matters worse, I thought I saw a momentary
reflection of metal as the group danced away.

At this point I decided I didn't care if they caught me
red-handed and accused me publicly of voyeurism. And if
things went from bad to worse, and they went hostile on
me, I would just run like crazy.

My quickly hatched plan was to pick Aurora out of this
nutty coven, make sure she was okay, and whisk her out of
there no matter how much she fought me (which actually
might be considerable based on her earlier enthusiasm).

I crept quickly through Dy's backyard, staying low in
the shadows, a feat in itself considering the bright moon
that appeared through the clouds to illuminate the sky.

Witches were splashing into the water from the bank, wading deeper into the river.

Apparently, throwing water on them would be useless. None of them were melting like the Wicked Witch had. Good to know.

From behind a maple tree, I tried to count witches again, had to start over several times, coming up short by one or two each time. If only they'd stop moving around so much and give me a chance to count properly! And to top things off, was this *really* a good time for the moon to disappear behind another cloud?

With the moonlight gone, I could barely see a thing. Good thing I'd grown up in this neighborhood, had played hide-and-seek in the dark, and still could have been able to get around blindfolded. I crept closer.

By now I was absolutely convinced that these women were up to no good. Their chanting was still going on, only the words had changed. It was now *Goddess from which we came, Power to the Blade.* Over and over.

I didn't stop to think about consequences or what-ifs. My only thought was for Aurora and what might possibly happen to her if I didn't intervene.

I didn't let myself even think about how cold that water must be.

The plan was to strip down to my underwear before diving in, but as I threw off my fleece and top, kicked out of my flip-flops, and unbuttoned my jeans, I realized my white underthings were standing out in the dark like Vegas neon signs.

So I had to strip those off, too, before I raced for the water. I skidded to a stop at the bank, forced myself forward, tiptoed in, gritted my teeth at the extreme temperature change, and waded as unobtrusively as possible toward the mass of bodies. Nobody even noticed as I joined them up to my armpits in murky, cold river water, hearing bullfrogs croaking all around me. Up close, visibility was much better, but if I wanted to stay anonymous (which I seriously did) I still had to hang back a little. Treading water with my face held low wasn't much of a problem, since it was pretty deep where the witches were now swaying and chanting. I finally spotted Aurora and slithered toward her. I gently took her arm and pulled her aside, placing a finger to my lips, the sign for silence.

"What? Oh, hi," she whispered in spite of my warning. "You came anyway." Aurora glanced toward the coven, but they were making enough noise to cover our little conversation. "Lucinda won't like it."

"We're getting out of here," I whispered back. "And we have to hurry."

Aurora was moving, but not toward shore. "I'm staying," she insisted, resisting.

So I said something that maybe sounded a little overly dramatic to anyone who hadn't spent the last several hours inside my head. I said, "They're preparing for a sacrifice and I'm pretty sure you're the chosen lamb."

Melodramatic, yes. Blurty, absolutely. But it sure did work.

I've never seen my neighbor move so fast.

And I was right behind her, noting that all the singing and chanting had come to an abrupt halt. All I could hear was my own rapid breathing and the sound of splashing water as Aurora and I tried to make our escape.

"Stop them!" Lucinda shouted. Mere seconds later, she appeared in my peripheral vision, on my left, splashing in the same direction, moving in to flank us. The rest of the witches were on our heels.

Running in water, I realized too late, was a great equalizer. I'd lost my edge.

"Hurry," I screamed at Aurora. "Faster!"

Five

&

We scrambled up the bank and took off running toward the house. It's amazing how much information your brain can process in a few seconds flat. Mine went wild trying to determine the right path.

A little more advanced plotting and planning on my part would have been beneficial. We were still in what my grandmother would call a pickle. For obvious reasons. Both of us were naked. We couldn't very well race down Main Street, shouting for help and calling all kinds of attention to ourselves. I'd have to leave town. My mother would see to that. And I'd be tarred and feathered on the way out, too.

Or . . . we could head for my house, or even Aurora's house, where we would beat them off with a broom and hold them at bay while we called for emergency backup.

If only our socially brainwashed brains hadn't demanded that we cover up. Automatically, both Aurora and I had first headed for our piles of clothing, and had almost made it, when we were surrounded by naked women. Two of us, twelve of them. How was I supposed to deal with the entire coven? Having Holly "Hulk Hogan" here at our side would have evened the odds considerably.

"You again," Lucinda snarled at me, one finger raised (I swear it was crooked), practically sticking it in my face. "What part of 'get lost' didn't you understand?" She turned to Aurora, who had scooped her clothes into a ball in her arms. "I thought you had potential," she said to Aurora, "until this happened."

I bent to pick up my clothes and get dressed, but Lucinda stepped down, grinding her heel into the back of my hand. I tugged it away and rose.

"We need to decide what to do about them." Surprisingly, this came from my new neighbor, not Lucinda. In the dark with the fire crackling and dying down to embers, Dy didn't have the same fresh, friendly expression that she'd had earlier today when we'd first met.

"I'll make that decision," Lucinda said. "Not you."

"We all will," Rosina said, as naked as the rest except for the pentacle around her neck.

Hunter, where are you? And where is that enormous knife?

Lucinda, Dy, and Rosina were in the grip of a witchy power play—glaring at one another. If their looks could kill, all three of them would be dead. Finally they broke the stalemate.

"Both of you," Lucinda said to Aurora and me with her judgelike authority restored intact, "get out of here and don't ever come back."

Get out! That was it?

Whew! What an enormous relief! Getting banned from the premises wasn't so bad. Maybe I'd misjudged this group after all. Maybe they weren't the demons I'd assumed they were.

Just then, without a single bit of warning, a beam of light brighter than the sun at high noon engulfed us. It was so brilliant I was momentarily blinded.

A voice called out from behind the light. "Freeze!" it said.

With the order to freeze, I realized I was freezing in more ways than one. God, it was cold.

Even worse (actually much, much worse), I recognized that voice.

Unfortunately, it wasn't my main man come to rescue me.

It was our police chief, Johnny Jay.

The entire bunch of us instinctively took several steps away from the light source. Being in the middle of them, I followed right along, staying low, realizing my fleece and other belongings were now out of reach.

So there I was in the witchy mix, feeling completely exposed in the industrial spotlight. How humiliating, to be nude in front of the absolute last person on earth I'd willingly bare myself before! How in the world had Johnny Jay known what was going on, and how did he manage to set up this sting operation without any of us spotting him?

Weren't witches supposed to know these things in advance? Then again, I'd managed to surprise them earlier, so I guess knowing the future wasn't this group's forte.

I peered around the people in front of me and noticed something that gave me hope:

Johnny Jay hadn't seen me yet. Maybe I could sneak out of this jam after all.

"What the hell is going on here?" Johnny roared, coming out from behind the light and really taking in the situation. "I almost dismissed the complaint out of hand since Patti Dwyre is a certifiable wacko, but this time she was actually firing on all cylinders."

Patti! I should have known. That woman manages to cause trouble for me nonstop. If I wasn't so cold, I'd be fuming.

I actually caught a hint of confusion in his statement, like he wasn't exactly sure what to do with so many women standing around in the buff. Johnny Jay, bully that he is, likes his prey to be isolated, no witnesses to his tactics, so this many of us really put him off his game.

A tiny part of me knew that if he'd shown up when I thought the witches were going to stab us to death, my reaction would have been more on the eternally grateful side rather than the extremely embarrassed side. But instead, the chief's appearance was untimely and unfortunate and a lot of other "un" words.

Johnny had backup with him. Several other officers came out from behind him and gawked. Geez, why couldn't it have been Sally Maylor? Come to think of it, why couldn't Sally have been in Johnny's shoes? That would have been so much better.

"We are going to get dressed now," Lucinda said to Johnny, with the right amount of demand in her voice.

"Cover up," the chief agreed, scowling at the other officers. "No funny stuff, though. Move nice and slow, then I want you to form an orderly line. I'm taking names."

I stayed low and crept quickly toward the very back of the group. I glanced longingly at my own clothes, knowing there was no way I could get to them without Johnny Jay getting a real eyeful. By the time the cluster of women broke apart, I was tucked safely in dense evergreens between Dy's house and mine. I felt safe enough to hang around for the big finale now that I no longer had an active role in it.

"As soon as you women are presentable," Johnny Jay went on to say, "we'll have a nice chat. Then you can give me your reasons for why I shouldn't book every last one of you."

Since the witches had been wearing nothing but loose gowns and flowing capes to begin with, they were all dressed again almost as quickly as they'd shed their clothes earlier. Lucinda stepped forward, and I noticed she had a few inches on the chief. I thought this should be a good showdown—one badass against another.

"I'm an attorney," Lucinda said to Johnny Jay, surprising me big-time. For some reason I just assumed she was a full-time witch. She went on, "I represent this group of women. We were invited to the home of Dyanna Crane, who moved in today, for a housewarming celebration. Isn't that right, Dy?"

"That's right," came the reply.

"My information says you were practicing witchcraft." Johnny Jay and Lucinda would've been nose to nose if the chief raised his chin and stretched his body up a little. "Is that correct?"

"Is it a crime to dance in this town? To celebrate the mystery of life? To bathe in the river?"

Johnny was definitely confused. "Uh, no, not exactly, but—"

"I don't see what harm they caused," one of the officers said, earning a hard look from the chief.

"Were we disturbing the peace?" the attorney wanted to know.

Johnny puffed up. "According to the neighbor's complaint, you were disturbing the peace, yes."

"And where is this aggrieved citizen?"

"I'm asking the questions here," Johnny Jay said. "I had a legitimate complaint about inappropriate activity at this address, and after investigating, I found a bunch of you . . . all of you . . . how many are there anyway? . . . running around bare-ass naked. We don't put up with that kind of behavior in my town."

From the safety of the pines, I saw the two warriors draw closer to each other while the rest of the coven kept a cautious distance. Pine needles from the trees that shielded me were poking into my arms, shoulders, and back end. One found its way into my big toe. I stifled a yelp and pulled it out.

"And you, Aurora," Johnny said after scanning the crowd more openly now that everybody was appropriately attired. "You should be ashamed of yourself."

"Nothing wrong with skinny-dipping," Aurora shot back at him. "Didn't you do a little of that yourself when you were young, before you turned into such a stick in the mud? In fact, I remember . . ."

This time I stifled a snort. The good old days came rushing back. I'd forgotten that Aurora had moved to Moraine during high school, and had even dated Johnny for a semester before realizing what a doofus he was. They must have gone skinny-dipping.

"That's enough out of you," Johnny barked at her, then paused to consider his next move. "I'm letting you off easy this time with a verbal warning," he told the group, "but I'll be watching all of you closely. If I were you, I'd get out of town immediately." That last part he addressed more to poor Dy than anybody else. She'd been right to worry about her standing in the new community. Once Johnny targeted you as trouble, he went at you like a pit bull. I should know.

Lucinda took the only step still between them, closing in. "Is that a threat, Chief?"

"Take it any way you want, but it behooves you to follow my advice."

I didn't stick around any longer, tiptoeing through stiff pine needles, then through a layer of crisp fallen leaves.

My skin itched like crazy from the pine needle episode, so before bed, I whipped up a mix of sweet antiseptic honey, water, and a dash of cinnamon to fight any bacteria that might be lounging in my pores, and applied the paste to my angry, irritated flesh.

I didn't realize that Hunter never came home that night until I woke up the next morning and found his side of the bed empty.

Six

Luckily, Hunter had been thoughtful enough to leave a message on my cell phone around four o'clock in the morning, which I hadn't even heard come in. "Don't worry," he'd reassured me, "I caught a case. Explain later."

Thursday morning the temperature plummeted into the middle thirties, something that happens on a regular basis in Wisconsin. Forty-degree swings aren't uncommon. Because of the cold, my honeybees were clustered in their hives, fanning all those tiny wings to create warmth for the queen bees and each queen's brood. I wished I could've hunkered down, too.

I would have been snug as a bug in a rug, or rather in my fleecy robe, if not for the itching on my back and nether regions. The rash on my arms felt and looked better, but certain areas needed another treatment. Part of me was extremely happy Hunter wasn't around to watch me with one of his amused smirks while I applied more salve to my butt.

Waiting for the honey concoction to do its magic, I tried

Hunter's cell, but again got no answer. We needed to have a talk ASAP regarding his cell phone etiquette. Or rather, his lack thereof.

I showered, dressed in jeans and a long-sleeved tee, and abandoned my precious flip-flops for something sturdier and warmer. Summers are wonderful, but there's also something special about that first crisp fall day when I pull on thick socks and a light jacket, and head out to breathe in the fresh smell of dried-out leaves. After a crumpet with honey and a travel mug of coffee, I strolled to The Wild Clover and began the process of opening for another day of business.

Carrie Ann, my cousin and the store's manager, arrived soon after, bundled up in a corduroy jacket and fashionable scarf. "Your mother asked me to help out with her wedding," she announced.

"WHAT?" Shocked didn't even come close to describing my reaction.

"I know," my cousin said, just as stunned as I was. "Until the very moment she called to include me in her preparations, I thought she really didn't like me at all."

That was an understatement if I'd ever heard one. My mother complained nonstop about Carrie Ann, even though my cousin had really cleaned up her act. Carrie Ann had had a wild side growing up and didn't bother hiding it from public view. She'd also had an alcohol problem, but she's recovering. Still, Mom isn't exactly the forgiving, forgetting type—she prefers to remember all the bad and none of the more recent good. "Just give it more time," Mom argues when I defend Carrie Ann. "She'll fall right back into her old ways."

And here was my mother asking Carrie Ann to help, before asking her own daughter first!

"What does she want you to do?" I asked, trying not to snort fire. Another jealousy episode threatened to erupt. Mixed with a pinch of resentment. And a dash of anger.

"It's not as though my mother has asked me for any assistance, and believe me, I've offered."

"Table decorations," Carrie Ann said, with an expression that told me she was sorry she'd brought it up. Geez, was that pity? "I'm thinking crystal bowls in the center of each table," she explained. "Filled with rose-shaped floating candles and scattered flower petals. What do you think?"

"It's okay with me," I lied, stomping into the back room and punching Mom's number into my cell phone.

"How are the wedding plans coming along?" I asked, managing through gritted teeth and a clenched jaw to sound pretty much normal. Or at least as normal as I ever was around Mom, suspicious and edgy from years of blind accusations and hurtful comments.

Judging by the upbeat pep in her tone today, though, I'd caught her in a good mood. "Everything is falling into place exactly as it should, thanks to your sister's role as my wedding planner. My younger daughter missed her true calling. I'm trying to convince her to go into business. We could call it Weddings and Honeymoons by Holly."

I rolled my eyes. Holly had treated college like husband hunting ground, shot her prey (Max) right through the heart, and has lived a life of leisure ever since. That had been her calling, not wedding planning.

I took a deep, cleansing breath and said, "I'd really like to help, you know? How about I go with you to pick out your wedding dress?"

"I found one months ago," Mom said. "Our wedding is only fourteen days away, and you think I don't have a dress yet?"

"Okay then, I know you are having trouble with the chapel for the wedding, something about a date mix-up or something. I could . . ."

"Taken care of, in spite of last-minute problems with a double booking. As it turns out, it will work for the best, because Tom and I decided to accept Holly's generous offer to get married at her house *and* have the reception there, too. But thanks for your offer, too, Story."

Okay, I need to deal with my disappointment once and for all. Granted, Holly has a mansion on a lake. But I have the family house and really felt that Mom should want her wedding there. Geez! See how sibling jealousy can zap the sense out of a woman? Grudgingly, I realized that of course Mom wouldn't want to get remarried in the same place she and Dad had raised us; she wanted a new start with Tom. Even I wasn't that insensitive once I got past my initial reaction.

"Holly and I could share the wedding planner role, then?" I wasn't about to give up.

"Holly has it handled, Story. Really."

"I could help her with flowers."

"Ordered yesterday."

"Food!" I run a market—of course I could handle the food.

"Did I forget to mention? Milly is catering our event."

Milly Hopticourt, a retired school teacher, handles The Wild Clover newsletter and creates one delectable recipe after another to include each month. I knew she'd been toying with the idea of starting a catering business. Guess she'd finally taken the plunge.

"I could help Milly," I suggested.

"That's between the two of you. I better go." Mom signed off with that breezy, happy voice, the one that hadn't included me in any of her wedding plans.

"We're out of apple cider," Carrie Ann announced when I joined her up front after my disappointing attempt to worm my way into my mother's wedding plans. "I called out to the farm for more, but Al can't deliver until this afternoon."

Moraine's business owners look out for one another. My store gives out little cups of cider from Country Delight Farm, after which we direct shoppers to the stand down the street where they can purchase quarts and gallons of cider as well as hot, buttery corn on the cob and caramel apples. Al returns the favor by promoting my honey products in a prominent display in his autumn shop, located adjacent to his wildly popular corn maze. The Mason family corn maze had been around for a long time, starting out as a little-bitty thing designed for their kids and the kids' friends. Over time it grew into a full-scale production, with a new design every year, created with the aid of GPS and tractors to flatten corn into the desired pattern. I've heard that it's best viewed from the air, but I haven't found anybody with a plane to take me up there yet.

"I'll go get a gallon from his stand," I said, slipping out and heading north, my mind on my mother's wedding and what I could offer to get a tiny chunk of her heartfelt appreciation. Why I keep trying is beyond me, but it's been ingrained since my formative years and I'm stuck with it.

I had to come up with something.

Maybe bride's honey? To be eaten right before the vows to bless the union with fruitfulness and fertility. Uh . . . wait . . . fertility? Maybe skip the fertility part. Mom is way too old and crabby for more children. But the bride's honey idea took root. I could use rosebuds from my backyard rose bushes, a little cinnamon, some cloves . . . I'd have to come up with a special recipe.

My creative side was going a mile a minute, which caused me to walk right past the country stand in deep thought. When I came back to earth, I found myself just before the bridge over the Oconomowoc River, where I noticed some active construction repair going on.

"Reinforcing the girders under the bridge," a buff guy wearing a hard hat told me when I inquired. Then I made a U-turn to retrace my steps to the farm stand and spent a few minutes eyeing up all the beautiful caramel apples while Joan Goodaller waited on a few customers ahead of me.

"Can you spare a gallon of cider for the tasting cups?" I asked after waiting my turn. "We're totally out."

"Sure thing. You've been sending quite a lot of business over here," Joan said. "You can have as many gallons as you need. Some excitement at your store. What was that all about?"

"I have a new neighbor. Apparently, those are some of her visitors." And that's all I said about them, and I was pretty proud of it. Exposing myself to gossip on a daily basis makes it difficult to stay above it. As a professional, I try to resist.

In her seventies, with a rosy, young-looking face, short and round like one of Country Delight's Cortland apples, Joan seemed to be thriving on small-town life. Two years ago, she'd found herself a widow, moved from the city of Waukesha to start a new life, and before we knew it, she and Al, who divorced way back, had become more than casual acquaintances. The locals chuckled about that a bit, because Al was a good ten years younger than Joan, but then everyone realized age didn't matter and forgot about it.

Joan had pitched right in, working the stand when one of Al's summer help couldn't make it, and even designing the corn maze this year. Both of the lovebirds insisted that they liked their relationship the way it was and weren't about to ruin it with legalities, so they kept their own places. I'd be much happier with someone more like Joan living on my street.

Instead, I had a neighbor with "trouble" tattooed on her forehead. Trouble on both sides, come to think of it. I was wedged between a rabid dog (Patti) and a feral cat (Dy).

Thinking of my neighbors reminded me of last night's bizarre ceremony and Johnny Jay's untimely appearance. Making a mental note to pick up the clothes I'd had to leave behind in my rush for cover, I took a moment to savor the Johnny Jay versus Lucinda Lighthouse bout. I thought she came out the overall winner. Although that would have changed if the chief had spotted me. He likes nothing better than to harass and bully me, and if he'd seen me, at least one of us would have been arrested.

Another customer came up, and I let him go first. As I waited, I noticed that Joan wasn't looking as rosy as usual. She looked a little under the weather, pale and tired.

"You might be working too hard," I told her when she finished up with the other customer. "You look like you could use a break."

"Hope I'm not coming down with that flu that's going around," she said.

"You and me both."

"I wasn't supposed to work the stand today, but Al's summer employees are young and pretty unreliable."

"Try to take it easy. By the way, I saw Al's son Greg yesterday. I didn't even recognize him, that's how much he's changed!"

"Al's grateful that he came out to help with the maze. So am I. It takes some of the pressure off."

After Joan gave me a gallon of cider, I did everything in my limited range of power to resist the farm's homemade caramel apples. My mind told me that corn on the cob was better for my waistline, but when the proper, healthy me also advised against all that salt and butter that I couldn't help adding, it lost its edge to the apples.

They were jumbo apples, bigger than I'd ever seen any-place else. And they were covered with so many tempting options. You could get your apple:

- coated in either dark or white Belgian chocolate

- rolled with nuts (pecans, cashews, peanuts, pistachios, walnuts, macadamias, or a mix)

- covered in crushed candy (Butterfingers, Snickers, M&M's, Oreos, toffee, or Reese's Pieces)

- and drizzled with caramel or more chocolate.

I caved to temptation and selected a walnut cherry

caramel apple, and walked slowly back toward the store carrying the cider in one hand and eating the enormous apple with the other.

My bliss was short-lived.

I fear I conjured up Johnny Jay. Never again will I think of that man for one second if this is what happens when I do. Now, however, there he was out in front of my store, pacing impatiently with what appeared to be . . . oh no . . . my clothes from last night, tucked in a ball under his arm. He looked tired and rumpled, as if he'd been up all night, but when he spotted me he still managed to smirk.

The smirk disappeared quickly and was replaced with pent-up anger when Hunter pulled up in his SUV and jumped out with Ben at his side.

Thank you, my hunk. Your timing is perfect.

"Wallace," the chief said to Hunter, "I'm going to tell you one more time since it doesn't seem to be sinking into your thick skull. This is my town and my case."

Case? My clothes were a case? Not good.

Hunter ignored him, came over to me, and gave me a kiss on my sticky lips. "You taste sweet," he said, though I noticed that his usual twinkle was missing. "Did you miss me in bed?"

"Every second," I fibbed, although if I'd known he wasn't there, I definitely would have missed him, and been worried sick that something had happened to him.

"Wallace!" Johnny Jay bellowed. "I'm talking to you!"

Hunter turned to give the chief more attention than he deserved.

"What case is Johnny talking about?" I asked Hunter, really, really hoping it didn't involve me or my clothes or my naked escape last night.

"It's Chief Jay to you, Fischer," Johnny pointed out for something like the millionth time. "Have some respect."

"What did I do now?" I asked anybody who cared to answer.

"That remains to be seen," Johnny snarled.

"What's going on?" I asked Hunter specifically.

That's when Hunter said, "There's been a death over at Country Delight Farm, very early this morning."

Seven

❦

It wasn't an easy matter to discover the specifics of who was dead and how and why. I put the cider down on the sidewalk—I had a feeling I'd want to watch what happened next between the two men, and the gallon jug was heavy. Hunter gave me a lopsided, here-we-go-again weak grin.

Johnny Jay and Hunter have gone more rounds about Waukesha law enforcement territory than professional boxers. Only without the physical part, up until now at least. The city of Waukesha is Hunter's turf, no question about it, but Waukesha County encompasses numerous towns and villages, and that's where things get murky between the local and county cops.

"It's my case!" Johnny Jay snarled, as menacing as I'd ever seen him, which is saying a lot. The chief can look downright scary.

But so can my man. K-9 star, Ben, wore his high-alert

expression, his sharp Belgian Malinois eyes never leaving his partner.

"Country Delight is over the town line," Hunter told him, moving closer, no trace of a snarl, but the look on his face said more than any caveman growl could. My guess was that the original emergency call came in to Moraine's police station and the chief took his sweet time notifying Waukesha County.

Hunter went on to add, "And as Moraine's chief of police you should already know where the town lines begin and end. You had no business taking over the crime scene before my team arrived. And you haven't fooled anybody. We know you sat on that call."

"Get out of my face!"

"Can somebody please tell me who's dead?" I blurted, too loudly since a few customers coming out of the store and several people on the sidewalk nearby heard me and made a beeline for our trio, their original plans taking second fiddle to our lively tune.

At this point I was getting pretty upset, because the dead person could be Al, or his son Greg, or one of the witches. I needed to know. Unfortunately, the two men were more focused on each other.

"Waukesha is handling this, Jay, and there's nothing you can do about it. I ought to have you brought up on charges for tampering with a crime scene."

"You couldn't solve a crime if it bit you in the ass."

"Getting personal now, are we?"

Nose to nose, the two law enforcement authorities weren't setting much of an example for our community members when it comes to peaceful communication and orderly conduct.

Thankfully, Ben had had enough and decided to give a menacing snarl that no human could duplicate in terms of serious intimidation. Johnny Jay has always been cautious around Ben, so he reacted first, backing up a few steps and shutting his big mouth. My man took that as concession.

Next, Hunter reached into the back pocket of his jeans, produced several sheets of paper rolled up into a circular tube, and tried to hand them to our chief. Johnny balked, but when Hunter continued to extend his arm, the chief reluctantly took them, giving Hunter a questioning expression.

"Now that lines have been established," Hunter said to him, "I'm requesting your assistance."

"What?" I burst out. "You can't be serious!"

Johnny Jay has never, ever allowed Hunter to assist in any criminal cases within his jurisdiction. In fact, he'd been downright rude to Hunter when he'd offered in the past. Now that the creep didn't have authority to interfere for a change, Hunter was actually inviting him to get involved? I wish he'd talked this over with me first. I'd have set him back on the straight and narrow. Instead, Hunter was setting himself up for a knife in his back, if you asked me.

What was my guy thinking?

Hunter and I had some information-sharing issues at first (okay, maybe we still do), sometimes forgetting that we were a partnership and that meant discussing topics and resolving any conflict issues. To tell the truth, I'd been worse at communicating than he was. Until now.

We needed to talk in the worst way.

I tossed the rest of my apple in a trash bin near the store door and asked again, "Who's dead?"

They both eyed the gathering crowd before turning to me as though they were only just now realizing they had attracted an audience. Which probably they just had.

Johnny was the one who answered. "It's going to come out soon anyway, and the family has been notified. We identified the body as that of Claudene Mason."

That certainly surprised me.

"Al's crazy sister?" I'd heard of Claudene but hadn't

actually known her personally. She'd moved away when I was just a kid. In the past, older locals had referred to her as Crazy Claudene, but with the passage of time, we all but forgot about her. I hadn't heard her name in years.

Hunter was grim. "Al's sister, yes," he said. "But she hadn't gone by Claudene for at least ten years. Apparently she legally changed her name after joining that witch coven that's in town."

"Witch coven?" somebody said, and I heard a few echoes. But I wanted to know, which witch?

"I saw them come into town in a van yesterday," somebody else said. "But I didn't know they were witches. Jehovah's Witnesses is what I thought."

Someone added, "They better keep right on passing through."

A few nodded in agreement.

"Was it foul play?" someone else wanted to know.

"All we are prepared to say at this time," Hunter answered, "is that the death is under investigation."

"Okay," Johnny Jay said, taking control, "let's break it up. Go about your business."

The crowd dispersed, and Johnny Jay and Hunter, with Ben sitting patiently at his side, put their heads together out by the curb like they'd worked cases together all along and hadn't just had a confrontation. That's men for you. I couldn't believe that one of the witches from last night's ceremony was dead and gone. I wanted more information, so I casually joined them, as though I belonged there.

I had to clear my throat several times before I got their attention.

"Lucinda was murdered, right?" I asked, thinking she was the most obvious as far as murder victims go. Overbearing, controlling, cold, and unyielding. She'd be my first choice if I was going to kill one of the coven members.

"No." Hunter turned, noticed me, and shook his head. "It wasn't Lucy Lighthouse."

"I thought her first name was Lucinda," I said, scratching an itchy arm through my fleece.

"Each of them has a special name selected during a ceremony of initiation," Hunter explained, although I already had suspected that. "It supposedly gives them special powers. Lucy's witch name is Lucinda."

"Well, whatever her name is, she's the head of the group."

The chief perked up his ears. "So you know these people?" he said, all insinuatingly.

"They came into the store," I told him. Then to Hunter, "Which one of them is dead?"

"Claudene legally changed her name to Rosina years ago."

The victim's identification surprised and saddened me. Rosina was dead? We'd barely spoken, but I'd liked the woman. I'd admired her pentacle necklace, and she'd gone on about how it protected her. I hadn't asked her why she thought she needed protection. Or from what. Not that the necklace's magic had been able to save her after all.

In a perfect world, only mean and nasty and unsalvageable people should die violent deaths, right? Although, now that I thought about it, in a perfect world everyone would be sweet and kind and good and no one would ever die by unnatural causes anyway.

"What happened exactly?" I asked, since the two cops hadn't kicked me out of their new club yet.

"That information isn't being made available yet," Johnny said.

Hunter stepped in. "Jay, the story is about to break anyway." Then his eyes met mine. "It appears that she died from multiple stab wounds," he said. "But the ME still needs to confirm cause of death."

"Not a pleasant way to go," Johnny added, keeping his voice low and narrowing his eyes to appear tough now that he was back on the case.

I've been around a few murders in the past, and they always hit me hard, even when I didn't know the victim.

Oh my God. I didn't feel so good. And I was pretty sure I'd seen the murder weapon, that big, sharp knife that had been on their altar, the one that vanished from view during the ceremony.

"That's horrible!" I said. "Have you arrested anyone?"

"Not yet," Johnny Jay told me, "but I'll see that this case is closed quickly."

I? My man caught it, too, because Hunter gave him a hard stare. "This is a team effort, Johnny Jay." Then to me, "We've been working the crime scene and interviewing everybody out at the farm. The killer's window of opportunity was very narrow. The victim had been with the entire coven up until about ninety minutes before her body was discovered. The time of death and cause will be announced within an hour or so. If any of your gossipy customers have something useful to report, they can talk privately with me or with the chief."

Johnny went off to his squad car, carting my clothes with him. They had taken a backseat to the paperwork Hunter had given him. But then he just sat there in his car, not starting his engine and driving off like he should. Not a good sign.

I took the private moment with Hunter to say, "You usually criticize my store for being a—what have you called it?—oh, I remember . . . a hotbed of gossip and innuendos. And I seem to recall a certain tone of distaste in your voice combined with a very negative attitude. Now you want me to talk this up with my customers and report back to you? I know what you're doing."

He rewarded me with a tired smile. "You're too smart for me," he said. Seeing how exhausted he was, I told him to go home and get some rest. I opened the passenger door for Ben, who hopped up and settled into the shotgun seat.

Hunter hugged me. "I'm gonna get a few hours of downtime. We'll talk more later. In the meantime, try to stay out of trouble."

"No problem," I said, kissing him and sending him off for a nap.

Then the police chief unfolded from his vehicle.

I turned to face Johnny Jay, who still had my clothes under his arm and that stupid smirk back on his face.

Eight

There was a very good reason why I didn't protest when Johnny demanded that I get into his squad car for a "little ride down to the station." The most convincing argument in favor of complying was his threat to go public with his "request." We'd gone viral in the past, and it never was pretty. If we faced off, my mother would find out, and that was unacceptable considering my efforts to stay on her good side. So would Hunter, who needed a few hours of shut-eye and tended to become snarky when overtired. Plus, I never win those rounds with the chief, so what was the use? I've learned to pick my battles.

Another important reason I capitulated is because I hate wearing handcuffs. Been there, done that, and Johnny promised I could go accessory free if I didn't put up what he called "a stink."

He opened the back passenger door. "I want to ride in the front," I demanded.

"Just shut up and get in," Johnny said, "before one of the

local snoops notices and you draw all that unwanted attention that gets you in trouble with your friends and family."

"Fine!"

But before I could move, Holly pulled in front of Johnny's car. My sister's Jag literally purred, and she had the top down. I envisioned her leaping over the top of the driver's door, but she opened it before pounding her way over to Johnny.

"Relax," I said to her. "It's voluntary on my part."

She stopped abruptly and gaped at me. "Did he drug you?"

"You two sisters crack me up," Johnny said. "Now make like a roadrunner and vamoose before I ticket your piece of junk vehicle."

"Don't tell Mom," I said, trying to keep the begging tone out of my voice. "And you need to help out inside. Tell them I'll be back in an hour."

Holly didn't believe a single word coming out of my mouth. She glared at Johnny, who grinned back at her. I could tell she was psyching herself up for a wrestling match, so I saved her from having to ride to the station with me by saying, "DeeDee was in the store. Stanley had her in his sights but he needs you."

That did the trick. Sure, I'd failed to mention that our most notorious local shoplifter was long gone by now, but Holly would find that out soon enough.

"You're sure you're okay?" she asked me, hesitating, but I could tell her interest had been piqued.

"I'm perfectly fine."

With that, she marched off, heading for the store.

I got in the back but crossed my arms with enough melodrama that he couldn't miss the fact that I was a hostile witness.

It appeared that the only way to handle the chief was with a whole lot of confrontational attitude. He'd backed off last night when Lucinda stood up to him. I'd try the same technique with him today.

On the way to the police station, I considered my options and responses. First of all, I took a moment to mentally forgive Hunter for including Johnny Jay in his investigation. Since Hunter hadn't come home last night, I hadn't had a chance to share with him what had happened over at our new neighbor's house. If he'd known, he'd have made sure Johnny and I stayed as far away from each other as possible. But he didn't, so he couldn't be blamed. Secondly, Hunter might have been trying to set an example for Johnny Jay, one of collaboration, teaching him how to be a team player. Too bad Hunter apparently didn't realize it was wasted effort, because the chief would never, ever get it.

We arrived and soon entered the same interrogation room where Johnny Jay always harasses and grills me. It was windowless and totally bare apart from a table, four chairs, and a heavy wood door with an unpickable lock (tried that once). This time it had a new feature, a mirror on the inside wall, and I had no doubt that there was an observation area behind it.

"I'm holding you," he announced when the door banged shut behind us.

"You're arresting me? For what?" I had my back against the mirror and my arms crossed in classic defiance.

"I didn't say that, now did I?" Johnny Jay threw my clothes on the table and sat down, swinging his feet up next to them. "I said I'm *holding* you. There's a difference. Legally I can hold you for forty-eight hours without charging you, which I intend to do. After that, we'll see what happens based on how cooperative you become."

"You can't do this!"

"Pretend you're back in high school," Johnny gloated. "Remember all those detentions you used to rack up? This will be pretty much the same thing, only with fewer amenities."

I gave up my stance at the mirrored wall and slumped down into a chair but kept my back to the mirror just in case someone was observing. This wasn't starting like usual. Normally Johnny charges in like the bull he is, wildly flinging accusations. Meanwhile, I wave my red flag to get him snorting mad before deftly stepping aside at the last minute. Dazed, he then regroups, redirects, and comes at me again.

Had the bull left the ring?

My eyes slid to the heap of clothes on the table.

"Recognize them?" he said when I shifted my attention back to him.

"Should I?" Dodging was our game, after all.

"You left a big clue behind. Imagine my surprise when all those naked women got dressed and . . . what do you know? . . . there was an extra pile of women's apparel on the ground."

"So what? You're implying what?"

"There were Queen Bee Honey business cards in one of the pockets."

"So?"

"And flip-flops on the ground, too."

I raised an eyebrow.

"Fischer," he said with a heavy sigh. "They ratted you out, so you might as well come clean."

Figures. If it isn't Patti snitching on me, it's somebody just like her. Couldn't the witches have covered for me? Although I guess I hadn't exactly endeared myself to them, had I?

Johnny really did look exhausted, dark circles under his eyes, tired lines around his mouth. So, in a weak moment of compassion and patriotic duty, I came clean.

"I only went over there because I was worried about Aurora. I'm the one who suggested her as an alternate to number thirteen and didn't consider at the time that those women could be evil witches and might sacrifice Aurora in some kind of cult ritual. When I got concerned, I went to get her."

My actions sounded sort of lame when expressed in words. Why is it that things seem so much more rational in your head than when you make your thoughts verbal? The act of talking about my motive brought on some pretty strong emotions—guilt and regret. A woman really had been murdered. If only I could have known and helped Rosina.

"So," Johnny said, removing his feet from the table and leaning in, "why did you decide to get naked?"

"Oh, that." I waved it off. "Only so I'd blend in."

"Let's hear the whole story."

Then an important fact struck me. Hunter was head investigator and would *not* be happy if Johnny Jay had information regarding the case before he did. Especially if it came from his live-in lover, who possibly could become his ex-live-in if she didn't handle this delicate situation with kid gloves. "I'd like Hunter to hear this, too."

"Hunter's not available," Johnny Jay had the nerve to say. I knew very well he'd be available if I asked.

"I demand Hunter Wallace be present," I said.

"You can demand all you want."

"I demand an attorney!"

"Tough luck."

What? This wasn't going well. Now I knew what it felt like to be caught between a rock and a hard place, or more accurately between Johnny Jay and Hunter. Let's see, what to do? What a no-brainer. Hunter trumped Jay anytime. "I'm not saying another word until Hunter is here," I announced, thinking my man would be so proud of me if he could just see me this very minute, going way out of my comfort zone to protect his position, even risking incarceration.

"Suit yourself." Johnny stood up and towered for effect.

"I want my phone call."

"Thanks for reminding me. Hand over the cell phone."

"No." Realization dawned—the phone had been in my pocket the whole time. I should have called Hunter from the police car when I had the chance. Or at least shot him a text message. Maybe Holly would become suspicious when I didn't return. Although I'd been so convincing.

This wasn't the first time Johnny Jay had pulled a stunt once he had me in lockdown. How many times before I learned? Apparently several. "You don't get my phone," I announced obstinately.

It made me feel slightly better to see how he was trying to control his temper. "I'll cuff you and leave you cuffed," he threatened. "Better yet, I'll get backup in here and physically remove the phone and anything else you might have on you that could be used as a weapon."

I handed over my only link to civilization.

"I want an attorney," I said again.

"You haven't been charged with a crime, so you have no rights." Johnny picked up my clothes from the table. A bit of panty lace peeked out.

Time for one final stance. "I have the right to contact Hunter, and I *demand* an attorney. And those clothes belong to me and I want them back. You're walking all over my rights as a citizen."

Which wouldn't be the first time.

Johnny rapped on the door, it swung open, and he and my clothes left the room.

Silence after that. I kept my back to Johnny's stupid mirror in case he was on the other side. After a certain amount of time (how much? I didn't know), a random idea struck me, one born of sheer desperation. Assuming that thinking bad thoughts about Johnny Jay earlier had actually conjured his control-freak presence at the store, why couldn't the same work to my advantage here? The chief isn't even the sensitive type, isn't attuned to what's happening in the universe, and still he'd appeared right in front of my store.

I bet witches are *really* tuned in.

Not that I necessarily believed in all that hocus-pocus,

but what else did I have to do with my time? There was no TV to watch or magazines to read; not even a toilet, which was going to become a problem very soon. Johnny was once again positioning himself to go down for abusing a prisoner. Wait until Patti got hold of this story.

Anyway, with my brain fired up for action combined with a positive attitude, plus total concentration, I sent out my appeal.

"Help," went my telepathic signal. "I've been detained at the police station. Get me the hell out of here!" I inserted *hell* for maximum effect.

After sending my plea into space over and over until my brain felt fried, I lowered my head on the table in defeat. This crapola didn't work, not one bit. My suspicions were confirmed. Call it what you want—ESP, clairvoyance, mind reading, whatever—if a bona fide witch couldn't pick up the signal, who could?

Just when I was seriously considering banging on the door in utter defeat, preparing to deal with more of Johnny Jay's gloating, just to have the opportunity to visit the little girl's room, came the sweet sound of a metal key clinking in the lock, the magical thud of the bolt releasing, the knob turning, the door swinging open slowly, a creak or two, and . . . the unbelievable happened.

One of the chief's deputies stepped through the doorway.

Right behind him, Lucinda Lighthouse walked into the room, holding my clothes and flip-flops.

"You're free to go," the deputy said.

My jaw slammed open.

Nine

&

"Really?"

"Really," Lucinda said, without a bit of friendliness, either fake or real. She tossed me my stuff.

Unbelievable! What was she doing here and what gave her so much power and authority?

My gaze shot past her to the open door. No police chief trailing in the ashes of his defeat. Just the witch. Then I recalled Lucinda telling Johnny Jay that she was an attorney. I smiled at the mirror. Johnny Jay wasn't anywhere in sight out front, either, when the deputy handed me my cell phone. What a coward.

Neither Lucinda nor I said a single unnecessary word to anyone or to each other until we walked out of the police station and she directed me to get into the coven van. Then, as we pulled away, I had lots of questions.

"You heard me calling for help?" I had to ask, thinking this appealing-into-space thing really was something I could see myself getting a handle on.

"Heard you what?" Her eyes were straight ahead as we drove toward downtown Moraine.

"Uh . . . I mean . . . how did you know where I was?"

"Aurora told me."

"How did she know?" I asked with less skepticism, though a little was still hanging on, clinging to the edge of reason and doubt.

"You'll have to ask her."

Either Aurora was a certified clairvoyant, or—a sudden thought with more potential—she had spotted me getting into Johnny's squad car and put two and two together. Yes, that had to be it. She must have been somewhere near the store and witnessed our departure.

I reined in my imagination and settled comfortably in that more reasonable explanation.

"Thank you for rescuing me," I told Lucinda with real, heartfelt gratitude. "The chief was going to leave me to rot." A bit melodramatic, but closer to the truth than not.

"What did you tell him?" She took her eyes off the road briefly to glance at me.

Was that wariness in her voice? This could be a tricky question to answer. It was obvious she had figured out why I was at the station, which wasn't too hard to guess since I'd joined their side the minute my bare toes touched river water. "Not much, really," I said, staying vague. "I asked for an attorney."

Lucinda nodded like I'd done the right thing.

"What did you say to spring me?" I asked her, letting a little awe into my voice. I loved that Lucinda could outmaneuver Johnny Jay.

"I educated your ignorant police chief on the letters of the law. After which, I offered to file a harassment complaint."

I grinned, wishing I'd been privy to that exchange.

"I'm sorry about Rosina," I told her.

"We all are."

I took a good look at Lucinda, still in black garb, even more appropriate now, considering the death of her friend or whatever they had been to each other. In the light of day, while concentrating on her driving (which she did deftly, by the way), the witch didn't appear nearly as intimidating as she had last night. More business-like, like how Hunter gets when he's working. It must be tough keeping that many witches in line. I had only a handful of employees and look how I'm managing them? Barely, that's how. Thank goodness for Carrie Ann and her patience with my other family members coming and going as they please.

About then, Lucinda shot right past my street and continued toward the bridge that was under construction. We had to stop and wait for oncoming traffic (three vehicles, if you can call that traffic—no big deal) to get first dibs on the one lane still open to the other side.

"My house is back there," I informed Lucinda, not too worried that she was kidnapping me since I could get out right now if I wanted to. If things got dicey once we picked up speed, I could always tuck and roll out the car door. Not that I've tried it, or wanted to, but I appreciate having options, albeit undesirable ones.

"I know where you live," Lucinda answered, "but since I did you a favor, I'd like to ask one in return."

Ah . . . a catch. Okay, though, anything (or almost anything) for the woman who pulled one over on Johnny Jay and rescued me from his clutches. I had plenty to offer her. Freebies from the store for the next ceremony? A lifetime of honey for their ritual crescent cakes? More garlic in case vampires came messing around?

But I was pretty sure she had her own idea of how I could repay her.

Now it was our turn to cross the bridge.

I saw Lori Spandle off to the side, talking to one of the hard hats, a young guy with a body to die for. The creepy real estate agent had her hands all over him, her tongue practically hanging out, the woman's fat little round face flushed with excitement.

In her fantasies.

What hot young stud wanted that has-been?

I tried to get a picture of them with my cell phone but didn't react fast enough. Rats!

"Where are we going?" I asked next, hoping it wasn't someplace isolated and witness free. My confidence threatened to jump out the window, leaving me alone in the passenger seat. I pulled it back. But believe me, I was perfectly aware that I was riding next to a woman who might possibly have one of her coven member's blood on her hands. If anyone was the main suspect, it was the woman sitting next to me.

It's amazing how fast one can replace gratitude with suspicion. In my mind's eye, I could see Lucinda plunging that knife into Rosina. Had I considered that she might have a weapon this very moment? After a fast glance around the front of the van, I didn't spot one. And she wouldn't have dared enter the station armed.

"To Country Delight Farm," came the reply.

Whew.

We sped along on Creamery Road, then slowed to enter the driveway leading to the farm. A sign out by the road announced the opening of the corn maze this coming Friday, which I realized was tomorrow. A wagon filled with pumpkins, gourds, Indian corn, and winter squash enticed passersby to stop and browse the barn with all its fall treats and decorative items. And while they were at it, they could go into a big fenced area and pet and feed the farm animals.

Al has a menagerie of animals for his visitors' enjoyment:

- pygmy goats
- a Tom turkey and a flock of hens and young ones

- a pink potbellied pig named Ms. Piggy
- two white geese who honked their heads off
- a miniature donkey named Dusty
- one struttin' peacock called Pretty

Instead of turning left toward the barnyard and the entry to Al's corn maze, though, we veered to the right and drove down a grassy lane next to the apple orchard until we came to the witchy guests' campground.

Three enormous canvas tents and a cluster of smaller ones encircled a fire pit not that much different than the one they'd danced around last night. The witches were crowded around a picnic bench and watched as I got out of the van. A familiar face would have been a welcoming sight, but Dy and Aurora weren't with them. I felt like I'd just entered enemy territory without a squad of Marines to back me up.

Instead of joining the others, Lucinda led me to one of the large tents and ducked in. Just to be on the safe side, I silently threw another bit of information up to the universe. "I'm going into Lucinda Lighthouse's tent. Should I go inside or run the other way?"

"What are you waiting for?" Lucinda called out.

An answer to my question didn't present itself, so I ducked through the flap and found myself inside a room at least the size of my bedroom. And furnished just as well (or nearly). These women knew something about outdoor living in comfort. If the world as we know it ever ended, they would be the survivors.

"Sit down," Lucinda said, taking one of two chairs at a small square table.

I sat, wondering where Rosina had met her maker. Hunter already told me it had happened at the farm. But was it here, in the coven's campground? In one of the tents?

"About this favor," I began with some nervous chatter. "I sure do owe you one, no question about that." I gave her some suggestions, the ones I'd thought about on the way over—honey, garlic, whatever.

When I ran out of ideas, Lucinda said, "The local authorities are forcing us to stay here longer than we had anticipated. Until they are satisfied that none of us were involved in Rosina's tragic death, we can't go home, and that is inconvenient at best."

"I'm so sorry about your troubles and about Rosina," I said again.

"Nothing could be worse," she agreed. "Tabitha found her in the corn maze, you know, and it was a horribly shocking experience for the young woman."

Tabitha! Which witch was she?

So Rosina had been killed in the corn maze, stabbed with a jagged-edged knife. Yikes. Lucinda continued, "The lead investigator wants the actual scene of her murder to remain confidential information." She studied me intensely before continuing, "If word got out that it happened in the corn maze, Al's financial future could be at stake."

Stake? The burning kind popped into my head. "You mean he'd lose customers if they found out the maze was the scene of a murder." That would not be good for any of us. What hurt one local business impacted all.

"Families come to play in the maze. A situation like this could significantly harm his business. Or, since Halloween is right around the corner, it might bring out the worst kind of imitators."

That was a nasty thought. "Copycats."

Lucinda nodded. "It's important that Rosina's murder is solved as quickly as possible for many reasons. Detective Wallace hopes to wrap this up quickly, but who knows if he actually will."

So the witches didn't know about my relationship with

Hunter. That was good to know. Lucinda went on, "We intend to invoke the presence of the high priestess, who will give us the name of the person Rosina went to meet right before her death, the one who did this awful thing."

"Uh, um, okay," I said, because I didn't know what to say, and I didn't want to alienate Lucinda with a snide remark or by laughing out loud. Instead I just had to ask, since the question had been on my mind since Dy's first wand sighting, "Are you Wiccans?"

Lucinda snorted derisively. "Wicca is a religion like any other. We believe in a higher power, but we leave religion to the insecure."

Okay then. By higher power did she mean God? Or the devil? Or was there some deity in between, in the gray zone? This time I was afraid to ask.

"How did you know Rosina was meeting someone?" I asked instead.

"She told Tabitha, her tent mate, but Tabitha didn't think to ask her for a name, and Rosina didn't offer one. When she didn't come back, Tabitha went to find her and discovered her body."

"But this priestess knows who did it?"

"That's where you come in," Lucinda said. "We need you in the circle."

What?

Turned out, the gist was that they needed a thirteenth member, since one of the original twelve (not counting Aurora) had been stabbed to death. In the corn maze with a big knife, I might add. Not exactly a tempting offer. My flight instinct revved up.

"What happened to the original number thirteen?" I needed to know. If she'd been murdered, too, I was so out of here.

"Retired to Florida," was the response, which was unexpected and refreshingly innocuous. "Well?"

"Have you tried reaching out to Lori Spandle?" I suggested, feeling much less guilty throwing her just about anywhere—under a bus, over a cliff, into the rapids of a river. "She's been a witch her entire life."

"You," Lucinda said, shaking her head. "It has to be you. You already have some experience from last night."

Did I have a choice? What if Lucinda actually cast a spell and forced me to do it? Not that I believed in that (I kept telling myself). On the other hand, as she'd indicated, I did owe her for springing me from Johnny Jay's trap. And since there was no such thing as a high priestess that could be invoked at Lucinda's whim, nothing was going to come of this anyway. Right?

I weighed the risks.

The very least that could happen would be another strip-down around a campfire, which wouldn't be the end of the world. And even if Johnny Jay crashed the party again, he already knew he couldn't arrest us. Lucinda would see to that.

"Where is the ritual knife you used last night during your ceremony?" I asked her.

"The police have it," she said.

Ah, good, that was one wicked knife out of circulation.

I couldn't rule out the idea that Lucinda had ulterior motives for inviting me, but impulsively, I decided that I'd deal with that by staying close to the group and keeping my eyes open for trouble. I wouldn't trot off for any clandestine meetings in the corn maze. Plus, I'd make certain Hunter knew exactly where I was. Heck, he might even agree to back me up in some way.

At the moment, Lucinda and the others didn't know about my relationship with the lead investigator, and I intended to keep it that way. They wouldn't suspect that I was working for the other side. Yes, it would be the perfect opportunity to do a little investigating, maybe figure out which witch did what.

"When?" I asked.

"Tomorrow night," came the reply. She bent down over a plastic bin and hauled out a black cape. "Here," she said, thrusting it at me. "Wear this when you come."

She didn't have to mention not to wear any undergarments. That part I'd figured out.

"But the corn maze opens tomorrow," I told her. "That won't work."

"That won't interfere with our plan. It closes before dark."

She thought I was worried about her, but my concern was more for Al Mason. He would have a fit if he heard about this. "What's wrong with tonight?"

"It's going to start raining soon."

Ha! There wasn't a cloud in the sky. But why should I care, I reasoned. That gave me one more day to get my act in order. With any luck, Hunter would have a suspect in custody before then and the witches could get the heck out of town before I had to do anything.

I grinned. I'd successfully infiltrated the enemy camp. Hunter was going to be so proud.

"Okay," I said. "I'll do it."

Ten

After Lucinda drove me back to town, I paused before entering the store. My gaze fell on the old cemetery beside The Wild Clover. The building that housed my store had once been a Lutheran church, until the congregation grew and the church needed to expand. Lots of local Lutherans had been buried in this graveyard, but it had filled up long before my time, and a new one had been built on the outskirts of town close to the new church. The stones here were weathered, many of the names faded with age and almost indecipherable.

Religion. Funny that Lucinda would group Wiccans in with traditional religions. I bet the head of the Lutheran church would beg to differ with her on that point.

I'd arrived just in time for a rush of customers. That was life in this business. Dead as a doornail one minute; flooded with customers the next. Lori Spandle chose that exact time (planned, I'm sure, for maximum effect) to make a grand entrance and start stirring the pot.

"One of my best friends is at the doctor's office right now," she said in a loud voice. "And she might have swine flu." Her evil little face turned to the register, where I had begun checking out customers. "Has anybody been in Story's back-yard recently? I bet she's raising swine back there."

A few locals snickered at her attempt to ruffle my feath-ers. Seeing a showdown between the two of us was like having ringside seats at a wrestling match.

"Laugh all you want," Lori said to them, "but I'm going to prove Story is to blame and that my friend got it right inside this very store because of poor hygiene practices."

"That's nonsense and you know it," somebody said.

"Throw her out, Story," came another. Advice I would have gladly followed, except my customers were doing a mighty fine job of defending me and my store.

"Lori has a friend?" I heard someone mutter. I wanted to answer that question with a big fat "no," but I bit my lip.

This was going great.

They kept it up. "Spandle, are you trying to start some-thing again?"

"Yah, what are you up to?"

How the woman makes a living selling properties in this town is truly remarkable, considering Johnny Jay would beat her in a popularity contest, and nobody in Moraine likes him one bit.

"Just remember," I thought I'd better remind folks all the same, "nothing contagious ever started in my store, and it's never going to, either. We take pride in cleanliness. Isn't that right, everybody? Have you ever seen my store dirty?"

Everybody had to agree that they hadn't.

Which reminded me that I'd better dust the choir loft before the seniors' next card game up there. If anybody *was* going to find a fingertip of dust, it would be one of those women.

"Besides," I blurted out. It just flew at her in spite of my effort to control myself. "The only pig in this town is inside my store."

Lori's face went even redder as she caught my implication. "You'll pay for that remark!"

"You'll pay for your products or get out of my store," I replied.

After Lori stormed out and the rush of business slowed, I tried to call Aurora, but she didn't answer her phone. Starving, since I'd missed lunch, I grabbed a yogurt from the cooler and wolfed it down while taking a break outside, where I was surprised to discover dark clouds moving in from the northwest, just like Lucinda had predicted. How had she called that one so right?

Stanley came in later and told us that Aurora had been called down to the police station to give a written statement. He said he'd been walking down Main Street when he saw the chief turn onto my block. "I thought he might be after you," Stanley said to me, "but nope, he was being more sneaky than usual and was aiming for Aurora's place. I hung around long enough to watch him pull out with her in the back of his squad car."

"Why Aurora?" I wanted to know, but Stanley didn't have any additional information. He did have some other good news for me though.

"Now that your mother is preoccupied and isn't on the schedule, I'm willing to come back part-time," he announced.

"Yes! Please! That would be wonderful." Poor Stanley had endured more than his fair share of my mother's verbal abuse and deserved the peaceful work environment I could now give him. That is, if we could just keep Lori out of the store.

"I've already cleared it with Carrie Ann," he added.

Oh, right, I forgot about my manager. Old habits die hard, and I've done some impulsive decision making that Carrie Ann called me on later for not including her in the process. I'm trying to do better.

"I'll see you tomorrow," Stanley said.

Then I called home and woke Hunter. "Johnny Jay is out

of control," I told him after apologizing for disturbing his rest, only this was too important to ignore. "He hauled me down to the station and locked me up without benefit of even a phone call. I'd still be there if it weren't for one of the witches being an attorney. Now Johnny has Aurora. Stanley said he saw the chief creep his car down Willow Street, probably so he wouldn't wake you. Then he took off with Aurora in the back."

Hunter offered up a few select swear words for the chief. I had some I-told-you-sos at the ready but kept them in reserve for our "talk" later. That's what he gets for being nice to the jerk.

"And answer your phone if I call," I instructed him before hanging up, having successfully sicced him on Johnny Jay.

Next Dy came into the store. She wore jeans and a long-sleeved tee just like I wore and looked perfectly normal like the rest of us. No witch garb or magic wands. "I'm so sorry about Rosina," I said. "Were you there when it happened?"

Dy shook her head. "I went to bed as soon as they left. I'm so glad I wasn't there since I would have freaked out."

The twins had arrived to take over for what was left of the afternoon and into the evening. Usually on Thursdays, I'd spend the next hour or two catching up with paperwork, but I had other things on my mind. "Want me to show you around town?" I asked Dy, thinking it might take her mind off the death of one of her friends.

"Another time maybe," she said. "It's going to rain soon anyway."

"Come on then. Let me make you some tea at my house."

We walked the short distance back to Willow Street together. I saw that my man and his dog had taken off, probably after the chief. I couldn't help thinking about how empty Willow Street seemed. Patti had been nowhere in sight since our standoff yesterday, and Aurora was at the police station being grilled. It was just me and the new neighbor.

Before putting the kettle on, we toured the beeyard. Most of my bees were sticking close to home today, either inside their hives or hanging around the last blooms on the fall flowers.

"Honeybees don't make honey for us," I explained. "We are robbers just like bears are. They make it for themselves to supply winter calories."

Dy laughed. "Why am I surprised that bees eat honey?"

"You aren't alone," I said with a grin. "The general population is pretty ignorant when it comes to the life of bees. Beekeepers work hard to educate people. Come on, let's get that tea I promised you."

Hands wrapped around our teacups, hearing thunder rumble in the distance, we sat at my kitchen table.

"So how is Greg taking this?" I asked, just for the sake of having something to talk about.

"He's devastated, as you would expect, but he's also riddled with guilt."

"Guilt?"

"His dad and aunt were estranged."

I nodded. "Everybody in town knew that."

"I first met Greg through Rosina. He and his aunt secretly kept in touch. When I moved to Moraine, he came up with a plan to reconcile his two closest family members."

"Did Rosina agree to his plan?" I asked.

"She did. Welcomed the opportunity, in fact."

I took a sip of my tea and thought about that. "I can't believe Al went for it. He's stubborn and pretty unyielding."

"Greg didn't tell him." She smiled sadly. "Perhaps he thought once Rosina arrived at the farm, she could charm him."

Her magic hadn't helped. Instead, she was dead. No wonder Greg felt guilty. He'd brought her here, to her death.

"It isn't his fault," I said. "His intentions were good. The one to blame is the one who stabbed her to death."

"In the meantime, he's thrown himself into working on the corn maze," Dy said with a sigh. "They're scrambling to finish by tomorrow, but Greg says they found extra help for the corn stand. He claims they're going to make it. I bet they work right through this approaching bad weather."

"It's really opening as planned then?"

"Greg says this is the time of year the farm makes most of its profits. The corn maze is a big part of that. He and Al argued that point with the authorities when they were considering closing it down. The police have cordoned off the section where Rosina died, but they will try to be through with that part of the investigation in time for the grand opening."

"So you know where her body was found, too? I assumed that information was being withheld."

"Greg told me."

Of course, the farm belonged to his family, so he'd be one of the first to know. But he shouldn't have gone blabbing it around. This could spread like wildfire if somebody didn't contain it soon. "Please don't tell anyone else about that. It could hurt Al's business."

"It's a closely held secret."

"But you just told me," I replied with a major amount of frustration.

Dy gave me a mysterious Mona Lisa smile. "You're one of us now," she told me.

Not wanting to get in deeper than I already was with this group, I got firm. "I am not one of you. Not even close. I don't believe in witchcraft or magic spells." There!

"Relax," Dy said, not looking offended in the least, so I suspected that my reaction was a common one. "I didn't offer any more information than you already had from your conversation with Lucinda."

"So you talked to her?"

She nodded. "A little while ago. On the phone. See, nothing magical about it."

"Lucinda wants me to help with the ritual tomorrow," I said. "You'll be there, right?"

Dy looked pained and grudgingly said, "Of course. When Lucinda tells us to jump, we ask how high. How did she talk you into joining us?"

"I owe her a favor." I told Dy about the lockup, and how Lucinda rescued me after Aurora alerted her. I finished with, "Aurora must have seen me get into the chief's car," convinced that was the most logical explanation.

Then we got into a discussion about witch names, and I found out that Dyanna was born Susan, that Tabitha was Karen, that Lucinda really is Lucy (which I already knew through Hunter), and all the other coven members' names until my head started to spin.

"How am I ever going to remember all that?" I said.

"You don't have to." Dy took a sip of her tea. "Our witch names are all you really need."

"Do you change them legally?" I asked since Hunter had mentioned that Claudene had officially changed hers.

"No, why would we bother? And besides, we use our given names all the time—at our jobs, filing taxes, mortgages. Only our close friends call us by our witch names, and as the first neighbor to welcome me to town, you certainly qualify."

If the witches weren't in the habit of legally changing their names, why had Claudene gone to all the trouble to officially change hers? And did it matter?

After Dy went home, I called Grams.

"I heard about that poor Mason woman's death," she said, which was a given considering my grandmother's honored position in the community.

"Why was she called Crazy Claudene?" I asked after the usual pleasantries.

"That poor girl just wasn't normal from the very beginning," my sweet grandmother said. "She went to school with your mother, you know, so she came to our house a few times, but Claudene just wasn't quite right."

"So what does that mean?" I asked. "In the scheme of things are any of us actually 'normal'? And who gets to decide? Normal in Moraine is way different than normal is in a big city, right?"

"Story, sweetie, Claudene talked to animals."

I've done my share of that, too. Hasn't everyone? "So?"

"So she listened to them, and they talked back. She had conversations with ghosts, too."

"Ghosts?" I might have my doubts about witches, but I believed in ghosts. "She talked to ghosts?"

"I thought her interest in the paranormal was harmless at first. Until she talked the other girls, your mother included, into a séance using a Ouija board and scared those young people almost out of their minds. The other girls insisted she'd let evil spirits into the room, and the stories about that night got wilder and wilder. The other parents and I began keeping a closer eye on that Claudene.

"Then," Grams continued, "things got really dicey, and she almost killed one of the girls after convincing her to drink a love potion to get the boy she had a big crush on. Claudene claimed it would make her irresistible. You know how young girls are about boys!"

Did I ever! That's all we thought about. Boys.

Grams went on, "And there was a popular song at the time, about love and potions. I forget the title."

"Love Potion No. 9."

"That's it. Claudene mixed up a brew of some sort for the girl. One of the ingredients was rhubarb. I'm sure she didn't mean any harm when she added the leaves."

"Rhubarb leaves are poisonous!" In this area of the countryside, we all pretty much know that. But had I known it when I was in high school? Probably not, because I was pining over one boy after the other and was way too busy for that kind of trivia.

"After that, none of the girls were allowed near her,"

Grams continued her story, "and soon, the family decided she needed a fresh start and sent her to live with relatives in Milwaukee."

So Claudene had had witch tendencies from an early age. Interesting. "I wonder if anyone from those days kept in touch with her," I said out loud. "I think I'll ask Mom a few questions."

"You should talk to Mabel's niece, Iris," Grams said. Mabel was Grams's best friend, but I didn't want her to get involved; she'd start making phone calls, setting up a meeting, et cetera. Then every last detail, every question and answer, would hit the grapevine.

"I'll just call Mom tomorrow," I decided.

"Your mother is busy with her wedding plans and is a complete airhead right now. Tom, Tom, Tom, that's all she can focus on!" Grams chuckled and I joined in, thinking of my pragmatic mother becoming a ditz. Stranger things have happened, but at the moment I couldn't think of a single example.

"Besides," Grams said, "don't you want to hear it from the horse's mouth?"

"The horse's mouth?" I repeated.

"Iris was the one who drank the love potion. She's the one who almost died."

Eleven

I puzzled over the story Grams had told me until Hunter finally came home. I'd just about pinned him down for our "talk" when we became distracted by the approaching storm, which slammed into town with such fury that the lights flickered and the electricity went out. So we stood together at a window watching bolts of lightning illuminate the sky like fireworks and listening to rain beat the ground, turning to hail at one point. Not much use having a serious conversation with all that going on.

I couldn't help thinking of the campers, wondering if they were safe and dry inside their tents. If Lucinda's work as an attorney ever fell through, she should apply for a position as weather woman on a local network television station. She was way more accurate than the current weather guy, who hadn't warned us about any of this.

The worst of the storm eventually moved on but left my neighborhood without power and with a steady chilly rain falling.

What else to do in weather like this but to go to bed early, right? Hunter was fully on board with this plan, which I thought was a good indicator of exciting things to come my way.

Only he fell asleep immediately.

That hadn't been *my* plan.

Ben had followed us upstairs, and he, too, snorted in his sleep from his bed on the floor. Not even the canine was going to keep me company.

Darn! Now what?

I got up and went into the kitchen where I called my sister Holly from my cell phone. I had to tell someone the story of the visiting witches, including my brief foray into the world of bare-naked rituals. I so love having a sister to share confidences with. We've had our problems, but I couldn't image life without her.

During my tale of derring-do, Holly made all the appropriate responses—gasps, chuckles, *oh no*s, and *oh my God*s when I got to the part about the witches chasing us out of the water, another gasp about the spotlight and Johnny Jay stepping onto the stage.

Holly really ratcheted up her dramatic responses when I got to the part about how one of them died, which she'd heard about at the store, but I had some pretty exciting filler to add.

"What does Hunter say about all this?" she asked when I finally wound down.

"I'd tell him everything if I ever had the chance. Either he's off investigating and not answering my calls or he's sound asleep from exhaustion. It's been like living alone lately."

"Welcome to my world," Holly said. With hubby Max on the road all the time, my sister was almost like a widow, a business widow, if there is such a thing. Then she added, "You two should tie the knot. Why haven't you? Doesn't he want to?"

"It's both of us," I told her. "I'm afraid to tie any more noose knots. Once was once too many, so this time I have to be absolutely sure."

"You *are* sure."

"Just agreeing to live with him was traumatic." And it had been. I almost drove myself crazy going back and forth, one day thinking it was the best idea ever, the next deciding absolutely not.

"But you made the right decision. You seem so much happier since he moved in."

Which was true. Hunter is a fine man, and yes, I *had* made the right decision to have him move in. But one day at a time, I tell myself. The two of us need a little more time.

"So what's going on with Patti?" Holly asked, changing the subject, which was a relief because I was starting to think I might still have residual issues from disastrous marriage number one.

It was then that I thought I heard movement on the stairs. Was Hunter up? But then Ben walked in and greeted me with a knee lick. "She's still avoiding me," I said, letting Ben outside. "Hasn't even been in the store, hasn't stopped at the house. In fact, now that I think about it, she hasn't been slinking around in the shadows spying, either. Or at least, not that I've been aware of. Maybe she's gotten better at it."

"That's not like her not to sneak around."

"I know, right? But get this, it turns out she's deathly afraid of the witches and witchcraft. She's the one who called Johnny Jay about the ritual. It's obvious she really believes in all that stuff." I walked over to a window and peered through the dark. "I see a light on in her lookout tower," I told my sister. "Probably plotting against the new neighbor."

Patti has a room in her upstairs set up with all kinds of surveillance equipment. When she isn't snooping on the neighbors, she surfs the Internet for bits and pieces of our private lives to put together haphazardly and then present as facts through the gossip mill. Patti isn't the town darling, that's for sure. By now, she would know about the murder, so it was only a matter of time before she resurfaced, once more back in my life.

"I'll have to make peace with her," I said. "And find out how much she knows about the witches and the murder."

Right after we hung up, I heard a masculine throat clearing coming from the vicinity of the stairs. Hunter walked out into the light, and judging by the expression on his face, he'd heard some of my conversation with my sister. But how much?

"So . . ." he began. Any sentence that begins with "so" has the potential for trouble. "What a surprise. You're getting involved in this case, which is exactly where you don't belong." I gave him a cheesy grin. I would have edited the conversation if I'd known he was listening. What a sneak!

"I could point out that I've helped solve a few cases along the way." He couldn't deny it. I'd been in the right place (or wrong place, depending upon the point of view) at the right time on more than one occasion.

"And you can't even blame Patti Dwyre this time like you usually do," he said. "Even *she* knows when to stay out of the way."

"That remains to be seen," I shot back. "Besides, I thought you'd be proud of me. I can spy for you, find out where all the witches were when Rosina was murdered."

Hunter had his arms crossed. Not a good sign. "That's my job," he said. "I've interviewed each of them."

"And what did they say?"

"I have nothing more to divulge. You and I aren't partners . . ." He saw my face darken. Or maybe it was the dagger eyes I was giving him, those little slits that mean I'm getting ticked off. "In a professional sense, I meant." He took my hand. "Look, I just don't want to see you hurt. A murderer is still on the loose."

"I'll be careful."

"If you need incentive, I can go into graphic, gory details about what a knife like that does to a body."

I tried not to gulp. "You're starting to sound like Johnny Jay." That reminded me. "The coven had a knife during their ritual. Lucinda was waving it around in the air, calling on who-knows-what. Was it her knife? She did it, didn't she?"

"You don't give up, do you?" Hunter sighed, deep and heavy. Good, I was winning. I could tell by that sigh. He went on, "Jackson has the body and the knife, which had been left at the crime scene. The women acknowledge that the knife belongs to them, but they also claim it went missing at some point during the night." Jackson Davis was the local medical examiner. He and I go way back, and we've helped each other out in the past. Or rather, he's helped me.

"The knife *did* vanish," I said, going into a brief overview of my involvement. "Lucinda had it one minute, but it was nowhere in sight when they all went swimming. And it's not like they could've been hiding it anywhere."

"Promise me you'll stay away from that whole bunch from now on."

"I'd feel safer," I said, avoiding making any promises, "if you'd answer my phone calls. You know I don't call to chitchat when you're working."

"You want me to keep my phone on?"

"Yes!"

"So . . ."—here we went again with the so—". . . Ben and I are on surveillance. Let's just pretend for a moment we have a violent suspect involved. Maybe he's armed, but I'm not sure. We're about to make an arrest. And just then, my phone rings. Now he's alerted to our presence, and the danger has intensified for me and Ben as well."

"Then put it on vibrate."

"I sometimes hear yours when it vibrates. I wouldn't risk it."

Visions of my man and our best canine friend in serious

danger did it. "Since you put it that way, I guess I can learn to live with being ignored. But what about Johnny Jay? You have to get rid of him. And what happened with Aurora?"

"He questioned both of you without passing it by me first. I made sure she was released."

"And Johnny's out, right?"

Hunter really knows how to shut me up when he wants to. And right now, he wanted to. I was relieved that he hadn't brought up the first part of my conversation with Holly. Hunter wasn't a dodger; he liked to face things head-on, so if he'd heard the part about how agreeing to let him live with me was so traumatic, he would have brought it up. I'd have to be much more careful in the future.

We never did get back to the subject of the chief and covens.

Twelve

Friday morning arrived cool, crisp, and sunny. Hunter was still sleeping, and I left him that way, quietly tiptoeing out of the bedroom. I was relieved to discover that the rash I'd suffered because of the pine tree had faded and stopped itching. While I was making coffee, Stanley Peck called my cell phone with an offer. "How about I open up this morning, take your place today, and give you a much-needed break from responsibility?"

Bless the ground that man walked on. "Yes, thank you, you are an absolute peach," I told him, signing off with an improved outlook. It was going to be a great day.

I went outside to check on my honeybees, who were lounging, too, inside their hives, waiting for the day to warm up enough to launch in search of what might be their last quest for nectar before cold weather grounded them until spring.

Looking up at Patti's window from my hives, I caught a

flash of motion. Even with a murder and these weird visitors in town, life had been much less stressful without her around creating fireworks. Then I felt guilty for thinking that, because the woman didn't have any other friends and considered me her best friend. As annoying as she could be at times, I couldn't wish her away forever. Not that that was an option for the future anyway. From past experience, I knew that eventually Patti would show up out of the blue and go back to sticking to me like duct tape.

Dy came over as I finished checking the hives and finding them healthy and in good working order.

"Hey," I greeted her, moving toward the door. "Come on inside. I have a hot cup of coffee with your name on it."

Once we were settled at the kitchen table with steaming cups in front of us, I asked, "How well did you know Rosina?"

"Pretty well. She was one of the original members. Lucinda, Rosina, me, we're the only three left from the original group. Or rather were before Rosina died. Now it's only Lucinda and me. Most of the original thirteen left in the past year."

"Why the high turnover?" I asked.

Dy considered before answering. "When we originally formed the coven, we all agreed to certain terms, especially that it was unethical to manipulate others with our magic. That was a hard-and-fast rule. Our intention toward others is what colors us one way or the other."

"As in black or white."

Dy nodded, and I noticed that she had tensed up along the way, a scowl etched on her face. She seemed edgy, nervous, not at all the same cheerful woman I'd met two days ago. "Exactly. And Lucinda has been moving into decidedly gray areas, going places with her craft that concern me."

"In what way?"

"It's hard to describe to someone from the outside, but sometimes there's a fine line between a curse and a charm."

I held my tongue (for once). I could see her point—both were intended to manipulate others, or at least to control circumstances and outcomes. Who got to decide where that fine line was? "How did Rosina feel about the new direction?" I asked.

"She had concerns and voiced them in private, among the three of us. I felt caught in the middle. But eventually Rosina usually gave in and went along with whatever Lucinda decided. I and most of the others couldn't agree. One of the reasons I moved out here was to make a clean break. Apparently, I didn't go far enough away."

I had a flash of insight regarding the conversation I'd overheard between Dy and Greg that night beside the fire. He'd encouraged her to be patient, said they would leave her alone soon enough, go back where they came from. Now it made sense.

There could only be one queen bee, and this coven had three who had been duking it out for the supreme position. With Rosina dead and Dy moving on, Lucinda would be the only one left to rule the workers. Sort of like a beehive and the reigning queen. There could be only one.

After Dy went home, I sat and pondered the situation. My impulsive, quick-to-judge side was suspicious of Lucinda, mainly because I hadn't liked her from the moment I met her. There was something dark about her, and I didn't mean dark arts, either. She had secrets. I was sure of it.

And what about my new neighbor? Dy was the one who had been trying to escape the coven, and she hadn't been too happy about hosting a ritual, based on her conversation with Greg. But if she was the killer, wouldn't she have stabbed the leader to death instead of the follower?

What about all the rest of the coven? I hadn't even touched the tip of the iceberg as far as the others were concerned. And there were simply too many witches to watch with the two eyes I had, so narrowing my focus was a given. Anyway, instinct told me answers to Rosina's murder were with the original members, not the newbies. Something from their past, perhaps. I needed to look into Claudene Mason's personal history, and a good place to start would be with Mabel's relative, Iris, the woman who had been her girlhood friend—or victim.

Before I could plot my day, Hunter came into the kitchen. He let Ben outside and sat down to the cup of coffee I'd poured for him. I proceeded to tell him about my recent conversation with Dy.

"Yeah, that's almost word for word what she said in her statement."

"Oh," I said, a bit deflated.

Hunter studied me across the table. "I've been thinking," he said, "about taking you on as a partner after all. You presented a solid case, and I should be utilizing your talents."

My eyebrows shot up in stunned amazement, and if they could have morphed into question marks, they would have. "Partner? Really?"

He nodded. "Yes, but with conditions." He laid it all out on the table (figuratively, of course). "You own your own den of deceit and dubious dealings," he said, watching with an amused grin as my eyes rolled up in my head. "Lots of rumors fly around down at The Wild Clover. Most of them are outrageously inaccurate, but occasionally you get a good one that has some validity."

Oh geez. Can we say patronizing? Hunter wanted me to just sit down there at the store and listen to the customers, maybe prod and poke them into relating a useful tidbit? Really?

Sure enough . . .

"Keep your ears open," he went on, his tone ultra-professional and secretive, laying it on thick. "Ask questions about Claudene's past. Absorb. You have a unique position, one I can't fill as the detective on the case. Your customers trust you and might open up."

I had a better idea. Hunter could sit at the store for the day while Ben and I would hunt down bad guys. "And what will you be doing during all this espionage on my part?" *How dumb does he think I am?*

"My job, as usual."

"So this is your partnership offer?" Can you believe the guy? "Tell me more. What's the condition you mentioned that goes along with this amazing opportunity?"

"You stay away from the farm. No trespassing there, no dancing around flames, nothing."

I couldn't help myself, and I was miffed that he knew so much about my whereabouts on a constant basis. "You have got to be kidding! This is your deal?"

He actually looked surprised. "I'm making concessions here. Usually my requests are for you to keep the locals from going off on tangents. I'm condoning this one. Gossip away."

Right before I saw nothing but red and started snorting fire, Hunter's face relaxed and he grinned. He'd been kidding around, messing with me in that boyish way I had loved up until right this minute. He burst out laughing when he saw my expression change.

"That wasn't funny!" I exclaimed, really annoyed that he'd gotten the best of me. "Be serious."

"Okay, let's start over," Hunter said. "How about this— I'll tell you everything I know, you keep me in your loop, and we'll decide together how to proceed. How does that sound?"

Much, much better.

"Besides," he said, "anybody who would strip down to nothing and wade into the thick of things to protect a friend like you did has to be really, really brave."

He laughed out loud. "Or," he added, "really, really reckless and foolhardy."

Okay, then. I was going with "gutsy, bold, and courageous." Whatever, Hunter had invited me into the inner circle. I was in.

Thirteen

"The emergency call was rerouted from Moraine to Waukesha at approximately four o'clock in the morning," Hunter told me. "One of the camping guests found the body right inside the entrance to the corn maze. She immediately recognized the deceased as one of her group and went screaming back to camp. Everyone was alerted. Lucinda took over, rousing Al and Greg Mason and contacting the police."

"What was Tabitha doing up and about at that time of the night?" I asked.

"Wandering." He gave me a puzzled look. "But I don't recall mentioning her name just now."

I kept going since Hunter hadn't had a second cup of coffee and that was to my advantage. If I told him I'd been out at the farm asking questions, he would *not* be happy with me. "Johnny must've told me. If she was alone, then she doesn't have an alibi."

Hunter looked frustrated. "Not a single one of them has

an alibi that I can accept at face value, not from the time they left our neighborhood until we responded to the emergency call. A few local residents don't have alibis, either."

"Aurora? It's my fault she was even over at Dy's. I suggested her. Aurora had never met any of them before that night."

"As far as I'm concerned, Aurora isn't one of our top suspects."

"Oh, good."

"In fact, it was your name as a potential suspect that came up on my radar, when the police chief asked me to identify several articles of clothing."

I came close to snorting coffee onto the table.

Hunter gave me a hard stare. "Johnny Jay says you denied any involvement at all, didn't even admit to being with the witches."

"You know how he gets. All belligerent and accusatory. He would have locked me up."

"But your clothes *were* right there."

"Maybe I forgot them earlier. I do live next door. Johnny was just fishing as usual."

Hunter's eyes held a certain criticism I didn't appreciate, but I let it pass. "Anyway," he went on, "Dyanna Crane says that she stayed home and spent the rest of the night alone. Lucinda says she was alone in her own tent. All the others shared tents and vouched for one another, but none of their claims are exactly rock-solid alibis." He shook his head. "Women!"

I gave him a glare. "What's that supposed to mean? Are you saying women are big liars?"

"No more than men. But this bunch all claimed they were together every single minute—except then I asked them if they'd visited the restroom, and of course every one of them said yes."

Oh, right, potty stops, that's true. Females are prone to

that, proven repeatedly by the long lines at public restrooms. Why is that?

"More than one of them might be involved," I suggested. "You never know."

"I was home alone, too, but that's only because you worked all night."

"And I'm almost positive you didn't kill the woman."

"Thanks for the vote of confidence."

I poured more coffee for both of us, feeling for once like I was actually part of a real investigation. Finally, I was getting the respect I deserve. At least from one law enforcement official. Johnny Jay didn't count one way or the other.

"And the knife that was used?" I asked.

"Jackson established that the knife found at the scene was the murder weapon. We figured as much, but the ME has to scientifically confirm even the obvious. And yes, it's the same knife that belonged to the coven."

We sat in comfortable silence for a few minutes. But since Hunter was cooperating and sharing information so freely, I didn't want to interrupt the flow by changing the topic, so I said, "The only positive in this whole mess is that Al gets to open the corn maze today right on schedule. But the poor man must be distraught."

Hunter was grim. "If the murder weapon hadn't been found with the body, he'd have a financial crisis to deal with as well as a dead sister. If it hadn't been there, we would have had to go over every inch of the maze, and that would have taken significantly more time."

"Didn't you have to anyway?"

"Sure, but if we didn't have a weapon we would have had to rip the entire thing apart. It wouldn't have resembled a corn maze by the time we finished."

"I wonder who she went to meet," I said, thinking out loud.

"What makes you think she was meeting someone?"

"Lucinda mentioned it."

"Speculation," Hunter scoffed. "Unless the leader of that group has information she hasn't shared with us."

"It stands to reason, though, that Rosina went to meet someone, otherwise why would she have been away from the camp? I bet whoever killed her *summoned* her to the maze."

I put finger quotes around the word *summoned* just for effect.

Hunter cocked his head to the right (a habit I think is cute) and appraised me. "Summoned? As in invoked? Don't tell me you believe in all that stuff."

"No, of course not," I said, not sure whether I was being truthful. The jury was still out on my beliefs. "Dy said that most of the coven members are new, that there were some power issues going on between them."

"Dyanna Crane is on my list of follow-ups for today. We talked yesterday, but I'm going to ask all of them to repeat their stories, starting with her."

"I'd like to find out more about Rosina's past."

"That's on my agenda today, too."

"Well then that's one thing you won't have to do. I'll take care of it."

I felt a small flame of excitement at the thought of delving into the dead woman's past. Genealogy has always intrigued me, so I know a little about digging for details on a person's life. Before I opened the store and started the bee business, Grams and I had traced our family history way back to the colonial days. There was something magical (not the witchcraft kind) about searching through old documents—birth certificates, death notices, census logs—and hanging out in historical sections of libraries, not to even mention the wealth of information to be found online. Our own town librarians had been a huge help in our research.

Not that I'd have to go that far back with Rosina, but

researching her recent past could be fascinating. And might even lead to the one clue that solved this case. Someone wanted her dead and that someone had a reason. What if it was buried in her past?

I told Hunter what Grams had told me about Rosina's teenage antics, and how her family had shipped her out. "Grams said that my mother hung around with her and some others, including another girl named Iris." I went on to tell Hunter about the love potion. "I'm going to see what Iris has to say."

"Good idea."

Music to my ears!

Hunter stood up, ready to conquer the world with Ben at his side.

"Any more information you want to share with me before I go off to solve this case?" I asked with a wide smile.

Hunter grinned. "Let's see what we each come up with and meet later at Stu's Bar and Grill. And for now, remember our deal. I did my part; you do yours by staying away from the farm and those witches. We still have a killer loose, and more than likely that person is at the farm."

"Of course," I responded, avoiding eye contact with him when I realized he still expected that to be part of the deal.

After that, I watched Hunter walk over to Dy's house and knock on the door. She opened it and he disappeared inside.

I walked down to the store, where I'd left my truck . . . and took off for Country Delight Farm for one more go-around with the witches before immersing myself in the dead woman's past.

Hunter, as should be apparent by now, is not the boss of me.

Fourteen

❀

I was waylaid on the way through town.

I didn't make it even one block before I pulled over at the Country Delight farm stand. I had two valid reasons—one of them personal, the other professional, due to my new position as Hunter's right hand. (Was that going overboard? Maybe.) Anyway, the first had to do with thirst. I'd overdone the coffee between chatting with Dy and picking Hunter's brain in the kitchen and hadn't had any other fluids before or since. And apple cider is the perfect antidote to dehydration.

The second reason was that I saw it was Al Mason himself manning the stand, which struck me as unusual. He wasn't a sit-down type of guy, although after what had happened to his sister, he had every right to be weak-kneed. Besides, wasn't the maze opening soon?

And I really needed to offer him my condolences.

I couldn't imagine how awful it must feel to lose your sister. Just the thought of not having Holly made me want to break down and bawl. I steeled my resolve and pulled over before I'd barely started out.

Al Mason wore overalls and a straw hat and looked every bit the country bumpkin, which worked to his advantage during the fall season. City visitors to the corn maze expected to run into clodhoppers, and Al didn't disappoint them. He's the spitting image of Captain Kangaroo's sidekick Mr. Green Jeans.

Underneath the hillbilly stereotype, though, Al is a shrewd businessman who cares about the community. On the downside, I feel he takes life a little too seriously and has a low tolerance for nonconformity, especially in family members who go off to delve into magic. Diversity is not his bag. If Al were a political animal (which he isn't) he'd definitely be a right-right-right-wing ultra-conservative.

By now he must have discovered his lodgers weren't exactly what a voter would label as moderate conservatives. The witches leaned so heavily to the left of center, they were in jeopardy of tipping over. Al threatened to go over the opposite way. Not a good combo.

"Hey, Al," I greeted him while surveying all the goodies on his table. Then I noticed he hadn't sprung up from the lawn chair he occupied and that his right leg was propped up on a stool, the ankle encased in an ACE bandage. "What happened to you?"

"Story, good to see you again." Al actually lifted his straw hat in an act of old-fashioned courtesy. "Just clumsy on my part. Tripped and fell, somehow landed on my ankle, all two hundred pounds of me. Lucky I didn't snap it in two."

"When did this happen?"

"Few days ago."

"Did you see a doctor?"

"No sense in that. It's only a sprain. What would he do but tape it up just the same as I did?"

"That's too bad what with the corn maze opening and all."

"Yah, nothing like this happens at a good time. But my family insists they can open just fine without me and since I need to sit, this is as good a place as any. I've been taking some painkillers I saved up, but they knock me out cold. Only use them at night."

"You really should go to the doctor," I suggested.

There was a pause in our conversation while I got ready to offer my condolences. What does a person say under these circumstances? What possible words could I speak that would comfort the man? Al filled the awkward space with small talk.

"Since we're on the subject of doctors, that friend of Lori Spandle's doesn't have swine flu," Al announced. "The fat mouth realtor has been shouting from the treetops. I told her to shut it up or she's going to scare away all the tourists and visitors to my farm."

"That's good news." At least on that topic, Spandle would have to stop breathing down my neck like the blood-sucker she is. "And anytime you want help stuffing Lori with sawdust and mounting her in the field as a scarecrow, let me know. I'd be happy to assist."

Al gave me a little smile, then said, "I don't know how I would have managed without Joan. That woman is a saint. She's over at the farm putting the final touches on the corn maze before it opens at ten. She and Greg have everything ready to go. Me?" He glanced at his leg. "All I'm good for is sitting around. Like you said, bad timing on my part."

"I'm glad to hear that you're opening for business, after what happened and all," I said, finally seeing an opening. "I'm so sorry for the loss of your sister. I met her at the store and she seemed nice." There—not much, but something.

"Thank you kindly. It's been quite a shock." Al shook his head sadly. "I wanted to shut down the whole thing after what happened, but Greg talked sense into me. The maze and the fall events at the farm are my bread and butter. I wouldn't stay above water without the profits from this part of the year. I'd lose it all. The farm operates on a tight margin."

"Do the police have a suspect in mind?"

Al's face clouded over, and his jawline hardened into an angry line as he said, "Those witches did it—trust me. And they did it where they did it for a reason. What was Claudene thinking by bringing those people to my farm? And then going and getting murdered in some kind of cult ritual practically in front of my nose. If I didn't know better, I'd say she planned it on purpose to hurt me."

"Hunter didn't mention anything about a ritual," I told him, a bit taken aback by his reaction. Was he actually blaming his sister for her own murder?

Al was off on a tangent. He leaned forward. "The lot of them should be burned at the stake for what they did." Al paused and thought about that idea for a few seconds as though he might arrange for it to happen. After all, he had plenty of flammable cornstalks. Then he said, "Claudene always was a problem, from the very beginning right until the bitter end. No love lost there." He blinked at me. "Sorry, Story, but it's true and it's been true from way back."

"Easy now, Al. Nobody in their right mind would actually plan their own murder. Hunter will find whoever did this and punish them according to the law. We don't have to take justice into our own hands."

"And Greg!" Al was gaining steam like a runaway locomotive on a downward slope. He hadn't heard a word I'd said. "He failed to mention the witchcraft part when he came to me about letting them camp on the farm. Never mentioned that my sister was coming, too. Just said they were friends of his, and all the time scheming to get us face-to-face. Some friends they turned out to be. If I didn't need the help, I'd send him packing right along with the bloody-handed coven of evil witches."

Al crossed himself, reminding me of his Catholic roots. Then he slumped back in the lawn chair and rearranged his injured leg.

"It's a hard time," I reassured him. "But things will get better. You'll see."

Al humphed like he didn't believe it. "The worst part is that I can't even run them off. That detective boyfriend of yours ordered them to stay right where they are, in my apple orchard."

"Hunter's only doing his job. You'll see. He'll find the person who did this fast enough and they'll be gone from town for good." As I said it, I saw Hunter and Ben drive past, heading toward the farm, which had been *my* next stop. I'd have to rearrange my plans for the day, because I wasn't about to blatantly flaunt my total disregard for that addendum he'd concocted as a condition to my being involved in the case. Why aggravate him right out of the gate?

Hunter saw me and waved.

Ben spotted me, too, and his ears perked up in what I've come to realize is a friendly salute.

"What a mess." That was Al's parting comment.

He could say that again.

I returned to my truck with the apple cider and revised my to-do list while satisfying my thirst with the pure, sweetly tart beverage.

My sister called my cell phone.

"We're having a meeting at Grams's house right after lunch."

"About?"

"The wedding, silly. What else could it be about?"

I don't know, I could have said, maybe to commiserate over one of Mom's old schoolmates having been stabbed to death? Sometimes my family can be so insensitive. Instead I said, "And you're telling me this because . . . ?"

"You need to be there, too."

"Since when?"

"Since I made you my assistant."

"You did?" I felt annoyed and pleased all at once. Annoyed that my younger sister had the lead position and it was in her power to decide who got to play along and who didn't (I'm used to being the one in that position). But also pleased that I was finally a member of the team.

I let the annoyance go, just shook it right off like a pesky insect. Holly could be the pre-wedding queen bee as planner, and during the marriage ceremony Mom would be queen for the day. I'd take a backseat to both of them, and be perfectly happy there. Sort of like being the vice president. Having an important position without any of the responsibility.

See? Absolute proof that I'm not a control freak like my mother. I can follow really well if I want to.

"Grams says make sure you have room for dessert when you come." And with that we disconnected.

Since I couldn't go to the farm, I decided to leave the truck parked where it was and walk back to Willow Street, where I headed up Aurora's driveway. I found her in her garden center getting ready for her ten o'clock opening.

Don't I wish The Wild Clover opened mid-morning like the garden center and the corn maze? What a treat that would be. But my customers depend on me to be open for them as they come and go from work, so the store has to open at the crack of dawn.

"Story," Aurora said when the door chime alerted her. "I was hoping we'd see each other soon."

"Me, too," I said, leaning against the counter while she fired up her computerized receipt system from the other side. "Thank you so much for coming to my rescue yesterday. The chief had me in lockup."

Aurora grinned. "It's the least I could do after you cared so much about me the other night."

"I'll never admit this publicly," I told her, "but Johnny Jay played a part in your rescue. Mine, too, even though he doesn't know it. Showing up like that. When they chased us from the river, I thought we were goners."

"And then instead of working us over, Lucinda simply ordered us away," Aurora added. "Being surrounded like that . . . it was freaky."

"Looking back, I might have overreacted," I said. "Sometimes my imagination gets the best of me, and it was working overtime watching all those witches dancing around."

It wouldn't be the first time I'd plowed right into a situation thinking it was worse than it was. But as the old saying goes, better safe than sorry.

Aurora shook her head adamantly and said, "Something alerted you to danger. Look what happened to Rosina later. If you hadn't sensed something wrong, I would have been out at their camp. That could have been me."

Now it was my turn to shake my head. "I don't think so. Rosina went into the corn maze to meet someone. It certainly wasn't a random act."

We thought about that for a few seconds, then Aurora said, "I'm not going back. Lucinda called and practically ordered me to appear for the next big event, but I've had my fill of them. After your warning and what happened to Rosina, I don't want anything to do with that bunch."

"Did you tell Lucinda that?" I couldn't imagine the witch being the type who took no for an answer.

"I couldn't bring myself to," Aurora admitted. "I'm just going to be a no-show. If Lucinda confronts me later, I'll come up with an excuse. Like my car broke down on the way."

Originally I'd planned to discuss my own participation in the upcoming ceremony, but I reconsidered quickly after finding out she was afraid to go back. I didn't want her to worry about me or to try to talk me out of it, or pull the whole clairvoyance thing and tell me my future. Instead I said, "You better disappear for the entire night. Lucinda will be out on her broom with her flying monkeys searching for you."

"That's what I'm afraid of, but don't worry about me. I know how to blend into the woodwork." I had my doubts. As much as I like and admire Aurora, she is NOT blending material. She literally shines with her own special uniqueness.

I asked the one question that had been on my mind ever since Lucinda marched into Johnny's interrogation room. "How did you know I was in need of a jailbreak?"

Aurora thought about that for a minute or two—brows knit together, concentration showing on her face, then puzzlement, like the question was too big and complex for her. "I guess the same way you knew I needed rescue from the witches."

What kind of answer was that? I'd expected something profound. Like she'd used her sixth sense, she'd heard my voice wafting through space, pleading for help, after which she would repeat my exact words back to me to prove she had, then go on to convince me of the existence of an alternate reality that interacts with our physical world.

Proof one way or the other would be a welcome relief instead of so much doubt. Why couldn't I just take a position regarding the practice of magic and stick with it?

Why had I been so sure Aurora was in trouble?

"It was instinct on my part," I told her. "A scary thought popped into my head and it grew and grew and I just had to get you out of there."

Aurora nodded in understanding. "We'll never know if you were right or not."

I leaned over the counter. "You're playing me, right? Come on, admit it. You saw me get into Johnny's car."

"No, I didn't." Now she was shaking her head. "Absolutely not."

"Then how?"

"A scary thought popped into my head . . ."

"And it grew and grew," I finished for her. "That's my line."

"The truth is that I don't know how I knew. I just did. And I was right."

No way could I deny that!

Walking back to the truck, I thought about all the times I'd had "feelings." Call it intuition or telepathy or whatever, any way you look at it, it's totally undefinable and inexplicable. I'd have to pay more attention in the future, tune in to those little knocks that happen inside my brain when they call out for my attention.

I'd had one of those sensations while watching the ritual preparation. I'd thought Aurora was in danger, but maybe it was Rosina who was the one actually in trouble. After all, one of the thirteen women really had died.

What if I could fine-tune and sharpen my instincts into something really cool?

Who knew? Maybe I could turn a gift like that into something useful. Like powering up my mind and sending Lori Spandle off into outer space. To the moon, Lori.

Yes, I definitely could see a whole lot of exciting possibilities.

Fifteen

✥

Mabel Whelan's niece, Iris, lived in the town of Erin on a road that ended abruptly in a parking lot at Loew Lake. I've dipped my kayak's paddle into the Oconomowoc River behind my house and made my way upstream to that lake many times. Today, with an agenda, a vehicle with wheels had to take the place of a glide along the river with all its secret beauty unfolding only to those traveling within its banks.

Sigh.

I needed one of those silent journeys ASAP.

I found Iris in her backyard, behind a modest and aging ranch, where she was burning leaves in a rusted-out drum barrel. Iris was shorter than me and carried more weight. And was at an age where distrusting other people's motives sometimes became a way of life. She didn't recognize me, even though she came into the store occasionally and I'd chatted her up like I do all my customers.

She swung around, startled by my approach, and it

would be a huge understatement to say she wasn't one bit friendly. "You Jehovah Witnesses were warned last time you came around," she snarled. "Stay away from my house."

"I'm Story Fischer."

"I don't care what your name is, you've already worn out your welcome. I'm not going to tolerate you people sneaking up on me and trying to convert me. I'm a Lutheran, and that's that."

"But I'm not a Jehovah. I'm Helen Fischer's daughter."

"Helen?" Iris, still suspicious, stood down from attack mode, but only slightly. "Prove it."

So to ease her mind and gain her confidence before she ran me off her property with a makeshift torch from her fire, I had to relate my family genealogy, going all the way back to two generations prior to Grams's time, before Iris decided that I was legit.

"Fischer? You must be the one who's shacking up with Hunter Wallace," she said, grabbing the rake and jabbing it into a pile of leaves then shaking it into the fire. This batch of leaves must have been damper than the others, because thick smoke rolled out of the barrel. "You've made your bed," she advised me, "now lie in it."

What the heck did that mean? This woman was like a clone of my mother before Mom fell in love with Tom and went all soft around the edges. Well, "soft" compared to the old Mom.

My brain wanted to tell her about Rosina first thing, but I had the same problem as I'd had with Al. My mouth didn't want to spit it out. Instead I sidestepped a plume of smoke that headed directly for me. Figures. It doesn't matter where I'm standing, smoke always targets me when a fire is in the vicinity. Par for the course, smoke curled around me, making me cough.

"Stand upwind," Iris said, shaking her head in a certain way that meant I was a big dumbo, so I moved again, worrying over how to broach Rosina's death.

Which gave me a few seconds to fashion a response to her weird (and snarly, if you ask me) comment.

You've made your bed, now lie in it. I was pretty sure I'd just been insulted.

For a split second I considered denying the charges against me and letting Holly take the rap. My sister would never find out. As tempting as it was, I couldn't pull it off. "That's me," I admitted, reluctantly sparing Holly's good name and taking what I had coming (I guess).

You never know how someone from older generations will react to that kind of news, that two people are living together without benefit of marriage, but all Iris said next was, "How's your mother these days?"

"Getting married."

"So I heard. I never got married, and I'm happy that way." Iris stopped raking leaves to look me in the eye. "And I never shacked up, either."

"Oh, we're getting married," I fibbed. Sort of. After all, it could happen someday.

"Just as foolish as your mother."

I wanted to tell her how much my mother had changed since finding the right man, but I had a pretty good idea that Iris wouldn't listen anyway and might even run me off her property before I could ask questions and get answers.

"Claudene Mason passed on," I forced myself to say, but gently, really hoping she had read the local paper or watched the news and already knew.

"So I heard."

"I learned that you used to be good friends with Claudene and my mom when you were young," I pointed out.

Iris kept adding leaves. At this rate, the fire would smother out under all the dampness. Then she stopped, leaned on the rake, and said, "For a little while we had our own schoolgirl clique, just the three of us—me, your mother, and Claudene Mason. But it was short-lived. A word of warning to you— girls are better off running around in even numbers. Two of

them, or four. But three? Three will fight like cats and dogs
and have lots of personality issues. So will five."

Uh, okay. "Grams told me about the love potion incident."

"Did she now? I always liked that woman. She was the
best mom in the whole school." Then a faraway look came
into Iris's eyes and she stared into the smoky fire. A hint of
a smile touched her lips. "I was in love with an older boy, a
senior. But I was just a starry-eyed freshman, and he didn't
even know I existed. Claudene was reading up on potions
and such, making out like she had special powers. Your
mother didn't approve and told us so, but we were convinced it would work. Where there's a will, there's a way, I
always say. I thought I was supposed to get him to drink it,
but Claudene said no, I was the one who was supposed to
drink it, and after that he'd find me irresistible and he'd be
putty in my hands."

Iris laughed, which made her look ten years younger.
"Like I always say, fools rush in where angels fear to tread,"
she exclaimed. "Unfortunately the stuff almost killed me."

"And you didn't get the boy."

"No, plus Claudene was sent away to live with some
relatives in Milwaukee, which seemed harsh to me. I never
thought she intended me any harm. We stayed in touch all
these years, and she must have apologized at least a hundred times for what happened that day."

Iris's expression turned grave. "And now she's gone. I
read that the police suspect murder. But they need to look
into that more carefully. Claudene had been battling depres-
sion for some time. I wouldn't be surprised if she took her
own life."

I was about to open my big fat mouth and inform Iris that
Rosina couldn't possibly have committed suicide, since
stabbing herself to death wasn't at all realistic. In fact, was
it even humanly possible? Then I remembered that the
police were withholding most of the details. I had more

information than the average citizen (for a change) and caught myself just in time.

Wait, had Iris said Rosina had been depressed? I should follow up, right, if I was going to be an investigator on this case?

"She was depressed?" I said. "About what?"

"She lost a man she cared about very much. She'd been so sure they would live happily ever after." Iris snorted. "Men! They really can mess up a woman's head. It was too late for me to stop the involvement anyway by the time I found out. She was in over her head. But a friend in need is a friend indeed, so I didn't share my personal opinion of their relationship."

What was with this woman and all the old sayings? And she acted like she'd thought them up herself. By now, I was pretty sure that Iris had memorized every proverb out there.

"Was he that bad, that you considered interfering? Was he an ex-con or something?"

"He was . . . well . . . a *man*," Iris said with distaste, "and men break hearts all the time. I didn't want that fate for Claudene."

Okay, I was in the presence of a certified (or certifiable) man hater who wasn't afraid to make her opinions public. Maybe that love potion had soured her for life.

But in any event, I had new news! Rosina had been in a relationship and it hadn't worked out. She had loved and lost. Plus, she'd been depressed. That could mean something, but I didn't know what. Maybe she'd shared certain concerns with him that could lead to her killer. "Do you remember the man's name?"

Iris peered at me, slyly, suspiciously, I thought. "Why?"

"Uh . . ." I shrugged. "No reason, just curious."

"You know what I always say," Iris said. "Curiosity killed the cat."

Well, wasn't that a creepy thing to say. Was she threatening me? Suddenly this detective business didn't seem like so much fun. I could see where it might get dicey as I went around asking questions. "Thanks for your time," I said, taking a few steps backward toward the truck, suddenly in a hurry to get away.

"Wait a minute," Iris called out, following me. "Let's see. I think I do remember his name. It was unusual. Maniac? No, that's not it." She paused.

I did, too.

"Martini?" I suggested. "Mantese?"

"No, no . . ." Then she snapped her fingers. "I've got it. Marciniak."

That really was a mouthful. No wonder it took her a few tries to get it right. "And his first name?"

"Claudene just called him Buddy."

Okay, I had a lead. My next step would be to locate Buddy Marciniak. He'd be easy to find with a name like that. Hunter was going to be so proud of me. "Thanks for taking the time to talk with me," I told her, heading for my truck. "It was a pleasure."

"All good things must come to an end," she called out before going back to her pile of leaves and the smoky fire.

As I hurried out, I countered to myself, *and a rolling stone gathers no moss.*

Sixteen

"But why do we need two wedding planners?" Mom said from her favorite spot at the head of the table. Grams had her offering ready—hot tea, apple crisp just out of the oven, and heavy cream to pour over the crisp. "And besides," Mom went on, "all the details have been worked out already. What's left to do?"

"I can make a wedding honey cake," I piped up as I devoured a big, gooey piece of apple crisp. I couldn't mention that I'd missed lunch or my mother would have a field day with me.

Mom shot my cake idea right down. "Milly has the wedding cake handled," she said. "It's a traditional cake, with white layers and a little bride and groom on top. But it was a nice offer, Story."

"Well, can I at least supply the bride's honey?"

"You are a real sweetie," Grams added, before my mother could reject that, too. "I can't wait to try some." Then to Mom, "Something old, something new. Bride's honey is the new." She smiled while she took a picture of Mom, Holly, and me. Unfortunately, she caught me with my cheeks packed and the fork on its way up to my mouth again.

Holly sounded firm about her decision, which didn't happen often. My sister could be pretty wishy-washy. "The day before and day of will be very busy," she reminded Mom. "Lots of errands to run, flowers to pick up, last-minute consultation with the caterer to make sure everything is on track, decorations to put up, lots of little details to remember. Everything will go smoother with two of us splitting the workload," she told Mom. "I can't do it without Story's help."

I looked up from my plate.

Aha! So that was why I'd been recruited. My work-phobic sister planned to use and abuse me. Here I'd thought she was being generous and considerate by including me, and all she wanted was a gopher while she was out having her nails and hair done for the wedding. I should have guessed. Instead I had walked right into it.

"I suppose," Mom relented.

Grams said to me, "The guest list is still a hot topic."

"That list was a done deal months and months ago." Mom scowled as she said, "Your grandmother wants to disrupt everything by inviting the entire town."

"And why not?" Grams argued. "We have a whole lot of friends from way back. They should help us celebrate."

"Family and close friends only," Mom told her.

"Another piece of apple crisp?" Grams asked me.

"I'll never fit into my dress if I do," I told her.

Holly and I were going to be our mother's only bridesmaids. Mom had snuck off on her own to pick out *our* dresses. No advance warning at all. That's how controlling she is. It would have been nice if she'd included us in the decision-making process, but that's not who she is. Even Holly hadn't been able to talk Mom out of the puce bridesmaid's dresses from hell once she had her mind set on them. We looked like replicas of Pollyanna: poofy sleeves, a sash with a big velvet bow taking up most of the front of the dress—not a good look for an adult. My sister and I are in agreement that the god-awful dresses are going to charity the minute this wedding is over.

"Speaking of dresses," Mom said, "I think it would be fun to dress up in our wedding outfits every year on the anniversary of our marriage, don't you, girls?"

"And every year I'll take the pictures," Grams offered, adding momentum to this terrible idea. Holly looked the color of . . . well . . . puce. We shared eye contact agony.

Okay, if donating the things wasn't an option, they would just have to have a fatal accident. A bottle of wine spilled, or a vicious dog snatching it out of my hands and ripping it to shreds. Or maybe it would be the victim of a robbery. Such a fine gown that a thief had run off with it. I had many more ideas where those came from if worst came to worst.

"I think I *will* have another piece of apple crisp," I told Grams. Not fitting into the dress suddenly sounded like another brilliant plan and the most fun of the bunch.

Grams beamed, scooped a generous helping onto my plate, and passed the cream.

My visit with Iris popped into my head as I made short work of apple crisp number two.

"I ran into Iris Whelan today," I told my family, nonchalantly, as though she'd popped into the store and we'd had a little chat. "She said to say hi, Mom."

"Was anybody hurt when you ran into her?" Grams asked. At my grandmother's advancing age and with the limited driving ability I'd witnessed from her, this wasn't an unusual assumption on her part.

"That whack job?" Mom sputtered. "What did you talk about?"

"Who is Iris Whelan?" Holly wanted to know.

"Mom's old chum," I replied to Holly. And to Grams,

"The other kind of ran into. Not ran over, ran into as in while out and about. Anyway, I ran into her."

"I find that hard to believe," Mom said suspiciously, sniffing like a pig after a truffle. "Where exactly did this conversation take place?"

I can't pull anything over on the woman, even something as small as this. "Actually," I said, not wanting Mabel to find out I went over her head on this one, "I paid her a visit."

"Mabel and I were looking forward to going over with you," Grams said, disappointed.

"A real whack job," Mom repeated.

"Whack job, Mom? That's a little extreme." Although I'd been thinking something along the same lines myself.

Mom's lips curled in distaste. "All those pithy little sayings. If I had to hear one more of them, I'd go crazy myself. She isn't still doing it, is she?"

"Yup," I said. "But you should be more tolerant. You know, as they say, you can catch more flies with honey than you can with vinegar."

"Don't annoy me, Story."

I did an internal pleased-as-punch high five for getting Mom's goat (is that one of those Iris sayings?), although let's face it, Mom is pretty easy to annoy.

Suddenly, I realized that we hadn't even mentioned the demise of a former local resident who had gone to school with my mother, one who was related to a family who went far back to the early days of Moraine. And that wasn't like us. So I said, "It's terrible what happened at Al's farm. Mom, you were friends with Claudene and Iris, right?"

"Yes, briefly, until I realized that they both had issues." Like she didn't?

"They fought over your mother," Grams explained. "Both of them wanted her for themselves because she was always so gay."

Holly shot me an amused look at the unintentional

implication. Mom and Grams were always saying things that could be taken the wrong way. In fact, our mother still called flip-flops thongs. That always gets a reaction. And Grams didn't seem to realize that the definition of *gay* has changed over the years.

"Your grandmother means that they competed for my attention," Mom told us. "They didn't like each other much, but both of them wanted to be my best friend. I was always in the middle."

This was too weird. My mother was popular? Gay? As in happy and fun to be around?

"They broke the rule of three," Grams added. "Three girls together just can't get along."

"That's exactly what Iris said," I said.

"Why not?" Holly scrunched her eyebrows.

Grams answered, "They just can't. Four is okay, so is two, but three is the kiss of death."

Mom piped up, "Finally, I'd had enough of both of them. The final straw was when Claudene started experimenting with magic. You just didn't do that back then."

I was pretty sure witchcraft and magic went farther back than Mom's generation, but I knew what she meant. While I helped Grams clean up, I thought about the three-some. If Iris and Rosina hadn't liked each other, had the tainted love potion been more than an accident? Had Rosina done it on purpose? We'd never know since the concocter was dead and gone. Though why had the two women kept in touch all these years if that were true?

"Claudene had a boyfriend," I said after rinsing and stacking our dishes in the sink. "According to Iris, anyway."

Mom laughed. "Maybe she finally figured out how to brew up a decent love potion."

"What love potion?" asked Holly, which meant we had to share the whole bad poison story again, since she was the only one at the table who hadn't heard it yet.

As I was getting ready to leave, I pulled Holly aside for

a minute. "You're a good dancer," I said. "Want to join us for a dance around a fire? Aurora can't make it and I thought of you."

"Sounds like fun," she said.

"I'll pick up your . . . uh . . . costume from Aurora."

"We'll be wearing costumes? Trick-or-treating early?"

"Something like that."

Holly wouldn't normally have been my first choice as a sidekick. She's way too citified and wimpy. Although she's risen to some occasions, like whenever someone tries to shoplift from the store. Then the woman is like a Tasmanian devil on steroids, taking the thief down in seconds flat. And literally flattening the foolish person. But put her out in nature with crickets singing and frogs croaking, and Holly is afraid of her own shadow.

But my usual partner in crime had disowned me, and based on Patti's irrational fear of all things witchy, she wouldn't help out even if we were on good terms.

I'd given the invitation some thought, because I wasn't about to put Holly in harm's way. It was one thing to walk into an explosive situation and risk my own neck, but I couldn't do that to my sister. That's why I decided that the risk to us was minimal. All we had to worry about was tripping on the long capes and falling into the fire. And that wasn't going to happen.

I'd reasoned this out like a real investigator.

If the killer was in their midst, she would be more worried about Lucinda actually conjuring up a spirit who might really be able to point a finger in her direction. Holly and I would be perfectly safe to observe the whole coven for suspicious behavior and possibly learn something useful about the witches. To be extra cautious, though (just in case I was wrong), we wouldn't wander off from the group.

Originally I thought Hunter could spot us, but that was before the condition that I stay away from the witches in exchange for information. Hunter could never, ever find out about this. That would be very bad for our relationship. I didn't think Lucinda would tell the investigator on the case about her plan for this evening. Definitely not. She wouldn't want cops busting in and ruining the ritual. Maybe someday when he and I were old and gray, I'd fess up. Or after the bad guy (or woman) was behind bars. If he found out before that, I was in such trouble. Which reminded me.

"Don't mention any of this around Hunter," I told Holly. "He's been acting weird lately."

After giving her the when and where details (my house, five o'clock) and heading out, I realized that I'd have to tell her more about what she'd be walking (or rather dancing) into on our way over to the farm. But I'd wait until after it was too late for her to have second thoughts. Because if thirteen bodies didn't show up, we'd have to postpone the big event for another time, and I didn't have an overabundance of extra patience in this matter.

And with the hooded cape as a disguise, the witches wouldn't even be able to tell that Aurora was really Holly. Unless we did the naked thing again. I hadn't thought that particular part through very well, which wasn't anything new, but things had a way of turning out.

As Iris would say, "We'll cross that bridge when we come to it."

Seventeen

I made a few phone calls on the way back to town.

Patti didn't answer, par for the course. She had caller ID and was snubbing me, I was sure of it. No answer. And no voice message option, either. She must be really ticked off. At this point, I wanted to make sure she was okay. Having her and her subterfuge out of my personal life had real advantages, but I wouldn't be able to stop thinking about how badly our last conversation ended until we reestablished a relationship of some sort.

What if Patti ended up moving away because of Dy? Not the most troubling idea in the world. That certainly had possibilities. I might actually get a normal neighbor for a change. Next I speed-dialed Jackson Davis, the ME. As the coroner, Jackson oversees all the autopsies in Waukesha County, which is spread over at least six hundred square miles with a population that has to be approaching half a mil. Good thing he has staff members to assist him, or he wouldn't have time for little old me.

"Hey, Story," Jackson said. "Let me guess why you're calling—Claudene Mason."

"You know me so well." I couldn't help grinning.

"And you know me just as well. Which means you have to know I can't tell you anything other than what's been released to the media."

"I'm on Hunter's team now," I told him. "And so are you. We are one big, happy family. So pass me the ball."

He chuckled. "I'm going to hog that ball. Sorry."

"Oh, come on, Jackson," I said, hearing myself give a Patti-style whine. "Do we have to go through this every time I call you?"

"I guess so."

I let the silence drag out after that. Unfortunately, so did he. I broke it first. "Call Hunter," I suggested. "He'll vouch for me."

"He might, but he doesn't have the final word on who gets inside information. I wouldn't be the professional that I am if I disregarded procedure. Sorry again."

Geez, he was being an uptight you-know-what. Maybe I should have invited him out for a drink first. Jackson was usually much more cooperative with a little of Stu's booze in his veins.

"Okay, I give up," I said with a big frustrated sigh. "But can you tell me anything about the pentacle she was wearing around her neck?"

There was a long pause on the other end.

Then Jackson said, "What pentacle?"

I had to pull over to the side of the road, that's how excited I was. Hunter actually answered his phone for a change. I skipped our usual small-talk opening that mostly deals with what we should do to each other's body parts and went right to the main topic. I practically shouted in my excitement, "Rosina, I mean Claudene, whatever, wore a pentacle necklace to protect herself from harm. Was it on her body?"

"No," was all Hunter said after a short pause. That one word was like gold.

"Then it's missing! This is so important. I can't believe I'm the one who found out it was missing. Maybe if you had included me from the very beginning, we'd be way ahead of . . ."

"Calm down," my man interrupted. "And start from the very beginning."

So I took a minute to catch my breath and then told him about meeting Rosina for the first time, and her cool necklace. "Then a few minutes ago I called Jackson and we got to talking and the piece of jewelry came up and he said, what pendant, which really threw me for a loop."

"How can you be absolutely sure she was wearing it at the time of her death?"

"Well, I can't, but she had it on both times I was around, and if she thought it would protect her, wouldn't she wear it to go out in the dark by herself?"

"So there's a possibility it's missing. That's interesting."

"Jackson wants me to try to draw it and make a copy for you, too."

"That should be worth watching," Hunter said, knowing that I can't draw a semi-straight line let alone something as complex as a piece of jewelry. "Where are you?"

"Where are you?" I asked back, prying to find out if he'd finished at the farm.

"Around," he said vaguely. "Why don't we meet and have a drawing session."

"I'm on my way to . . . um . . . Stanley Peck's to um . . . er . . . compare beekeeping notes." See how one little deceitful act like dancing with witches can turn into a full-blown cover-up? If I'd been more prepared, I would have told him something closer to the truth, like that my family was working on wedding plans.

The day was getting away from me. In a couple of hours it would be time to meet Holly at my house. I still had to get a cape for my sister from Aurora and work up a plan. Not to mention taking the time to give Holly all the details and then successfully handling the fallout from her. "This is more important," Hunter said. "Be at Stu's in ten minutes." And he hung up.

Reluctantly, I drove back to Moraine, pulling to the curb in front of Stu's Bar and Grill.

We arrived at the same time. Hunter and I drew together and kissed beside his passenger door, then I opened it so Ben could give me several warm, wet kisses, too, while I scratched his ears.

"You have to stay here, big guy," I told him, although Ben most likely already knew that. He's one smart canine. Ben has a special license, since technically he's a cop, too, but Hunter leaves him outside as a courtesy when he eats inside Stu's Bar and Grill, though the K-9 is always welcome in the back of my store.

And I'm here to say that Ben is much cleaner and better behaved than some of the drinkers I've encountered at the popular bar.

Stu's Bar and Grill was almost empty at this time of day, "sandwiched" between the lunch crowd and the late-afternoon drinking bunch that always bellies up around four o'clock and doesn't leave until they're thrown out at closing time.

Stu will be a real catch if anyone ever nails him down permanently. He's had an on-again, off-again relationship with his high school sweetheart that has been seeing more offs than ons, and some woman should swoop in and pluck him out of his sexy little pond once and for all.

If Hunter didn't exist (which would have been tragic), that woman might even have been me.

As we took a table near the window, several of the construction workers repairing the bridge walked in and headed for the bar.

Lori Spandle was right on their heels.

When she spotted me, we locked glares. Then she turned tail and hustled off down Main Street. What was that all about?

I noticed that the same guy she'd been hanging on when Lucinda and I drove over the bridge was one of those at the bar. And his eyes had followed her cheating backside out the building until she disappeared from sight.

"I think Lori Spandle is making time with that guy over there." I did a directional eye thing and Hunter followed my sight line, then he glanced back. And shrugged. Guys! They don't make a big deal of that sort of thing unless it's happening to them personally. Then it's a whole 'nother story.

I glanced out the window.

Oh no, was that Johnny Jay's squad car pulling up? What had I done now?

The chief walked in. First Lori, now Johnny, and all before we'd even placed our order. If this kept up I'd be too nauseous to eat.

"Same as usual?" Hunter asked me, and I nodded. "A diet coke, a lemonade, and chicken wings," he called to Stu. His eyes narrowed as Johnny Jay approached us.

"Are you absolutely sure you and your team checked every inch of the corn maze?" Hunter began as Johnny Jay sat down without an invitation.

The chief said, "Of course we did, Wallace."

"Because I ASS-umed"—special emphasis on the first three letters—"you had done so. My team came in after yours and did a cursory sweep based on your supposedly more thorough search. And for the record, you had no right to barge in on our crime scene like that."

"I smell a setup," Johnny said. "You needing a scapegoat, Wallace? What's happened?"

"Potentially, new evidence. But it might be nothing."

One of the things I've noticed by hanging around with

cops is how carefully they choose their words. And most of them begin with a P:

- potential

- probable

- possibly

- positive (I.D.)

- presumed

- process

- produce (as in produce an alibi)

- procedure (I really hate that one)

"I presume you searched the witches and their tents," I said to both of them, using lingo they'd recognize.

"Are you trying to interrogate me, Fischer?" That from Johnny, of course.

"Settle down, Jay," Hunter said. "Don't go all defensive on us."

"What would I have to be defensive over?"

"Maybe a poor excuse for a search."

"You better watch it, Wallace. Besides, what does it matter? We have the murder weapon."

That was just like Johnny to make a bunch of lazy assumptions. These two were going to go at it again if something wasn't done to stop it.

Stu delivered our drinks and wings. "Take it outside," he said. "Or I'll call nine-one-one. I don't care if both of you are cops. I won't have my bar busted up."

Then he winked at me. See? What a heartthrob! I reassured him, "Nothing to worry about, Stu."

He sort of rolled his eyeballs and went back behind the bar.

Hunter said to me, "With the assistance of the local police department"—I could hear the sneer—"the grounds were searched. That included Claudene's tent and belongings. And no, the item in question wasn't located."

"What item in question?" the chief asked, slow on the uptake. Hunter had already mentioned new evidence. How many clues did the guy need?

Instead of answering, Hunter countered with, "Why are you sitting at my table?"

Johnny's self-importance was palpable. "I just came from the library. Seems like someone has been stealing books from the romance section. You know, all those pornographic, explicit novels, total trash, but the library director filed a complaint, so I'm investigating."

"And that involves me how?" Hunter sure was doing a good job of handling the chief. I didn't even have to help out with my usual sass.

Johnny stood up and towered. "It doesn't involve you in the least," he said. "I just thought I'd spend a few friendly minutes shooting the breeze while I waited for the town chairman. We're going to set up a sting operation over at the library. Cameras and all."

Just then, Lori Spandle's husband, Grant Spandle, our town chairman, came in. He and Johnny moved off into another corner out of earshot, which was just as well. I'd have loved to be a fly on the wall, though. "It's probably just some kid," Hunter said. "And look at them, acting like it's some big crime."

After we ate the wings and wiped the stickies away with those little wet napkins, Hunter produced a sketch pad, a pencil, and a big eraser, and I went to work. We almost ran out of paper (and eraser) before I got it close to right. Which would have happened sooner if I hadn't been in such a hurry to get it done so I could get myself out of there. It doesn't pay to rush, that's for sure.

Eventually, I handed over the final copy. "The crystal in

the middle is blue," I added. "We really need some colored pencils, too."

Hunter turned the paper sideways. "That's a crystal?"

"A blue one."

"A blue crystal and a five-pointed star within a circle."

I nodded. "She said she wore it for protection."

"The big question is, who was she afraid of?"

It was my turn to shrug. "Evil spirits?"

"Or evil humans?"

"She'd have done better with a whistle around her neck," I said.

After creating my masterpiece, I told Hunter about my conversation with one of Rosina's classmates. "Iris mentioned a man Claudene had been involved with by the name of Buddy Marciniak."

"Do you want to follow up on it?"

I grinned. "You bet I do."

If Hunter ever left his job, we could open a private investigation business. We would call it Fischer and Wallace.

Eighteen

❦

Next, Hunter dropped what could have been a real bombshell, except I saw it coming. "I'm going to have to restrict access to the corn maze," he said. "I'm calling my team back in for another search of the entire property. Thanks to you."

I can't read Hunter when he snaps into professional mode, so I wasn't sure whether he was actually grateful or meant that in a sarcastic way, like thanks for totally complicating this case.

He saw my confusion. "Thanks. I really mean that."

"It's the right decision," I said, wanting to support him all the way.

"It'll take me an hour or so to assemble the team," Hunter said, checking the time. "And I need to get on the phone for that warrant. Until now I didn't have enough to conduct a thorough search—the weapon was left at the scene, nothing in her tent appeared out of place, her purse was there with enough money inside that robbery wasn't a motive. Now we have a pentacle to find. Good work, Fischer. You might be detective material after all."

I really liked that, a compliment for a change, but had more pressing issues on my mind. "Al's going to be upset."

"When would he usually close up for the evening?"

"Around five," I said after thinking back to last year. "The maze isn't lit up. Al doesn't want anybody lost in there after dark."

"If we're lucky and find what we're looking for, it'll be business as usual for him tomorrow."

I really hoped so, for Al's sake and for all the families looking forward to what had become a tradition. But would I want to take my family to a place where a murder had occurred? Probably not. I sent a silent message into the sky. Please keep this contained as much as possible.

"I could kick myself for letting personal feelings interfere with my professional duty," Hunter said. "I should never have agreed to let Al open up, and I shouldn't have taken Johnny at his word when he said they'd searched the maze. This was my responsibility and I blew it."

"It's fixable," I said, trying to be as comforting as possible.

"We're going to tear apart every inch of the place, and if it's there, we'll find that pentacle. Unless some customer already has. If that happens let's hope they're honest and turn it in. In light of this new evidence, I'm sure I can get a search warrant for the entire farm."

I nodded, still thrilled to be a contributing member. "Rosina could have lost it during the assault. She must have struggled. Maybe it was ripped from her neck."

"Or it could have been what the killer was after in the first place."

"Was Ben around during the initial search?" I asked. Hunter's K-9 partner was one fine tracer.

"He was there," Hunter told me. "Ben got her scent and we did a sweep, and we came up with nothing. But I'm thinking he might not have been able to detect something like that. Metal isn't porous the way clothing is. Although if it had blood on it, he would have found it."

I've seen Ben in action. He's amazing. My bet was that the pentacle wasn't in the maze or he would have found it. But police work isn't decided on bets and hunches.

The construction workers were long gone from the bar by the time Hunter had made his phone calls and we rose to leave. We walked past Johnny Jay and Grant Spandle's table on our way out, but they were still immersed in their sting operation plans and didn't notice us. At least the chief had something to keep him out of Hunter's hair. And the town chairman would be preoccupied with stolen library books while his skanky wife slithered through the weeds under the bridge.

An idea began growing in my head. It was a terribly awful, wonderful idea:

What if I could get Lori and her latest target to put on a show for the hidden cameras in the romance section at the library?

You wouldn't do that! said Good Me.

Sure I would, replied Not-So-Good Me, thinking of all the mean-spirited things Lori had done to me over the years.

Don't even think it. Shame on you.

I dumped the other me (the fun evil twin) out of my head and kissed my man good-bye.

It was only after Hunter and Ben drove off that I realized tonight's ceremony wasn't going to happen. With investigators all over the place, Lucinda would have to put her ritual on hold again. What rotten luck for her. First it rained cats and dogs, then it poured cops.

I felt a huge relief. No dancing, no getting naked, no having to convince Holly, no black magic. I hadn't even been aware of how much stress and tension I was carrying until it disappeared.

Most days, I know exactly what I'll be doing—taking care of my bees and customers. But Hunter's professional life is prone to lots of stops, starts, and U-turns. Realizing in a flash of insight how flexible and prepared Hunter has to be twenty-four/seven was a revelation for me.

As I pulled away in my truck, I realized just how much I valued my steady, predictable little world. Stepping outside of it once in a while was exciting, but I knew I could always return anytime I wanted to. Not so with Hunter. It was what it was.

I loved and appreciated him more than ever. I couldn't imagine life without that hot guy. And Ben, of course.

I was one lucky woman.

Since the witch's ceremony was a no-go, I went home and called Holly. She didn't answer my call, so I sent her a short text. *Plans cancelled. Talk to you tomorrow.*

I spotted Dy leaving her house a little while later, probably on her way to the farm since she didn't know that the ritual was about to be cancelled. I had been indecisive up until then. I debated informing her of the turn of events but figured she really ought to be there with the other witches when their little circle of fire was surrounded by law enforcers asking more questions and taking careful inventory. Why not? Dy hadn't managed to come up with an alibi. Therefore she was just as suspect as anybody else.

I walked down to the store and slipped into the back room without anyone noticing. Carrie Ann was up front, turning the reins over to the twins, and the back door was unlocked. That's a small town for you. We don't sweat the small stuff.

From my desk, I surfed for any information on Buddy Marciniak, the man Rosina had been seeing. Even with the unusual last name, several Marciniaks popped up in the Milwaukee area, but none of them were named Buddy, so that had to be a nickname. I wasn't sure how to proceed, so I filed this task for tomorrow. The chances that he had anything to offer that would move the case forward were slim to none anyway.

I slipped back out and went home again. Seeing my new neighbor's house empty, I was startled by the obvious. Why not check out Dy's house?

I knew the place like the back of my hand, including which window didn't close correctly (I'd jimmied it so I could get inside easily back when my ex-husband had lived there). Dy wouldn't have had time to fix it, probably hadn't even discovered it yet.

So I let myself in.

And thought, *Now what?*

What would Hunter do? What would Patti do? She and I had done some B and E in the past. And what did we do? Just started snooping. So that's what I did.

I found mostly unpacked moving boxes, stacks of them.

Starting in the kitchen, opening cupboards and drawers, I realized that any ritual supplies would be over at the farm, not here, since the witches still expected to perform a ceremony tonight.

I moved on to Dy's bedroom, where very little had been unpacked. Just odds and ends on her nightstand.

By now, the day's light was fading. It was darker inside the house than outside, and I really wanted to turn on a light. Instead, I picked a few things up from the nightstand and went over to a window where visibility was a little better.

Just then, I thought I heard a creak, like someone was walking over a loose floorboard. Listening hard, holding my breath, I told myself the sound was probably just the house settling in for the night.

Back to the task at hand, my prizes included a necklace with a pentacle much like the one Claudene had worn only with a black crystal in the center instead of a blue one.

Another spooky creaking sound and I quickly returned everything to its original place and hustled home.

Inside the dark entryway of my own home, before I could flip on a light, something heavy and cumbersome descended on me.

After that my world went completely dark.

Nineteen

I fought hard against my assailant, but he had surprise on his side. The attack came out of nowhere, and it came with lightning speed. And I had to assume this was a male because he was really, really strong. A sack of some sort had been shoved over my head, a thick, scratchy material that smelled strongly of farm—straw, animals—and it was tightening around my neck. Was that rope? Or piano wire?

I couldn't see what was going on around me. I was in total darkness. My hands instinctively went up to defend my airway. I recognized the coarse texture of garden twine.

I tried to get a few fingers between it and my throat, and failed. Was this really how I was going to leave this world— strangled to death in my own home without even a hint as to who would do such a thing to me? And why?

Abandoning efforts to throw off the noose, I punched wildly, first above, then behind, scared now. My right fist made contact, but not very effectively. One arm was wrenched behind my back.

I tried to land a hard and solid kick but met with dead air.

My heart was beating a mile a minute, I couldn't breathe, and I felt myself falling sideways, not sure if I was disoriented from lack of oxygen or was experiencing vertigo from the bag on my head. Either way, I went down.

Now he was on top of me, smashing my face against the floor, my other arm wedged under me. As hopeless as the situation had become, I couldn't just give up. I twisted and heaved.

Hunter had offered me defense instructions recently, so that he could teach me how to get out of various holds. But the timing never seemed right. Why oh why hadn't I made the time? Instead, here I was, facedown with my head inside a bag. I twisted and managed to free the left arm I'd fallen on, only to have it wrenched behind my back, too, in some kind of wrestling hold.

If I didn't know better, I'd think my own sister, who is just as strong as any man, had taken me down. "Holly? Let go," I managed to squeak, just in case it really was her instead of some death demon.

No answer.

I tried to flip my assailant off my back. His thighs clamped my sides and squeezed until I stopped struggling.

Visions of Rosina popped into my head. Had she been taken from this earth in the same way? Caught unaware in the corn maze, blinded by a hangman's hood?

By now, I really couldn't catch my breath between the pressure along my sides, the exertion, and the fear that I would soon feel a steel blade plunged into my back. It all contributed to some serious panic.

Then I felt something cool and wet on one of my trapped palms. My attacker shoved me on my side and slammed that hand against the wall, holding it firmly pressed.

I fought, but my attacker held my hand in place. Finally he released it.

What the heck! The skin of my palm with my fingers spread wide open was stuck to the wall. I tugged. My hand, palm, and fingers didn't budge.

Okay, so my head was still in a bag. And one of my hands was stuck on the wall. But I still had feet and a fist, which I used to lash out.

Only to have the other arm grabbed, my hand doused, and anchored as well. This guy was superhuman.

I was distracted by the thought that I was going to die soon, so it took a few minutes for me to react to a distinctly strong and obnoxious odor in the air.

I recognized that smell.

Unbelievable!

I'd just been superglued to my own wall.

So here I was, both palms flat against the wall, fingers splayed, head hooded. Helpless and horrified.

But the human spirit doesn't give up easily. I still had feet, and although I'm no kung fu expert, I managed to land a pretty solid twisted body, bent knee, followed by a thrust kick. My foot connected with a mass of flesh. I heard a moan, felt a momentary ray of hope, and tried again, but without the same luck.

Finally my attacker spoke up, or rather gasped, giving me a small little pleasure. I hadn't been a total pushover, had done at least a little damage. "Hold still and let me free your head."

What? I couldn't believe my ears! I recognized that voice.

I was going to kill Patti when I got loose.

And since I now knew where she was based on the direction of her recent utterance, I let her have another good swift kick with the side of my foot.

She grunted and let out a choking sound. Yeah, for me! Boot to the throat.

"If I were you," I said to my pathetic excuse for a neighbor, "I'd run for a different state and never, ever dare to come back."

She'd have a reason for a pity party when I got done with her.

Patti fumbled with the hood, releasing the twine, and drew it up and over my head. Static electricity zapped my hair, and I felt it stand out in all directions from the charge.

"I figured you wouldn't appreciate my efforts, and that you'd get all abusive. How well I know you, and how predictable. All I care about is keeping you safe, and look how you thank me."

"What the hell do you think you're doing?" I had to twist my head around as far as possible to see the woman because she was wisely keeping her distance while I bellowed, "Are you insane?"

I yanked my arms in an attempt to break free.

"I wouldn't do that if I were you," she said. "You're going to rip off all the skin on your palms."

"I'm going to rip off your head, is what I'm going to do."

So, I admit it, I wasn't exactly handling the situation with grace and understanding. But I'd just been scared out of my wits, and I really meant every single violent word that spewed from my mouth in the next few minutes. *Kill. Rip. Maim.* All very active verbs that defined my emotions really well.

"I'm here to save you against your will," Patti informed me when I ran down. She was not one bit affected by my outburst. What was she? A sociopath? Where were her human feelings?

She continued while I fumed more quietly, already plotting my escape, "The only way to reverse the witch's spell is first to isolate you from the coven. Since you're under their control, you can't think straight to help yourself. That's where I come in."

"I'm perfectly fine!"

"You've been associating with them, right? In fact, right this minute, you have a black witch robe in your truck."

"I can explain that."

"You don't need to. You've been bewitched by those witches."

I had a long list of criminal charges against Patti besides assault:

- abuse—gluing my hands to the wall certainly qualified

- kidnapping—holding me against my will

- trespassing—she hadn't been invited into my house or given permission to search my truck

- breaking and entering—maybe the door wasn't locked, but in the sane world, that is not an open invitation

"There's nail polish remover in my bathroom," I demanded. "Go get it." My hands might as well be encased in concrete for all the movement I could muster out of them.

"I'm going to do one better," Patti said. "Now that I've removed you from danger, the next step is to track down the Lutheran minister and have him perform an exorcism."

"I am not possessed!" I shouted. "And you need a Catholic priest for that anyway."

"Really? Oh, you're right, thanks."

That ought to slow her down. The closest Catholic priest was a whole lot farther away than the Lutheran minister. That would give me more time to figure out how to escape.

"Don't try to go anywhere," were Patti's parting words, leaving me to consider whether or not a priest would believe her. Wouldn't he be more likely to blow her off as the kook she is, or tell her to make an appointment? What if I was stuck (no pun intended) here for hours while she searched for the proper religious leader to perform a . . .

This was so ridiculous!

After what seemed like forever, I heard someone rattle a key in the front door lock. The door opened and closed. The only ones who had keys to the front and actually used that entrance were Grams and Mom. Mom, because even though this used to be her house, she insisted on being treated like a visitor, and according to her, guests always use the front, never the back. And Grams came in that way because she's usually with my mother and it's become a habit.

Oh geez, if this was my mother, I was just going to die. How in the world would I explain? Plus I'd get a blistering about how irresponsible I am and what terrible influences my friends are.

Thankfully, it was my grandmother who stepped into the room, holding her little rat-looking dog Dinky. I almost cried with relief. She saw me splayed and let out a gasp.

"What in heaven's name happened?" She said in her surprised-but-sweet grandmother voice, putting down Dinky, who began crawling all over me.

"You can't imagine how happy I am to see you," I gushed, meaning Grams, not the dog. "You're like an angel. Help me please. Patti superglued me to the wall."

"I superglued my fingers together once," she told me. "And your mother has had a few encounters with the stuff, but your situation takes the cake." Was that a giggle she was trying to smother? "Let me get a picture of this. Nobody would believe it otherwise."

"No, please." I tried to hide my face.

The shutter clicked.

"Mom will never let me live it down if she finds out," I told Grams.

"I didn't think of that. I'd never put you in that position. Don't worry. See? I deleted it."

That was better.

Dinky, past our greeting, went off exploring.

After giving Grams the location of the nail polish remover and guiding her through the slow application process, while enlightening her as to Patti's latest insanity, I was once again a free woman, though my hands felt raw and stiff.

Bits and pieces of drywall had crumbled where I'd attempted to break free. "And look, she's messed up my wall," I complained, although that was the least of my worries.

"I suppose she meant well," Grams said, always looking for the good in every situation.

I wasn't ready to agree. I'd like to glue Patti's butt cheeks together, that's how mad I was.

"Want to drive me out to Al Mason's farm on your way home?" I asked Grams, deciding that I could hang with Hunter until he was finished and come home with him. I couldn't drive myself, since my fingers wouldn't bend, let alone wrap around a steering wheel.

Of course, Grams said yes.

And we were off.

Twenty

✤

In the passenger seat of Grams's Cadillac Fleetwood, tiny Dinky planted herself firmly on my lap after giving me a friendly neck washing. I'd been her foster mom for a brief time, and she hadn't forgotten.

There just wasn't enough bend in my hands yet to manage, so I had to ask Grams to put my cell phone on speaker and then call Patti's cell, whose number (believe it or not) was in my friend list. It went directly to voice mail.

"We have two options to consider," I began recording. "The first, and my personal favorite, is for me to file assault and kidnapping charges against you and have you thrown in the clinker. After which I will testify in a court of law before a jury of my peers to the emotional and physical trauma you put me through. Notice I said *my* peers, not *your* peers, because you are one of a kind. And that isn't a compliment, Patti."

Grams gave me a disapproving tsk, but that didn't even slow me down.

I kept going, "And trust me when I tell you that lots of people in this town have voiced angry complaints over your total disregard for the law and personal rights. I'll get statements from every single one of them. Plus, I'll get a restraining order. You won't be allowed in my yard or in my store."

That's when a beep told me I'd run out of message time, and I had to figure out how to call Patti back myself, since Grams had her hands full just staying on the road. I tried not to look out the window. By now, feeling was coming back into my hands, and it wasn't a pleasant sensation. But at least I was able to bend my fingers enough to hit the right keys.

I presented option two on Patti's voice mail.

"*Or* your other choice is for you to put your nosy little body in gear and work off your debt to me, beginning with a full breakdown of Claudene Mason's personal life, every single detail going back at least two years. That's only for starters. I have more service orders where that came from."

I knew Patti would go with option two, because she's a big snoop and this was right up her alley. Besides, she'd think all was forgiven and that we were back in the old days when I actually went along with her ridiculous escapades. Buds again. Ha!

Once Patti gave me whatever information she could dig up on Rosina (and I have to admit that the woman is really good at uncovering juicy details), I planned on going for the restraining order anyway. So I lied, so shoot me. All's fair when it comes to skirmishes with Patti. And as far as I was concerned, her recent actions had turned our relationship into a full-blown war.

Grams's Cadillac Fleetwood coasted up Main Street at about five miles an hour. Grams never seems to notice when she has an impatient parade behind her. This time she had a doozy; it was rush hour, so all those poor souls were trying to get home from work, dying to change into more comfortable clothes and pour themselves a much-anticipated beverage. And wasn't it just their bad luck to encounter a grandma in a Caddie and, even worse, a solid yellow no-passing line?

The jerk directly behind us blasted his horn, which rattled Grams, causing her to slam on the brakes. Dinky, used to her sudden stops, managed to stay put on my lap. I did fine, too, unlike the horn blower, whose car brakes squealed. Looking in my rearview mirror, I saw him veer in a frantic defensive maneuver, coming to a stop sideways.

Then I saw him get out. Not good.

"Take off right now," I shouted to Grams. If I had to choose between Grams's driving and this guy's road rage, I'd pick the known over the unknown.

Grams put the pedal to the metal and we fishtailed out of there, leaving behind a wild man shaking his fist.

"Turn right here," I advised her, "onto this side road. Then park and turn off your lights."

"Everybody's in such a big hurry these days," she said, turning where I'd advised. "Maybe I should have listened to Mabel. She tucks a tire iron under her front seat just in case she has to defend herself. There are a lot of lost souls running loose."

I thought that was a really bad idea and told her so. If you stacked Grams and Mabel up like two dominos, they'd be almost as tall as your average person. Whacking an irate driver over the head just wasn't doable for either of them. "I'll get you a can of pepper spray if you think you need protection," I told her.

"I've already forgiven that rude boy behind us," Grams said, reverting to form. "I'm sure he had his reasons. He could have had an emergency at home and felt desperate. Or had to go to the bathroom. You never know."

We crept out and hit the road again, and the farm came into view up ahead. I said, "You can drop me at the road and I'll walk up. You don't want to get trapped up there by other cars."

What I meant was that I wanted to save Grams from herself. If she had to maneuver around police cars, something was bound to go seriously wrong. She'd had more than one run-in (run-into) with Johnny Jay, and one of these days he was going to attempt to revoke her license. "Pull over right here."

"Nonsense," she replied, heading straight up the drive. Her car crawled along slower than I could have walked that distance. We pulled up next to Hunter's cop vehicle without incident. But from past experience, it's foolish to let your guard down around my grandmother.

Grams saw me struggling with the door latch, so she came around and opened the passenger door for me. She scooped Dinky from my lap.

"We should have pasted some honey on your hands," she said, the word *paste* reminding me of glue and how ticked off I was at Patti. "And if we encased them in cotton socks, they'd be good as new in no time."

I imagined myself running around the crime scene with socks over my honeyed hands. It wasn't a pretty picture.

"I'll be as good as new soon anyway," I reassured her, feeling impatient to get to the action. "Thanks for the ride."

"There sure is a lot of activity going on here," Grams observed, glancing around at the parked cars. I recognized a few as the Critical Incident Team's vehicles, Hunter's team. Nobody was around, though we could hear voices coming from the direction of the corn maze. The sky over there was lit up with searchlights.

"They're still looking for clues to Claudene's murder," I told her. "Some possible new evidence."

I love my grandmother. She never pries. Anybody else would have started grilling me for information, threatening, pleading . . . Okay, maybe only Patti would have done those things. The rest wouldn't have bothered because they just weren't that interested. But by Grams's quick glance at my face, I could tell she knew something was up.

"You be careful, sweetie," Grams warned, getting on her tiptoes to give me a quick kiss on the cheek.

Then I helped her back her car up and turn around to head home.

Accident free for a change.

Sometimes miracles really do happen.

Twenty-one

I walked along in the dark, dodging vehicles parked haphazardly up the driveway and on the lawn. Johnny Jay's squad car was off to the side. I just had to go over and try the doors. Locked. Not that I had any idea what I would have done if one of the doors had been open. Find some donkey manure maybe and leave it on his driver's seat? I kicked a tire instead.

The farm animals weren't braying and honking like they usually did during the day; they were bedded down for the night, tucked snugly in their stalls, safe from harm. Not that we had many big predators in this part of Wisconsin. No bears, moose, or wolves. Just the occasional coyote, which didn't cause much trouble unless he was traveling in a pack, and critters like foxes or raccoons. That was about it. Oh, and skunks, which I've had some close encounters with when they raided my beehives for honey.

Tonight, though, all was quiet except for the sound of human voices drifting on the light breeze.

I found Greg, Al, and Joan Goodaller bunched together near the corn maze, blinking in the blindingly bright spotlights. After we greeted each other, Hunter came out of the maze with two other cops and joined us. I could tell he was in professional mode, because he barely even acknowledged my presence.

"Did you find anything?" Greg asked Hunter. The two men stood eye to eye, both as handsome as men get.

Hunter didn't respond to Greg's question, another clue that he was taking his job ultra-seriously. Cops don't share information with just anybody, especially if that person might be on a list referred to in cop talk as "persons of interest." Unfortunately, that was pretty much everybody.

"Al," Hunter said, zeroing in on the farm's owner and the dead woman's brother, "we'll take a look inside your house next."

Al's back got ramrod stiff with indignation. His jaw jutted out as he said, "You're kidding me, right?"

Nothing about Hunter implied joking around. "It's standard procedure when a murder occurs on someone's property," he told Al. "Routine."

I've heard cops use the old "standard" and "routine" speech so often, I have to wonder if that's the story they've been trained to feed to every private citizen who challenges them in any way.

"You need a search warrant for that," Al said, sticking to his legal rights.

Hunter presented the warrant. "Sorry, Al, but we have to take a look. We won't be long."

Without another word, Al stomped off toward his house with the cops trailing behind him.

I'd absolutely hate to have Hunter's job. When something bad happens, he's forced to interrogate people he's known his entire life. Hopefully, Al would understand that Hunter was only doing his job.

I much preferred my new position as sidekick.

"So," I said to Greg and Joan, making small talk while I massaged my hands, feeling them start to loosen up. "They must not have found anything interesting in the corn maze."

"I don't know what they expected to find, since they already went through there with a fine-tooth comb," Greg replied. "But this time is different. They're searching everything." He gave me a studied look. "Do you know what they're after?"

I couldn't blurt the truth, which was that they were searching for a pentacle necklace. Was there such a thing as a professional lie? Or only professional liars? I tried to follow Hunter's lead in how to dodge these kinds of bullets without stooping to untruths, but instead Johnny Jay popped into my mind. I knew exactly how he'd handle questions.

"I'm asking the questions here, Fischer," he would have said. "Not you." So predictable.

But bullying wasn't my style.

"I don't have any idea," I lied. Oh well. It was time for redirection. "Where's the police chief? I saw his squad car down the drive."

"He's over with the campers," Joan told me. "It's obvious that the detective on the case and the police chief are having some territorial issues with each other."

Tell me about it, I could have said, but I didn't want to get into it.

"Detective Wallace ordered the chief to leave," Greg said. "Only not in those exact words. More forceful."

"But," Joan added, "we saw the police chief sneak down the drive on foot and head toward the apple orchard."

I needed to get over there and throw a wrench in Johnny Jay's plan, whatever it was. But first things first.

"Greg, I'm sorry about your aunt. I know you were only trying to get the family back together. Then this had to happen."

Greg looked tired—I guess from working so hard to get the corn maze open, from the murder of his aunt, from the stress and tension of the investigation. "Thanks, Story," he said.

Joan reached over, took one of his hands, and gave it an affectionate squeeze of reassurance. "You did everything right. Don't be so hard on yourself."

"Can you tell me anything about your aunt that might shed some light on her death?" I asked.

"I can't imagine any of the witches doing this," Greg said, to my amazement. If not one of them, then who? "I got to know them pretty well. Sure, they had some conflicts here and there, but none of them are capable of murder."

I thought about the rule of three. Iris and Grams had both mentioned that three girls just can't get along together. The original three were Lucinda, Dy, and Rosina. Did that rule apply to grown women as well?

"Who else was out here that night?" Joan asked.

"Besides us and the guest campers . . . ?" Greg paused in thought.

"That's the point," I mentioned. "It had to be one of the witches."

Greg looked shaken. "I guess you're right, but I really hope you aren't. I'd never forgive myself for bringing them here if one of them killed Aunt Claudene."

"There, there," Joan said. "You aren't to blame."

I had more questions. "What about your aunt? Any unusual situation in her past that might have been the cause of her death? Anyone out to get her?"

Before Greg could respond, Joan interrupted, addressing me, "I'm sure if Greg knew anything important he would have shared it with the detective."

"I'm sorry," I said, really meaning it. "Sometimes my timing is terrible."

"You're forgiven, dearie," Joan said, then glanced in the

direction of the apple orchard. "I wonder what's going on over there?"

Johnny Jay, that's what. "I'll be back," I said. "There's somebody I need to follow up with."

And with that, I made a beeline for the witches.

Twenty-two

❀

For once, I didn't barge right into the middle of a scene. Instead I stayed in the apple trees' shadows and slunk closer, trunk by trunk, until I was near enough to hear and see the action. And when I realized what was happening, it took every ounce of self-control not to burst out laughing.

Because Johnny Jay was trapped in the center of the witches. He was out of his element, and it showed.

"Back off," he ordered. "Don't crowd me."

Nobody moved forward or backward. Talk about intimidation. And knowing this bunch, they were doing it for exactly that purpose, to rattle him.

Lucinda was putting him through the wringer. "We are guests and won't be treated like common criminals . . . especially by such a . . ."—here she paused, then said with a whole lot of disgust—"common everyday bully. Besides, you're out of your jurisdiction."

Smart woman!

Dy stood right next to her.

"Dyanna," Lucinda said, "do you have that detective's phone number? I'd like to call him down here."

"Yes," Dy said, searching the folds of her gown. "It's here somewhere."

"That won't be necessary," Johnny said, abruptly deciding he'd had enough of Hunter's wrath. "If you women will just back off, I'm done with you for the night."

The masses parted, and the chief practically fled.

I wondered if he'd been hexed or bewitched. Wouldn't that be great?

Lucinda dismissed him from her mind. "Where are our two replacements?" she wanted to know.

It dawned on me that Holly and I were those replacements.

"We aren't prepared to go through with the ritual with all the extra commotion up at the main farm anyway," Dy said, "whether the other two show up or not."

"The authorities won't be coming to the orchard," Lucinda said to her, as confident as if she'd peered into a crystal ball and seen the future. "Let's give those two a little more time."

Another disturbing thought crossed my mind—what if Lucinda sensed my presence? What if the coven found me hiding behind a tree? What possible explanation could I give them? At least my sneakiness proved once and for all that I wasn't under any kind of spell. If that were the case, I'd be right in their midst, excited for the dance, right? At least it proved it to me. Patti was another issue.

The other witches were dispersing, some to their tents, others to the picnic table to converse in low voices. Only Dy and Lucinda remained at the fire.

Just as I was about to slink away, Dy said, "I learned that Rosina had changed her name."

"What's your point?" Lucinda asked, her tone a little snotty, but taking the words right out of my mouth. Sure,

Claudene had changed her name to Rosina, but I hadn't thought that much of it. People do it every day.

"We all take new names during initiation," Dy continued, ignoring Lucinda's attitude toward her, "but we don't go to the trouble of changing them through the legal process. Also, I'm pretty sure she originally told us her real name was Mary."

Lucinda looked annoyed. "Well, that is kind of odd, but I still don't follow."

"What if she changed her name to disappear, to start over? Someone might have tracked her down, someone from her past."

"Oh please," Lucinda said, "it's perfectly obvious that you wanted control of the coven and you'll do anything to get it. I've got my eyes on you."

"Are you accusing *me* of her murder? Really?" Dy's face contorted in anger. "I never had a problem with Rosina. If any of us had a motive it was you!"

Oh my gosh, was I about to witness a real witch fight, flashing wands and all? My money was on Lucinda if it came to blows. She was scary, strong-willed, and forceful. Yet, this Dy was also dramatically different from the sunny person I'd met for the first time a couple of days ago. Her voice exuded almost as much power and confidence as Lucinda's.

They were so preoccupied with their little argument (which was surprisingly similar to what went on between Hunter and Johnny Jay) that I spotted movement before they did. Someone was running toward them.

"You'll never guess!" the shadowy figure shouted, coming up to the fire, panting from the exertion.

"Tabitha," Lucinda said. "Calm down."

Ah, so Tabitha was the witch with the pointy glasses, the one who had found Rosina's body. Where had she come from? In all the drama I'd forgotten to count heads.

"I was almost ready to give up for the night and come back," she gasped. "Then it happened. It's over."

Considering the direction Tabitha came from, they must have sent her up to the corn maze to spy.

"What's over?" Dy asked.

"They're arresting Rosina's murderer. We can go home!"

At that breaking news, I backed away from my vantage point and reversed my steps, creeping off the same way I'd arrived.

Only to find the unthinkable: Hunter had Al Mason in handcuffs!

"They found whatever they were looking for," Joan whispered to me, a catch in her voice and tears in her eyes. "Inside the house."

"You have the wrong man," I heard Al say as members of the Critical Incident Team escorted him to an awaiting vehicle, while Joan followed behind, crying. Greg caught up and helped support her or I think she might have collapsed.

Hunter came over and pulled me aside. "Is this it?" He held up a baggie. The blue crystal caught my attention.

I nodded, sad that I was the one who had to identify Rosina's pentacle. Even sadder about where it had been found.

A little later, I suddenly realized I didn't have transportation. I wasn't about to call my grandmother for a return wild ride, and Hunter would be busy after this unexpected arrest, so I caught a ride home with one of his team members.

Several hours after that, Hunter called to say that Al's fingerprints were all over their new piece of evidence.

What more did the cops need after that?

Al had motive—he'd always disliked his sister. If only he hadn't been so open about his feelings. Al also had opportunity, at least as much as anybody else. And Claudene wouldn't have thought twice about meeting her brother in the corn maze, probably hoping for a reconciliation. Plus Al had means; he could have easily taken the witches' ritual knife.

What had the guy been thinking, keeping the pentacle?

Al Mason didn't have to worry about keeping the farm going, at this rate.

Because Al was going to have free room and board for the rest of his life.

Twenty-three

"I still can't believe Al killed his sister," I said early Saturday morning as Patti Dwyre and I sat on a bench outside The Wild Clover wearing light jackets. I was enjoying the crisp fall air in spite of present company. The more I thought of Al as his sister's killer, the less I believed it.

Earlier, I'd walked through the quiet beeyard, thinking how lucky I'd been this year. None of my hives had gone rogue on me. Bees in the wild have a tough time surviving. They might find a nice nesting cavity in a hollow tree that's as good as any hive I could provide, but diseases and parasites take a toll on them. So I'm major relieved that I can provide medical care as well as happy homes.

Then I'd walked to the store and P. P. Patti called, saying she had "important classified information" that she refused to divulge over the phone, and since she also wouldn't come near my house with the witch next door at home, we had arranged this meeting. Which I fervently hoped would be our last.

From her point of view, though, we were back to business as usual. But not from mine. She'd crossed the line when she assaulted me, and I wasn't about to forgive and forget. I saw a restraining order in her immediate future. Since Al would be charged soon, if he hadn't been already, Patti's expertise (prying where she doesn't belong and digging up dirt best left buried) was no longer needed. Her usefulness was a thing of the past, and the bruise on my arm where I'd hit the floor was a motivating reminder of her outrageous attack on me.

I went on, just thinking out loud, "Why would Al hide incriminating evidence in his house? And if he did something as dumb as hanging on to the necklace, wouldn't he have at least wiped it clean of prints?"

"You suspect a setup?" Patti asked.

"I don't know what to think. Al sprained his ankle recently. How could he have been able to pull off something so physically violent?"

"Unless he injured it during the struggle."

What was she? The devil's advocate?

"What was so important that we couldn't discuss on the phone?" I asked her.

"You never know who might be listening in."

"Geez, Patti, that's really paranoid. In your world, this bench we're sitting on could be wired."

"It's not. I checked."

"Fine. But anything you have to offer me is moot at this point. The cops have their killer. End of story."

Patti smirked. "You're right," she said. "The name of the boy involved in that love potion . . . you remember? . . . the one the witch concocted that almost killed her friend? . . . isn't important anymore. It doesn't matter."

No, it didn't really matter. My search into Claudene Mason's past was over before it began. Still . . . I was human, and we humans are n-o-s-y.

Patti knew that and waited me out.

"Who was it?" I couldn't help asking.

"Never mind," Patti said, baiting me, which I realized right away. Was a name from the past worth a Patti in my future? No way.

Before we got any further, before I could announce my decision to exclude her from my life on a permanent basis, Greg Mason pulled up to the curb right in front of us, got out, and headed directly for our bench. After another round of condolences for all his family's troubles along with some statements such as *I can't believe this is really happening*, I asked Greg, "What will become of the farm?"

"The media can't legally release Dad's name until he's actually charged," Greg explained, "even though the staff at the *Reporter* has that information. And thankfully the cops haven't charged him yet. Everybody in town will find out, if they don't know already, but I'm praying it won't affect the out-of-town business, since that's where most of our visitors come from."

Greg went on, "I'll stay at the farm a little longer and run things. Joan has offered to help out until Dad is released. I'm not sure how to plan if he . . ."

He didn't complete the sentence, but it was easy to finish it for him. There was a possibility, a probable one, that Al wasn't coming back home.

Up until now, I'd been focusing all my attention on the witches. But with Al's arrest for the murder of his sister, and my own refusal to believe it, I took a good, hard look at Greg. With his aunt dead and his father in jail, he stood to take control of the farm. Hunh.

Right about then, Johnny Jay cruised by with Grant Spandle in the seat next to him. They were traveling in the direction of the library, probably puffed up like strutting roosters, plotting their current harebrained scheme. I'd bet the store that Johnny was really annoyed to be missing out on the bigger case. A normal person would learn their lesson, but not this guy. Let him stew and go chasing after book thieves.

"Dad asked for you, Story," Greg said. "He says he needs you. And from what I gather, you have a knack for helping in situations like these."

Patti piped up, "What about me, Greg? I should be on the case, too. I'm Story's partner."

"No, you're not," I said.

"Wasn't I right at your side every single time something went down? *We* cracked those cases together. You needed my talent then, and you need it now."

Yeah, right. Patti has a special talent all right—she disappears every time the going gets tough. And she gets me in plenty of hot water because she doesn't react to situations like a normal person. When they passed out common sense, Patti didn't get her fair share.

"In fact," she said with that grating whine of hers, "I saved your life." Then to Greg, "If it weren't for me, Story Fischer would be buried in a grave over there . . ."—here she gestured toward the cemetery on the side of the store—"and I'd be placing flowers over her instead of sitting next to her like now." Then to me, "I suppose you've forgotten that, haven't you?"

Darn, she was cashing in her one and only chip!

"I remember perfectly fine," I muttered, then said to Greg, "I'm not sure how I could be of any assistance."

"As much as I don't want to admit it, I guess it must've been one of the witches who stabbed my aunt to death," he said. "And Dad thinks whoever did it planted that pentacle inside his house to frame him."

I really hated to remind Greg of one very important, damning detail, but facts are facts. "Greg, his fingerprints were all over it!"

But Greg wasn't deterred by that. "You're already close to the witches. They trust you."

"No, they don't."

"If this involves fraternizing with those witches," Patti said, throwing in her unsolicited two cents, "we'll have to pass on the case. Story already has serious damage from her last association with them."

I turned to her. "If you continue to fear them," I advised her, "that fear will consume you. Nobody can harm you unless you believe they can. So get over it."

I wasn't sure what I meant by those words of wisdom, but they sure sounded good.

Patti glared. I glared right back. But my mind was on Country Delight Farm and what might happen to Al and his property if he stayed in jail.

In spite of evidence to the contrary, I still believed that Al Mason was an upstanding member of our community. He always reached out to those less fortunate, taking excess crops to the food pantry, inviting classrooms filled with kids to tour the farm, showing up with his toolbox when a neighbor needed to repair a fence. At least I could poke around a little, do my part for him the way he'd done for me and others in the past.

"What can you tell me about your aunt?" I asked, deciding to remain alert and cautious around Greg even while soliciting information from him. "Somebody said something about a man in her life at one time."

"I don't see how that's relevant," Greg said.

"I don't, either, but humor me."

Greg thought about that. "Aunt Claudene was very private about her personal life. Although . . . there was a rumor, but I really wasn't paying attention at the time."

Okay, now we were getting somewhere. "Go on."

"Something about an inquest. The family shushed it up. Nobody would talk about it, though, and I guess I was so busy with my own life that I didn't get any more details."

"Inquest?" Patti said, suddenly all ears. Then to me,

"That means a judge and jury were trying to determine how and why a person died. That means it was a suspicious death."

"I know what it means," I said, which was sort of true.

"Now that's something I could get my teeth into," Patti said.

"All right," I told Greg, making my decision. "Tell Al I'll see what I can do. But I'm not making any promises."

"That's all he's asking."

"I'm in, too," Patti said. "*We* will see what we can do."

Just for good measure, I added, "What if everything leads back to your dad?"

"Then we'll have to accept that."

After Greg left, customers began arriving, some walking up the street, others parking in front. I smiled to myself, glad to see how the store was becoming an integral part of their daily routines. Especially since last month when my smart manager Carrie Ann had suggested adding a coffee station to the store's offerings so locals could stop for a cup of coffee on their way to work.

My smile faded when I realized I couldn't give Patti the boot quite yet. Here we were, back at square one, thanks to a sudden appearance by the accused man's son. I was stuck.

"What was the name of that boy who was the focus of a love potion?" I demanded.

"You aren't going to believe it."

"Try me."

"The boy Iris was all gaga over was Stanley," she said. "Stanley Peck."

Patti was right. I hadn't expected to hear Stanley's name. My fellow beekeeper and aging friend had had girls chasing after him? Somehow I'd forgotten that he was young once. Stanley Peck? But I played it cool, no jaw slamming open or wide-eyed stare. All I said was, "You follow up on that inquest and meet me back here later."

Patti's eyes narrowed. "Stay away from that evil den of witches."

"I'm working at the store all day," I lied. "Don't worry about me. Focus on getting information that will clear Al's good name."

Twenty-four

❀

Not surprisingly, the locals were completely "up in arms" about our latest town visitors and the so-called wickedness they were spreading around Moraine. It wasn't even nine o'clock in the morning, yet here they were, all fired up and ready for a shootout. And as usual, Lori Spandle, the biggest troublemaker on the planet, was leading the pack.

I hung out with Carrie Ann at the checkout register, keeping an eye on Lori, who had a group gathered around the coffeepots. Lots of bad karma was in the air.

"Ew," Aurora said, coming in behind them. She was back to her normal self (if you could call Aurora normal) with her hair back in a ponytail instead of free falling. "Where did all the negative energy in your store come from, Story? What's going on?"

"I'm not exactly sure, but Lori has something to do with it."

"Witch hunt," Carrie Ann told her.

"Last I checked," Aurora said, a bit loudly, "we weren't in Salem. And this isn't the sixteen hundreds."

"Pact with the devil," I heard someone say.

"The mark of the devil will be on their buttocks," someone else announced. "We could check."

Aurora went a shade lighter than normal and her mouth shut in a firm, tight line.

"One of them has two pupils in each eye."

"Some of 'em can change forms. I saw one change into a black cat right before my eyes."

"They put a spell on Al, made him do their dirty work."

Oh geez, there's nothing worse than a pack of animals. Most critters are perfectly fine one-on-one, but just get them in a gang of others of their kind and they go berserk, acting out in ways they'd never consider on their own. Humans aren't a bit different than coyotes or wolves. I'd seen the same thing when Lori once led a mob over to my beeyard thinking she'd eliminate my honeybees. If Stanley Peck hadn't been around to fire a shot overhead, who knows what would have happened.

Where was Stanley, anyway? I really hoped he was on the schedule and soon, too. I needed to grill him about Iris. Not to mention that I might need backup.

"Is Stanley working today?" I asked Carrie Ann, watching Aurora fade down the least populated aisle of the store, the one where vegan products were shelved.

Carrie Ann nodded and glanced at the clock over the entry door. "He should be here any minute."

"Salt." They were still at it. "Sprinkle it around your doors and windows. They can't cross it."

"Turn a broom upside down next to your door and they can't enter."

Carrie Ann and I exchanged eye-rolls.

Some wiseacre piped up and made a suggestion. "Don't even own any brooms, that's the best way to stay safe. Vacuum instead. Throw your brooms out with the trash. That way they won't have any reason to break in and steal from you."

"Lord knows who will be next!"

"We have to take action!" Lori shouted, sensing the building of serious momentum.

I jumped in and addressed the ringleader. "One more yell in my store, Lori, and I'm kicking you out. Plus, you have no business instigating a mob in here."

"They brew up black magic in a cauldron," another gang member added. "Over a blazing fire. Then they dance wild around it. Naked!"

At least that stretch of the imagination had some semblance of truth to it. Okay, maybe a lot of truth. But really, I hadn't seen any magic brewing in a pot.

Lori's followers were getting worked up good. "Their master is a goat," I actually heard one of them say.

Well, weren't we descending into madness now?

Aurora's complexion when she came to the register to check out had gone fifty shades of pale. Which surprised me. She'd lived in Moraine long enough to witness enough displays of insanity that she should be more or less immune by now. Although this time things were much closer to home for her.

"Goats?" I scoffed from the register. "You have to be kidding!"

Nobody paid any attention.

"So that's why they're out at Al's," some dim bulb said. "His goat is the reason."

"That's ridiculous," Aurora said, breaking her silence. She opened her mouth to expand on that. But so many glares shot at her, she'd be dead and gone if those had been bullets. She shut right up.

"They bewitched Al," Lori said. "And you, too, Aurora. Who knows who will be next?"

"That's what he gets for inviting them onto his farm in the first place."

"He didn't know what they were," I said to a whole lot of closed minds. Then realized my comment didn't exactly make me any better. "I mean," I amended, "he wouldn't have cared if he knew." Which wasn't a bit true. Geez, what a narrow-minded bunch.

Everybody was really worked up at this point, ready to take the matter into their collective hands.

"I know what will scare those witches out of town," I called out in one last attempt to diffuse the situation. "And it's guaranteed, or your money back. Trust me, they'll run away for good."

Aurora gave me a confused look.

"Tell us!" Everybody wanted to know, all excited because I was joining their side, and (even better) I had a plan. Lori was the only one who looked ticked off that I was interfering.

So here it was. "The secret to rid the town of them once and for all is with great big displays of ignorance and intolerance."

Aurora's puzzlement turned into pleasure. She was the only one who got my sarcasm right away, followed by Carrie Ann.

The rest stared at me, and for a split second I thought at least a few of them understood what I was trying to tell them. Then Lori waved my comment aside. "Ignore her. She's been seen with them. She's as brainwashed as Al. Let's go out to the farm and run the whole lot of them out of town the good old-fashioned way."

I tried one more tactic. "The corn maze opens in less than an hour. You can't interfere with Al's business. You'll destroy it."

But nobody heard me. They made a unified rush for the door just as Stanley opened it. They almost trampled him.

"What the hay?" Stanley said, after he'd dodged the stampede.

"They're all going out to confront the witches," Carrie Ann told him. "Things are going to get ugly."

"Lori Spandle is a danger to this town," he said. "Should we call Grant? See if he can talk sense into her?"

"Her husband can't control her," I told him.

Aurora looked absolutely shell-shocked. "I've never seen them like this," she muttered.

While helplessly watching the mob head out to do damage, my animosity toward the coven vanished. I still believed that one of them might be responsible for Rosina's death, but I couldn't hate and fear all of them just because of one bad apple in the apple orchard, just because their beliefs were different than mine, or my family's, or the entire town's for that matter.

I've seen examples of this collective mentality my whole life, both in Moraine and in Milwaukee when I lived there during college. Population size doesn't matter. Unfortunately intolerance and bigotry know no boundaries between nations, races, genders, or the size of a community. So the concept of small-town mentality is all rubbish in my book. Sometimes I think the whole world has come unhinged.

With a clearer understanding of my own need for improvement (even if the others didn't get it), I called my man. He actually picked up.

"Hey, sweet thing," he said, all cheery and upbeat.

Unfortunately, I didn't have time for sweet talk. Worse, I was about to destroy his good mood. "A lynch mob led by Lori Spandle is on the way out to the farm," I told him. "And I'm afraid for the campers. Lori has fired up at least twenty of the locals, maybe more." I'd seen a few gawkers outside the door when Lori made her exit. She'd enlist them, too. "Call out the guards."

"I'll see what I can do," he said. "The women out there have been cleared to leave today, but I doubt they're gone yet. Thanks for the tip."

And he was off. Good. If it came to a verbal argument between Lori and Lucinda, the witch would chew up Lori and spit her out. But if it turned physical, Lori had plenty of backup.

"I'm going out to the farm," I told Carrie Ann.

"I'm going with you," Stanley said.

Stanley is a good man to have around in times of trouble. He doesn't tolerate fools.

Carrie Ann looked around the almost empty store. "I can handle things here by myself," she said. "Apparently most of Moraine is out on this witch hunt. Get going."

I glanced at Aurora. "You might want to send one of your special telegraphs to the witches," I told her. "Tell them to get out of town now."

Just then, my sister sashayed in. "I'm getting a manicure and my hair done for the wedding. Want me to ask for an appointment for you, too?"

I brushed past her. "Whatever," I called back to Ms. Oblivious. Like I cared about my nails and hair at the moment. Sometimes, I'm convinced I was adopted into the Fischer family.

On second thought . . . I made a perfect one-eighty and grabbed my sister by the arm. "Hurry," I said. "We need your help."

"Wha . . ."

But Stanley and I had her flanked, with a grip under each arm, practically dragging her along. Holly was about to get a taste of reality.

We hustled to my truck, stuffed Holly between us, and shot out of the parking lot and up Main Street. We had to wait a few seconds at the bridge, which was still under construction, still down to one lane. Those ticking seconds felt like forever. In between ticks, Holly had a bunch of questions, which I answered in bullet points for both her and Stanley's benefit.

- Al Mason was in the process of being booked for the murder of his sister.

- Lori Spandle was stirring up a hornet's nest (not to be confused with my gentle honeybees' hive).

- She had a mob on their way out to the farm to run the witches out of town, or worse.

- We needed to offer backup assistance to the guests.

- But only until the cops arrived.

Traffic from the opposite direction passed by, and we were off again.

"Slow down," Stanley advised. "We want to get there all in one piece."

Adrenaline was steering the truck, not me. "But Lori has a head start," I argued. "And we're ahead of Hunter, not behind, so we're the rescue team." I had visions of a mass riot going on in the apple orchard. "Do you have a concealed weapon on you, Stanley? We might need it."

Holly squealed. "OMG! Let me out. Pull over right here. I'll walk back."

"Where's your sense of adventure?" I asked her. "It's about time you had some fun."

"Fun? Lori's instigating a mob into violent action, and Stanley needs a gun. You call this fun?"

"Much more interesting than having your nails done," I said with a wee bit of sarcasm.

"Manicures are loads of fun. Let me out."

"We need you." Holly certainly played the need card often enough. Now it was my turn. "You have special skills, ones we need. I need you."

"If you're talking about wrestling, I only use it if I absolutely have to." Did I detect a certain tone of pride? "To fight on the side of good, to vanquish evil."

Oh brother, weren't we full of ourselves today? Although her voice had that recognizable Fischer humor in it.

"You're the best," I laid it on thick. "Trust me, you don't have to get actively involved unless you want to. You can watch from the sidelines. But there's strength in numbers."

"How many of them are there?" she wanted to know. She was hooked.

"Believe me," I said, throwing my future credibility into the toilet and flushing it down without a moment's hesitation. "We're one on one."

"When you're packing," Stanley said. "The odds are in your favor. We'll end this peacefully."

Holly relaxed about the time we turned into the driveway leading to the farm. "Well, okay then," she agreed. "This doesn't sound so bad after all. But no shooting, Stanley."

I tried to veer off toward the orchard, but cars were scattered haphazardly across the path.

A moment later she said, "There sure are a lot of cars out here." Then, "OMG!" She added a few choice swear words to the mix, which indicated a significant spike in her level of apprehension.

Holly tends to exaggerate big-time. Everything in her world is ultra, supersized drama.

So most of the time her reaction to any given event can be discounted for what it is—Holly overreacting.

Except this time, there was really only one word for the situation: chaos!

Twenty-five

❀

The first tip-off that something was very wrong?

Al's potbellied pig ran straight for the front of my truck. I slammed on the brakes, threw the gears in park, and bolted out the door. Ms. Piggy usually is totally laid-back and greets visitors with a sweet little curly Q tail wag. Right now she looked plenty upset. I've never in my life seen a pig run that fast. At first I thought she was going to bowl right through me, but at the last second she dodged around my waving arms and kept on going toward the road.

"Who let the animals out?" I yelled, not expecting an answer and not getting one.

Right behind Ms. Piggy came a flock of turkeys, moving faster than Olympic runners, their scrawny, pea-brained heads bobbing like crazy. They were shouting something extremely important back and forth in their own language. Several of them took to the air over the truck, beating their wings and actually clearing the treetops. A pygmy goat ran across our path, heading in a totally different direction than the pig and turkeys.

The peacock named Pretty, dragging his tail instead of displaying it, zigzagged along without any obvious plan, all the while making a chilling noise that sounded suspiciously like a woman's scream—Holly's, to be exact.

"What the hay?" Stanley said for the second time in less than thirty minutes, but with a little more dramatic flair this time.

He stood at my side, just as dazed as me.

Holly did her usual shtick when it comes to wildlife (which means both domestic and wild animals as far as she's concerned)—she slunk down and cowered inside the truck.

I tried to drag her out. She kicked and screamed. "I'm telling Mom," she claimed, voicing her standard threat. Which she's never, ever actually made good on, so it had no effect on me whatsoever.

Stanley had to help me. Once we had her standing outside, I used my fob to lock the truck's doors so she wouldn't sneak back in.

Greg ran up, breathing hard.

"Most of them went that way. Toward town," I told him.

"Now what am I going to do?" Greg said. "Not only this, but there's a lynch mob in the orchard."

"Business as usual," I said. "Try to make catching the animals a game with prizes for the families. In the meantime call the store and have Carrie Ann organize a search party. We'll take care of the mob."

Stanley and I raced over to what was left of the campsite, with Holly dragging along at a distance. Gone were the tents and all other signs of habitation. All that was left were the smoldering remnants of a fire.

No sign of the van, either. Maybe Aurora had gotten through via telepathic radio, or Lucinda had zeroed in on

Lori on her own, or . . . whatever. The how didn't matter. Thankfully, the witches were gone.

Lori and her followers, however, still milled around, their ticking bomb defused for lack of a target.

"Who let the animals out?" I demanded. "Lori, you're responsible for this, aren't you?"

She ignored my accusation and said, "Where did your wand-carrying friends go, Fischer?"

"Watch how you talk to my sister," Holly said, with a whole lot of intimidation in her tone. She might be a whimpering mess when it comes to creatures on four legs or with feathers instead of flesh, or my busy buzzing bees, but she isn't one bit afraid of confrontations with her own kind. She joined right in, coming nose to nose with Lori. "You have some explaining to do," Holly said.

"I don't owe you two Fischer tramps a thing," said the biggest slut in town.

"Okay," Stanley interceded, sensing a fight on the way, "we'll sort this out when the cops get here."

I really wish he hadn't clued them in.

"Thanks for the tip, Stanley," Lori said. Then to her gang, "Our problem left town just in the nick of time. They got lucky. Let's get out of here."

I narrowed my eyes at Stanley. His met mine and appealed to me for forgiveness. My dream of watching Hunter cuff Lori went up in flames.

Behind Lori's backstabbing rear end something in motion caught my attention. There came Dusty, Al's miniature donkey, running at full speed right toward us. He would have missed Lori altogether if I hadn't given her a tiny push sideways.

It was a direct hit.

Since Dusty is only about three feet tall, his head connected with Lori's butt. What a glorious sight to behold!

Lori flew forward into Holly, who was standing next to

me. Holly went into ready mode, an instinct from her wrestling days. The most that happened was that my sister had to take a few steps back to maintain her equilibrium. The look on her face said it all. *Game on.*

"Clothesline her!" I suggested.

This wasn't going to be a fair fight. There was nothing tough about Lori Spandle. She's all smoke and mirrors. While Holly was taking down Lori, the rest of us stood around watching the instigator try to fight back. The smartest move to use with my sister in a situation like this is to call out something submissive, like 'surrender.' But Lori wouldn't. She's too dense.

"Don't even think of ending this," I said to Stanley.

Stanley grinned, catching my meaning. "And give up a ringside seat? No way."

Once Holly got Lori on the ground, it was all over but the singing. Holly straddled the loser, one arm holding her down, the other arm raised in a victory salute.

"Amazing," Stanley said, "and I didn't even have to pull the trigger."

Right after that, we were surrounded by Hunter's team of pros. Unlike Johnny Jay and his need to announce himself to the world with lots of bells and whistles, the C.I.T. operates covertly. Nobody realized they were there until they were.

"Holly, let Lori up," I whispered. My sister realized we had company and hopped off.

Lori got to her feet, unsteady and discombobulated, which made me snort with glee. Her hair stuck out like she'd been electrocuted, she wore most of her mascara under her eyes, and her face was twisted with rage. Downright scary. Nothing attractive about the woman now.

"I'm pressing assault charges!" she screamed at my sister, then addressed the people who had been following her, who were now backing away. "You saw what she did, right? Tell them what happened."

Lori's gang had had enough. It was one thing to bully strange, out-of-town women from the safety of the pack. It was another to get involved with the Waukesha police. They collectively stepped away, creating distance between them and their one-time leader, while Lori glared at them. She whipped around to Stanley. "You're a witness."

"I just got here," he said. "I didn't see a thing."

She directed her anger at me. "What a coincidence that Hunter Wallace just happened by. What a little snitch you are."

While I've never considered myself a tattletale, there was a bit of truth to her accusation this time. Only since this was more like an intervention, I felt guilt free.

Hunter whispered in my ear, "I thought we had agreed that you'd stay away from this camp."

"I agreed to stay away from the witches," I whispered back, keeping one eye on Lori, giving her a wide grin. "Do you see any of them here? No, you don't."

"I'm going to wipe that stupid smirk off your face," Lori said, getting even hotter, assuming Hunter and I were talking about her. "You and your sister are going down."

Which was sort of funny considering who had just been down.

"That's enough out of you for one day," Hunter said to Lori.

"I'm taking this to the town chairman," she threatened. As though her husband Grant had any influence over anybody other than Johnny Jay, and the chief didn't count. Out of his jurisdiction again.

"Grant will take care of you two," she warned.

"Your husband's too busy hanging out in the porno section of the library," I couldn't help saying.

One of her former followers snickered and said, "I saw him there yesterday. What, Lori? Can't you keep him satisfied at home?"

That got everybody cackling.

Which reminded me of the witches.

And Al's request for help.

Tomorrow I'd make a road trip.

It was time to pay a visit to my old stomping grounds on the east side of Milwaukee.

Twenty-six

🐝

Stanley and I were standing in the parking lot behind the store. Holly had hopped into her Jag and peeled out, recovered from her recent rabble-rousing (frankly looking rejuvenated if you asked me) but late for another planning meeting with Mom and Tom.

"What's the story with Claudene Mason and Iris Whelan?" I asked Stanley. "I hear Iris had the hots for you back in high school."

Stanley actually blushed. "I suspected as much."

I gave him a come-clean look.

"Okay, you got me there. She *did* have a crush on me."

"Something about a certain potion . . ."

"Well, it didn't work, now did it? Instead, Iris got really sick and almost died. She was a cute little number, but that was a long time ago. Claudene came up with one concoction after another, but most of us were smart enough not to sample her experiments. Those two girls sure learned their lesson the hard way."

I wasn't so sure Rosina had learned hers. Tomorrow I'd follow up on Greg's tip, find out if the dead woman had really been involved in an inquest. If there was some sort of hearing, and she'd testified, I'd bet the store it had something to do with mixing and matching.

"You know, Iris is single," I couldn't help pointing out. "Just like you."

"Playing matchmaker, are you?"

I laughed. Iris and Stanley were both odd ducks. I had a feeling that now, as adults, they'd hit it off famously. "She doesn't come into town much," I said. "But next time she does, I'll let you know."

"Why don't I open for you in the morning again?" Stanley offered, changing the subject to one we'd both appreciate. "With my bees bedded down for the winter, my days are long."

"You're the best!"

"Just trying to keep out of trouble."

I walked around to the front of the store and checked in with Carrie Ann, who told me that some of the locals had organized a search party to track down Al's escapees. "What a day!" she exclaimed.

She didn't even know the half of it.

"By the way," I told her, "I'm going to Milwaukee tomorrow. Stanley offered to open for me again. And the twins are on the schedule, so we'll be in fine shape. You should take the day off. Relax for a change."

Carrie Ann agreed enthusiastically.

When I opened the back storage/office door, I found a familiar potbellied pig sprawled in my path. I almost fell over her. Not only was Ms. Piggy in my space, she'd gotten into a box of plastic honey bears, rooted around, managed to break into some of them, and was wallowing in a puddle of honey.

"Carrie Ann!" I shouted, temporarily forgetting my professional, public manners. "Get in here!"

"Oops, I forgot to mention the pig," she said, poking her head around the corner.

Before I could turn into my mother and read her the riot act, Hunter and Ben came in the back door. Ben trotted over to Ms. Piggy, who wagged her curly tail. Ben wagged his own. Then Ben took a lick of her sticky pink skin, briefly considered her sweet flavor, and took a few more appreciative licks. Since bears and raccoons like their honey, why not canines?

"The health department will close us down if they find a pig in here," I whispered, remembering to lower my voice so customers wouldn't hear. "Get her out. Now!"

"But Ben comes into the store all the time," Carrie Ann argued.

"He's special."

Carrie Ann's eyes flicked to Hunter, who nodded his agreement. "Fine," Carrie Ann said. She pried Ms. Piggy up from the floor and added, "Yuck, she's all sticky."

"Did you find out how the animals got loose?" I asked, watching as she stuck paper toweling all over Ms. Piggy, who seemed to enjoy the attention.

"No. I asked Greg when he called about getting the word out about his missing animals," she answered, "but he said he has no idea who would have opened the gate, let alone set them off like that."

"Lori Spandle, I bet," I said.

Hunter shook his head. "Not possible. If she left The Wild Clover with you hot on her heels, she wouldn't have had time. Besides, she had her mind on other things."

Which was probably true. Lori didn't have enough mental range to focus on more than one thing at a time.

"Animals escape from enclosures all the time," Hunter informed us. "Maybe Greg didn't latch the gate properly. Or one of the farm's visitors left it ajar, and the animals spooked when they found out they weren't confined."

Leave it to my man to offer up a perfectly rational explanation.

When we were alone, Hunter said, "Think I'll take the rest of the day off. Any ideas for the remainder of the afternoon?"

I knew that look.

"Maybe I'll join you," I said.

He took my hand in reply, and we snuck out the back door.

On the way home, he filled me in on Al. "We haven't booked him yet, but we'll have to soon," he said.

"Any chance you can hold off another twenty-four hours?" I asked, thinking about Greg's plea to me to assist his dad. "If you can wait until Sunday evening, at least the farm will get some cash from the weekend's corn maze. You *did* clear that, right?"

Hunter nodded. "We found what we were looking for."

"The guy needs to pay for an attorney, you know. Please wait just a little longer."

"What makes you assume I have that kind of power?"

"I know you do." Hunter was the lead detective on the case.

"We aren't formally charging him until Monday morning," he admitted.

Even better. "Do you really think Al murdered his sister?" Hunter has known Al Mason as long as I have. Al hasn't so much as had a speeding ticket. I doubt the guy even jaywalks.

"Everything points to it," Hunter told me. "And at this stage in the game, it doesn't matter what I think. Do I wish we hadn't found his fingerprints all over the dead woman's piece of jewelry? Of course I do."

I stopped and searched his eyes. "You really deal in absolutes, don't you?"

"That's my job. I don't have the luxury of doubt."

"But you can't always be right."

"That's where a judge and jury step in and take over. I believe in the system."

I could have mentioned how many times the legal system has failed, but that was one area we'd never agree on.

"Our partnership sure didn't last very long," I went on to observe instead. We started moving again, holding hands as we turned onto Willow. Ben strolled along at our side. "We'll have to try teaming up again some time."

"Yeah," he said. "Listen, why don't you continue to look into Claudene's past? The D.A. will have to have details of Al and his sister's estrangement. Unfortunately, Al's opinion of her wasn't a secret. He shared it with anyone who would listen."

Wasn't that the truth. Al had bent my ear, so I could only imagine what he'd told others about her. Not good for his case. Not good at all. "I really want to do something, but not to help the D.A.'s office gather evidence against Al," I told him. "It would be with the intention of helping Al and his family."

"Okay, that's fair enough. What do you have so far?" Hunter asked as I unlocked the back door.

That made me pause. No way could he find out Patti was working with me again. He'd totally flip out. Besides, then I'd have to share the little story about our altercation and what she'd attempted to do to me. Then he'd really lose it. So I was once again keeping things from him. Believe me, I've been there, done that, and every time I tell myself it's the last time.

But it never is.

Excuses came to mind. "Circumstances beyond my control" was the most believable. Except Hunter wouldn't buy it. It was all I could manage just convincing myself as to the truth of that. As my pragmatic mother would say, "Why is it, Story, that you always pick the wrong path?"

In my personal opinion, whether it's the right path or the wrong one is sometimes in the eye of the beholder. Hadn't

I solved a few cases in the past? The hard way, usually, but not necessarily because I took the wrong fork. Just because I chose one over the other didn't mean my decision was the worst of all possibilities.

Back to Hunter. "I've got some leads," I hedged. "I'd rather wait until all the pieces are in place."

He paused inside the entryway. "What happened to the wall?" he asked, studying the supplies Grams had used to pry my hands free and the powdery drywall.

"I was repairing a few chips," I told him.

"Nothing was wrong with it in the first place."

"Men! You never notice anything!" I countered. That comment, he *did* buy.

"Maybe you should call a handyman with more experience," he suggested. "You might have made it worse."

Now Hunter took the lead, holding my hand, climbing slowly up the stairs, his eyes hooded and dreamy. My cell phone went off. It was Patti, so I didn't answer. I turned it off and left it on the steps, confident she wouldn't show up at the house with Hunter here. Patti planned her surprise visits around his absence. If he was home, she stayed away.

I heard Ben plop down behind us at the foot of the stairs, which made me feel extra safe from unwelcome interruptions. Between Hunter and Ben, nobody from the outside world would ever penetrate our personal space.

Speaking of personal, what came next was . . . well . . . personal.

Twenty-seven

Sunday morning at the crack of dawn, bundled up in a parka since the temperature hovered in the high thirties, I put my bees to bed for the winter. Indian summer had run its course. In the past, as a new beekeeper this had been a sad time for me. After the lively and busy spring, summer, and fall, the approach of cold weather had signaled an abrupt end to our activity as a team, and I missed them.

But with more experience under my belt, I realized just how much there still was to do, most importantly preparing the hive so that the bees would survive until next spring. Plenty of honey to feed on, protection from harsh northern winds, and a strong queen are the keys to success. Nothing causes a beekeeper more anguish than opening a hive in the spring and finding that the entire hive has perished.

So I do everything in my power to make sure that doesn't happen. This year I decided to build a northern windbreak, having already placed cedar posts in the ground earlier in the month before frost made that impossible. This morning, I nailed burlap between the posts, finishing it off.

Stanley's first thought as a newbie had been to wrap his hives in plastic, until I explained that honeybees need a certain amount of ventilation. Wrapping them, yet making sure they have the air they need, can get very tricky. The key is to have a sturdy hive box to begin with and to narrow the entryway so mice can't get in. If that happens, the mice build nests and eat up all the honey.

"See you in a few months," I told them. "I'll miss you." During the time we were apart I planned to experiment with a few new flavors, create one or two cosmetics I hadn't tried yet, and of course, make a big batch of mead.

Ben trotted here and there, sniffing whatever aromas we humans can't smell but sure do entice the canine population.

After letting Ben back inside, I swept up the incriminating drywall, put away the nail polish, and filled a travel mug with coffee. Then I drove out of town toward Grams's house. Breakfast with Grams was always special, and this time she'd promised a real treat.

I paused on her porch to take a deep breath. Was that really her homemade cinnamon rolls baking in the oven? My grandmother is the queen of bakers, winning every local competition hands down.

I hadn't expected Mom to be in the kitchen. She and Grams had lived together after Dad died, but that was before Mom moved in with Tom. But there she was, in her old spot. Head of the table.

"Hi, sweetie," Grams greeted me, bending down with pot holders to remove the rolls from the oven. "You're just in time. Help yourself to coffee."

"I brought my own," I said, holding up the travel mug. Grams makes decaf, and I needed high-test this morning. "Hi, Mom. What brings you by so early?"

"Your mother is staying here," Grams said.

"I can speak for myself, you know?" Mom said to her.

Then to me, "Tom and I thought it would make our wedding more special if we spent the days leading up to it apart."

"Absence makes the heart grow fonder," I pointed out, thinking of how grating those cutesy sayings are to my mother—thanks to Iris.

"Stuff it, Story," Mom said.

Sometimes I suspect I'm just as responsible as Mom for our relationship issues, but I avoid going there.

Grams set a bowl of hard-boiled eggs on the table and handed around plates of gooey cinnamon buns. While we ate, Mom carried the conversation. "Holly this" and "Holly that," and "guess what Holly found for my something blue?" Holly, Holly, Holly . . .

I could be the perfect daughter, too, if I had paid help with my house and yard, had all the money in the world, and didn't have to lift a finger to do any actual work. Personally, I'd rather shoot myself than stoop to being under Mom's thumb.

"Grams," I said when I couldn't take it any longer, "do you still have the pictures you took of the witches on your camera?"

My grandmother beamed. There is nothing she likes better than to be the center of attention, a position she rarely gets to enjoy when Mom's around. "You bet," she said.

"Mind if I look through them?"

"Not one little bit. Help yourself. My camera is right over there on the counter."

I stretched out to get it, teetering on the kitchen chair's back legs, thus earning a scowl from my mother. She hates when I do that. Mom effectively turned the topic of conversation back to herself while I tuned out. Grams had really gone to town on the pictures. There was Tabitha with her pointy glasses, and Lucinda and Rosina poking through the garlic basket, Rosina posing with a handful of garlic so Grams would have proof for Mabel that it didn't ward off witches. Her blue crystal pentacle was prominent in that photo. Another of Rosina in the corner talking on her cell phone. Then Stanley and other local busybodies arriving. Lori and Lucinda shaking hands (if only the witch had zapped Lori with a wart curse).

Grams had captured the entire store event.

"I bet you're looking for a clue," Grams said to me.

"A clue to what?" Mom asked.

"The murderer's identity," Grams told her.

"Rubbish. Al Mason has been arrested for his sister's murder."

"If only I were younger," Grams said with a longing sigh. "I'd be just like our Story, digging for the truth, making sure justice is served."

Mom snorted.

"Do I sound like that when I snort?" I asked my grandmother.

"Exactly."

I vowed never to snort again.

"Well, did you find a clue?" Grams wanted to know.

I shook my head. "Not yet, but I will."

"That's my granddaughter!"

"Hunter might want to see these," I mentioned. "Could you let him know you have them?"

"I always enjoy visiting with your boyfriend," she said. "I'll let him know."

"No hurry," I told her, since I hadn't seen anything out of the ordinary other than proof that the pentacle in Hunter's possession really belonged to Rosina. He already had my identification and drawing, if that poor example counted for anything.

"I'm spending the day out of the store," I told them as I walked out the door. "So if anybody needs me, call my cell phone."

I failed to mention the most important part: that I'd be on the streets of Milwaukee's east side, looking up a few witches.

Back in the truck with my hands ajitter from too much coffee and a boatload of sugar coursing through my veins, I put in a call to Patti as I made my way toward the highway leading to Milwaukee. Since I had a forty-five-minute drive ahead of me and the expressway didn't have any aesthetic value, I planned to use the time wisely by making a few hands-free phone calls.

This time, Patti was the one who didn't answer. I didn't leave a message, assuming she would contact me when she had information.

Besides, I should be relieved that I'd managed to evade her and get out of town without her carcass in the passenger seat, or behind me as a tail.

For good measure, I did a thorough survey behind me. Nothing.

From the highway, I called Iris Whelan.

After identifying myself, Iris made me trace my family history again to verify my association credentials. "You can never be too careful," she said, after I passed inspection. "Jehovahs, Mormons, Jews, Muslims, they're all out to take over the world and destroy our American ways."

Stanley and Iris were like a match made in heaven. Iris had the right amount of paranoia to feed Stanley's manly protection instincts. With her fear of religious persecution and his distrust of government, combined with his vast array of weapons, they could live happily ever after in anxious anticipation of the worst.

"Stanley Peck still lives in Moraine," I couldn't help mentioning.

"I know. I should call him sometime. Nothing ventured, nothing gained, as I always say."

I gave her his number, then said, "When you told me Claudene had lost a man, I thought you meant they broke up." Maybe it had been the way she had said it that made me leap to that conclusion, because until Greg had mentioned an inquest, I thought Rosina had been jilted by the man.

"No, he died on her."

"Literally, like he actually died on top of her?"

"What is it with you? Try to follow."

See? It was her weird speech pattern that had thrown me off.

"Claudene and Buddy dated each other . . . when was that? . . . about ten years ago I believe, then he passed away. That's what I said in the first place. She lost him."

"How did he die?" I asked, hoping to get a straight answer that I could understand.

Iris went on to tell the sad tale, and I followed along just fine. Buddy had suffered from asthma his entire life. Growing up he couldn't participate in sports or exercise, and he always had an inhaler with him. Rosina, who only wanted to be helpful, stirred up a brew, encouraged him to drink it, and then he died.

"What was in the drink?" I asked.

"I don't remember all the ingredients, but there was red wine, some garlic, cinnamon, red pepper, that's all I remember. She and I talked about the ingredients at the time, trying to figure out which one might have killed him."

"Then what happened?"

"Claudene was devastated, thinking she was responsible. Nobody made it easy for her, either. Eventually the official ruling was death due to an allergic reaction to an antibiotic he was taking at the same time. But people had it stuck in their brains that she was responsible, so she changed her name to Rosina to make a fresh start."

That's why she went to all the trouble to legally change her name. Dy had suggested that Rosina was hiding secrets from her past, but Lucinda had dismissed it out of hand. So the Queen Bee didn't know everything.

"You sure were a good friend to her," I said to Iris. "I thought you two didn't get along so well in the past."

"Who told you a thing like that?"

Mom had, but I couldn't tell on her. "I don't recall exactly. I might have misunderstood you last time we spoke."

"Helen said that, didn't she? Your mother was the problem. Once she was out of the picture, Claudene and I became bosom buddies."

The rule of three! There it was again. Or maybe the real reason was because Mom had always been a troublemaker. I'd never get the real story, because Mom's version and Iris's version weren't going to come close to matching, and the only one who could break the deadlock was no longer able to tell her side of the story.

"Are you still living with that man?" Iris asked.

When I didn't respond right away, she went on. "Men are a dime a dozen. Don't sell yourself short."

I'd forgotten about her opinion of the male species. "I thought you were considering looking up Stanley Peck."

"They aren't a dime a dozen at my age. But I'm not getting hooked up. I like an occasional conversation with one of them. They talk about interesting topics, not kids and cooking."

When we hung up, I spotted the tail.

Twenty-eight

P. P. Patti doesn't drive much, preferring to walk while she stalks, or if she has to expand her reach, she'll bum rides from whomever she corners, which is usually me. That doesn't mean she doesn't have her own wheels. She does. A black (of course) Chevy that's seen better days, probably dating back to the nineteen eighties.

Black cars all look pretty much alike to me. Unless they have other distinguishing features. And Patti's does.

Her pre-owned Chevy came with lots of added antennas, and she hadn't bothered to remove them. The previous owner must have been a ham radio fanatic. And a CB radio nut. And even had an antenna for a two-way radio.

That's how I spotted her behind me.

There isn't much highway traffic on Sunday morning, so I couldn't just dodge from lane to lane weaving among other vehicles until I lost her. And I didn't want to go much over the speed limit, since with my luck I'd be the one stopped, not her. Besides, I doubted that my truck could outpace her Chevy anyway. They both were on the slow side. And Patti is tenacious when she puts her mind to something.

What to do?

I ducked in between two fast-moving vehicles and got an angry horn blast as a reward. Looking in my rearview mirror, I didn't see Patti's pursuit car, but I did see a very red-faced driver and the middle finger he held up as a gift of gratitude for my existence.

I ducked back out and refused to look him in the eye as he passed, but I could feel his glare.

Now Patti was right behind me. I could see her sneaky beady little eyes over the steering wheel.

I did an exaggerated wave with my right hand.

She slowed to create distance.

At the last possible second I veered and took an exit. So did she, a sloppy maneuver but effective. I drove up the on-ramp and continued on, thinking and planning.

Now it was obvious. She knew I knew she was back there. We were playing a game of cat and mouse, and didn't it just figure that I was the mouse.

I called her cell. This time she answered.

"Where are you?" she asked me first thing.

"Don't play games. I can see you."

"I don't know what you're talking about."

Just to be on the safe side, I studied the other driver in the rearview mirror. That was most definitely Patti.

"Where are you going?" she wanted to know next.

"Keep following me and you'll find out."

"I'm not following you. What gave you such a silly idea?"

"Patti, I can see you, for cripes' sake." Cripes' sake? That was my mom's expression, not mine. I was becoming my mother!

When Patti didn't respond, I hung up. Once Patti discovered that I was going to pay a visit to the witches, she'd disappear into thin air. No point trying to talk sense into her when show, not tell, was about to work much better.

I didn't have much of a plan for the visit, only a thin outline. Online research revealed a witch/magic-type store on Brady, a busy bohemian street, running nine blocks long, framed on the east by Lake Michigan and on the west by the Milwaukee River.

I'd lived not far from here, when I lived in Milwaukee, and used to frequent Brady Street businesses on a regular basis. From the thrift shops and tattoo parlors to the best ethnic restaurants in the entire city, Brady Street draws as many young urbanites as it does aging hippies. It was sometimes known as Milwaukee's version of Haight-Ashbury, and you can still see remnants of its counterculture past.

This particular business establishment, called Little Shop of Magic, opened at noon on Sundays and was owned by a Tabitha Moon. Since the witch who discovered Rosina's body was also named Tabitha (why hadn't I found out her last name?), I was hoping they were one and the same person. How many Tabithas could there be anyway?

I had to circle the area several times before a parking spot opened up, but when one did it was right in front of the shop. I'd lost Patti on one of the circles, but she wasn't dumb. She'd figure out what I was up to.

With fifteen minutes to waste before the shop opened, I settled in to wait, studying the storefront. Black fringed awning, with "Little Shop of Magic" in large letters. An image of an eye stretched across the space directly below the name. Signage on every available inch of the window. Words like "Tarot," "Palmistry," "Spellcraft," "Runes," "Healing Arts," "Divinations," "Phone Readings Now Available." More signs announced sachets, poppets, and mojo bags inside the shop, most of which was totally foreign to me.

A familiar woman moved along the sidewalk and blocked my view, then tried to open the door on the passenger side of my car. Locked. Ha! Anticipation is an important part of dealing with Patti.

I slid down the window, but only a little.

"What do you have to report?" I asked her.

"Let me in and I'll tell you," she said through the opening.

"You're a dangerous woman, Patti. For all I know you have a rag full of chloroform waiting for me. I prefer to do our business by phone. And following me here is creepy, too, in case you don't realize that."

"We're partners." She tried the door again. "Open up." And again. See how mulish she is? Other descriptions popped into my head.

- Bullheaded

- Hardheaded

- Pigheaded

Patti is lots of different forms of "headed," and none of them are compliments.

"Notice where I parked?" I tried to point out.

She turned around and got an eyeful before whipping around and saying, "Please tell me you aren't going in there."

"See, this is exactly the problem. You have an unhealthy, uncontrollable fear when it comes to witchcraft. And this whole case is about witchcraft. That's why you're supposed to be working the history angle and I'm working the street."

"Fine!" she said, not fine at all, her lips pressed in a thin, unhappy line.

"So what have you got so far?" I expected her to blather on about the inquest and everything else that I already knew, so I started planning how, after her debriefing, I'd send her on some other wild goose chase to keep her out of my hair. "Let's hear it," I demanded.

Patti grinned with glee and surprised me by saying

something totally unpredictable. "I found the victim's apartment," she informed me. "And I also convinced the next-door neighbor to let us in."

Us?

"I thought I'd wait for you and we'd go together. I'm supposedly Rosina's niece. You can be my BFF."

Oh darn, this was just too good to pass up. And definitely not what I expected from Patti. But I should know better than to try to second-guess her. "What about the police?" Hunter would kill me if I crossed over any crime tape.

"According to the neighbor, the cops finished up days ago. There wasn't a 'do not enter' sign on the door when I chatted with her."

Geez, Hunter was thorough. Too bad he had to put so much stock in things like hidden evidence and fingerprints instead of flying by the seat of his pants with good old intuition like I was doing. "If the cops already searched," I said, "we won't find anything significant to the case."

Patti shrugged. "We'll never know unless we check it out."

Which was true.

"Okay," I said, "but I'm checking out this store first."

Patti looked self-satisfied and almost smirky, as though she'd anticipated my response. Was I that predictable? I hated being predictable. She also seemed nervous now that she realized she was right in front of a witch's shop.

"If you get into trouble in there," she warned me, "don't call me for help."

I rolled up the window, pulled the keys out of the ignition, and sighed.

It appeared that P. P. Patti had sucked me into one of her schemes again.

This time I was going to practice extreme caution and uncommon common sense.

Yeah, right.

Famous last words.

Twenty-nine

❧

Patti needed an excuse to avoid accompanying me into the magic shop, so she offered to go in search of lunch. I watched her slither down the street dressed all in black, down to her fatigue jacket and low-riding ball cap. She'd purchased the men's jacket in a secondhand store last year. All those little pockets meant she had to have it. But since it was green and she only wore jet-black, she'd dyed it. Patti might have made a good soldier if the military could have trained her to follow orders. That wasn't her strong suit.

I stepped through the doorway into the Little Shop of Magic. Tabitha with the pointy glasses greeted me by name. I almost missed her in the dazzling array of products—books, oils, candles, incense (which hung heavily in the air), tarot decks—it went on and on. And like the storefront window signage, stuff filled every spare inch of space.

"What are you doing in the big city?" she asked from behind a counter loaded with items for sale, sounding friendly enough. Glancing down in a front case, I spotted something called . . . dragon's blood. Really? And a bunch of jewelry on top of the counter, including pentacles on chains, necklaces similar to Rosina's.

"Just visiting old friends," I lied. "You have an amazing store," I went on. "Now that I'm here, I could use a potion for asthma."

I watched to see if my mentioning asthma would draw a reaction, like about the inquest into the death of Rosina's boyfriend.

But Tabitha didn't bat an eye, leading me to think either she hadn't been aware of it or she was a very skilled actress. I went with unaware. "Potions were Rosina's specialty," she said, wistfully, while consulting a book behind the counter. "You heard, didn't you, that she was killed?" Tabitha's voice was breaking up.

"And her brother is in custody," I added.

"It's so sad."

"I agree, such a shock. You two must have been close."

She looked up with tears in her eyes. "We got along really well. That's why we were sharing a tent. I'd asked her if she wanted me to go along with her, but she didn't want my company. If only I'd insisted."

Tabitha broke down completely at that point.

"You can't blame yourself," I tried to reassure her.

I waited a few minutes while she pulled herself together. "So you have asthma?" she asked, after wiping her tears away with a tissue.

"Not me. A friend." No way was I going to pretend that I had difficulty breathing.

She stopped paging and looked up. "I have to see your friend to help her. Does she live close by?"

I thought of Patti and how much fun it would be to drag her into the store to act out the role of asthmatic. "No," I said reluctantly. "She doesn't."

"Next time, bring her with you. Sorry, I can't be of any

use without the person." Then she perked up and said, "Why don't I make up a little magic for you? Let's see. How about a potion to make a wish come true?"

"That sounds like fun," I said.

"This is on me. A gift. First we need a mojo bag." She produced a small red flannel bag. "While I put it together, you think of a wish. But don't tell me. Keep it to yourself."

I had my secret wish pronto.

She put some beans in the bag. "Wishing beans," she explained. "And a rabbit's foot key chain—a fake one, just so you know, I'd never harm an animal—and a piece of parchment with a little of this and that added. There." She handed me the bag from the other side of the counter. "Carry it with you, but keep it out of sight. And don't let anyone else touch it."

"Thanks." I stuffed it into a pocket. "I'm sure you told the police everything you remembered from the night you discovered Rosina's body, but have you thought of anything else since?"

Tabitha adjusted her pointy glasses. "I told what happened, but I never thought that her brother was the one who killed her, and I still don't."

"Why not? All the evidence points to him."

"I was sharing a tent with her, remember? When she left that night, she was calm. If she had been meeting her brother, she would have been anxious, you know, really nervous. They hadn't spoken in years, and she told me she was worried that he'd make her leave."

"That's a good observation on your part," I said. "But not enough to get Al released, I'm afraid."

"There's more." She leaned forward. "A group of us consulted the high priestess when we came home. Lucinda said not to bother since a suspect was in custody, but we needed the practice so we did it without her." Tabitha tensed after that. "Please don't tell Lucinda. I shouldn't have told you. If she finds out . . ."

"Don't worry about me," I assured her quickly. "My lips are sealed. But weren't you short of the proper circle?"

"Some of us got together with a few witches who come into my shop. Actually, we were testing that ritual. Most of us didn't actually believe it worked."

So witches could doubt their magic, too. "And what happened?"

Tabitha brightened. "I think it worked just fine. The high priestess spoke through the written word. In fact, she picked me as her conduit, and I wrote her answers down on paper. It was pretty incredible because I didn't know I did it, but sure enough, it was my handwriting."

"And?" I had a lot more doubts than Tabitha did. This should be good. "What did she say?"

"That Rosina's killer wasn't her brother. I'd written *not brother*."

"Who was it then?"

"Unfortunately, the high priestess refused to tell us that."

Doesn't it just figure. An all-knowing being shows up and refuses to cooperate.

Back out on Brady Street with my mojo bag safely stowed away and my wish tucked back inside my short-term memory compartment, I took an incoming call from Hunter.

"What's up?" he wanted to know.

"Not much."

"Where are you?"

"Around."

"You sure are a Chatty Cathy this morning."

"I'm sort of busy right now."

"Okay, that's a good thing, right? Your store sure has been a success."

Hunter thought I was working. And I wasn't about to correct him. He'd burst a blood vessel if he knew I was hanging with Patti. And visiting with witches. And about to break and enter. Well, not exactly break and enter, but close enough. "Yes, The Wild Clover has been a huge success.

Chalk it up to all the gossip. We serve you rumors with your groceries."

"I like that. It would make a cool sound bite. Listen, let's meet up later this afternoon for a nap."

I did the math—a quick peek at Rosina's apartment and forty-five minutes back to Moraine. I could make it easily. "I like how you think," I told him.

We disconnected. Patti came at me from across the street, paper bag in hand, ball cap pulled down tight so her features were indistinguishable, a sort of stealthy manner about her. If I were a beat cop, I might consider stopping her with a few questions about her intentions.

And this was Brady Street where you expected to see just about anything.

Looking right then left, she jaywalked to my side.

With trepidation, I unlocked the passenger side door.

Patti slid in.

Within a heartbeat, she had reinserted herself into my life.

Thirty

&

We drove over to Farwell Street, where Patti directed me to pull over next to a run-down, dirty white Victorian. Then we ate traditional Wisconsin Sunday fare: hot ham and rolls.

I shared what I had learned about Claudene's legal situation, confirmed the inquest and how she had been cleared of any wrongdoing but had changed her name to Rosina to escape the stigma of those allegations.

"Who told you all this?" Patti asked, one cheek loaded up with ham.

"Mabel Whelan's niece Iris."

"Only heresy then!" Patti stated as though she were a litigation attorney.

"You mean *hearsay*."

"Whatever. Iris doesn't have any personal knowledge of the events you described. But don't worry. I have actual facts to back up her story. My information came from documents I found online. So my info trumps yours."

"Stop acting so cocky or you won't hear what the owner of the magic shop had to say."

Then I went on, wading through the details of the latest ritual.

"These witches didn't intend to go bad," Patti stated. "They might have started out innocent enough, but then the dark forces take control. That's why it's best to steer clear of them in the first place. Having one on the block is going to ruin property values and worse, jeopardize our healthy minds. I'm telling you, watch out."

"I just realized why you waited for me instead of going into Rosina's apartment alone. You're afraid."

"At least one of us has a clear head," she said, unzipping her jacket halfway and drawing out a DIY project. When Patti had worked for the newspaper, she'd crafted her very own press pass and wore it around her neck, even though as far as I know, it never gained her special access. This time she'd created another piece of neckwear by hanging a long, beaded chain with a large crucifix, the kind I've seen on people's walls. She noticed me appraising it. "I made it myself."

"Obviously."

"I drilled a hole for the chain. It's a little heavy but worth its weight in gold."

"Since when are you the religious type?"

"Since I found this witch's den and knew I'd have to go inside."

It's one thing to wear a cross as a symbol of love and sacrifice; it's another to use it like a bulletproof vest to ward off people who are different. I'm not Catholic, but I can respect their traditions. As far as I know Patti isn't Catholic, either. If she gets zapped by a lightning bolt, I just pray I'm not standing next to her.

"Keep your jacket zipped and the cross hidden away," I advised, "or someone is going to try to take you in for a mental health examination." And that somebody might be me.

We got out and approached the white Polish flat where

Rosina had lived. Most visitors to Milwaukee don't know what Polish flats are, because they aren't found anyplace else. When our early Polish immigrants arrived, they often built small cottages. Some years later, they raised their homes on jacks and constructed apartments below in the partially sunken basements, which they rented out to the constant influx of more immigrants. "The downstairs neighbor will let us in," Patti said, stopping at a door underneath the stairway leading to the top flat.

While we waited for an answer to our knock, I thought about Al Mason and how we probably were going through motions that wouldn't change the outcome one bit. If it weren't for the incriminating fingerprints on the dead woman's pentacle, and if it hadn't been discovered inside Al's home, I would have said, "no way would he kill his own sister." But I had to admit to myself that he probably really had killed her, and all our wishful thinking was just that. Wishful thinking.

The optimism I'd been clutching had all but fizzled out. What was there to find in Rosina's apartment? Nothing, that's what. Before I went totally negative, I found a ray of sunshine in the situation: It sure would be fun watching Patti squirm her way through a witch's den.

With that pleasurable thought, the door opened and my glee evaporated.

Because it was Lucinda Lighthouse who frowned at me from the entryway.

It made sense once I thought about it. Patti had never shown her face around the witches, so Lucinda wouldn't have had any reason to doubt it when Patti showed up claiming to be a niece. "You!" she exclaimed, still focused on me. "You're the best friend?!" Then her head swiveled to Patti. "I don't know what you're trying to pull, but it isn't going to work."

"We've met already," I explained to my confused partner. "Hi, Lucinda."

"We just need to pick up a few of the family heirlooms," Patti explained.

"*She*"—here Lucinda made sure there was no doubt that I was the *she*—"isn't going up."

So Patti's claim as one of Rosina's relatives was still going to work.

"But, but," Patti sputtered.

"Go on," Lucinda said to Patti, moving out onto the porch and unlocking a door leading up to the second floor. "But I'll have to inspect whatever items you intend to leave with."

Then she stepped in front of me and blocked my path.

Patti gave me a pleading pout from the other side of the witch. Then, with her fist tightly wound around the cross, she started up the steps to Rosina's flat alone.

Lucinda closed the door behind her and crossed her arms in a guarding pose. Then she said, "You are a busybody of the worst kind. Why don't you get a life and leave us alone?"

Lucinda continued to stare, glare, and flare at me.

"I'll wait in the truck," I decided.

She didn't discourage me.

While I sat inside the cab, Holly called me. "Mom's moved up the wedding," she said. "They're getting married Tuesday morning. That only gives us the rest of today and tomorrow to get ready."

"What? How is that even possible?"

"Story, Mom wants a quiet, small affair. Besides, everything's pretty much done. Since the big event is at my house, and we aren't dealing with a hall, the date is easy to move. And the minister, who could have been an obstacle, has agreed."

"Why the sudden rush?"

"Mom wants to get it over with before Grams invites the entire town. They've been butting heads nonstop. And Tom's been on her case for leaving to stay with her mother.

Mom's had it, and you know how she gets when she's had it."

Boy, did I ever.

"But what about the reception? All the food?" This was moving too fast. I wasn't even sure I was ready on an emotional level quite yet.

"Milly's on board, too, with the catering. It's a go."

"Fine with me," I said, since my opinion didn't count anyway. Then Holly was gone.

After that, I simply waited and thought about all the details leading up to this useless trip into Milwaukee. And about Greg. And Rosina losing her man and her life. And why in the world would Al kill his sister? Just because she had the nerve to show up in Moraine? I mean, couldn't he have just sent her packing? Why lure her to the corn maze, stab her to death in his own yard, and hide a piece of her jewelry where someone was sure to find it? At the very least, shouldn't he have wiped off his prints?

If it were me and I didn't want to get caught, I wouldn't have done it at the farm. And I certainly wouldn't have taken a souvenir. Al had definitely been set up.

Think back to the very first day, I said to myself. *Start there.*

I'd been pleasantly surprised to find out that the handsome man over at Dy's was a local I'd actually known from high school. Why, though, hadn't Greg been around during the years since? Sure, he might have visited without stopping in town at the shops. And a lot of kids left Moraine for bigger and better opportunities, many of them never returning. I'd done the same thing for a while.

But wasn't it a little suspicious that he showed up suddenly, after inserting himself in the middle between his dad and aunt? Then his aunt was murdered and his father is in a heap of trouble. Yes, Greg actually had a lot to gain.

Then there was the first witch meeting inside the store.

Grams taking photos. I'd scrolled through them this very morning. Nothing struck me as unusual, a precursor to murder. There'd been pictures of garlic. Lots of black garb. A pentacle that I'd admired. A brief exchange regarding the number thirteen. My offering of Aurora.

Wait just one minute. I had something, a flash of insight!

Unfortunately, Patti appeared back out on the porch, interrupting my reflections. She looked nervous and her hands were empty. I rolled down the passenger window so I could hear the conversation between the guarding witch and Patti. "I didn't find anything of value to the family," she told Lucinda. "Thank you for allowing me up."

Without a word in reply, Lucinda locked up the entrance to the upper flat, then vanished inside her own home.

Patti practically ran to the truck, leaped in, rolled up the window, and locked the door. "Not a single clue one way or the other," she panted. "I risked my life for nothing."

"It wasn't for nothing," I said to her, grinning.

And I really meant it.

Because I had a new question to answer and a new direction to explore, thanks to the short but fruitful opportunity for a quiet review of that very first day when the witches had come to town.

As I pulled away from the curb, I pondered silently, *Who in the world was Rosina talking to on the phone the day the witches stopped at The Wild Clover?*

All the way back to where we'd left Patti's car parked on Brady Street, she badgered me. "What's with the happy face? What's going on? Are you keeping things from me?" It was like the woman had a direct connection right into my brain.

So I filled her in on my first meeting with the women and finished with, "Rosina thought she had someone lined up to make the numbers work. Only the other woman canceled at the last minute. That's why Aurora ended up joining the group as a substitute. Would you look up the number for Dyanna Crane? I need to speak with her."

Unfortunately, Dy wasn't able to supply me with a name. "All I know is that Rosina assured us that she had a witch who was experienced and willing, someone she had met online and hit it off with. Then at the last minute the person backed out."

"But who was it?" I asked. "I need the name of the woman."

"Why does it matter?"

"Uh . . ." What could I say? Nothing came to mind, so I said, "Greg asked me . . ."—here I got the evil eye from Patti for not including her—". . . to do a little digging and maybe clear his dad."

"Poor Greg. He's having a hard time accepting this."

"So who did Rosina call from my store?"

"Sorry. I can't help you."

By now we were idling in a no-parking zone behind Patti's antenna-covered car. I disconnected, convinced that Rosina had been talking with witch number thirteen that first day in my store. Could it have been Iris? I had to chuckle at that. Somehow I couldn't imagine Iris in that role. Besides, Dy said she met this other woman online. Rosina had known Iris her whole life.

"Did you see a computer inside the house?" I asked Patti.

"A laptop on the coffee table."

"Perfect."

"Why?"

"I want you to stick around Milwaukee," I told Patti. "Watch for an opportunity to get back inside."

My big, bad partner groaned and whined, "Do I have to?"

I nodded. "You're the expert on picking locks. I need you to bring me that laptop."

"You want me to steal it?!"

"The word you're looking for is *borrow*, not steal. We'll put it back."

"You mean *I'll* have to put it back."

"Semantics, Patti. It's simply how you look at things."

But of course that was exactly right.

"What are you going to be doing," Patti said, "while I'm putting my life and freedom on the line—once again, I should remind you?"

I could have told her the truth, that I would be taking a nap with Hunter, but that wouldn't have gone over very well.

Patti would never, ever understand.

While driving back to Moraine, I called Greg Mason. "Have your aunt's things been released yet?"

"What things?"

"Whatever she had on her person that night." I hated to ask Greg, since he was on the suspect list, but he was the only family member available and the only one legally authorized to retrieve her belongings.

"I haven't thought about it," he answered, "what with my dad in jail. Why?"

"I'll find out. You might have to go get them. It might be important."

"All right, let me know."

There! Let's see what he'll do with that.

It was a long shot, might amount to nothing, probably *would* amount to nothing, but it was all I had. If her laptop didn't reveal anything new and the identity of the woman on the other end of Rosina's phone call dead-ended, at least I would have given it my best.

Hunter was waiting for me at home. Our nap was everything I'd imagined. Not only did I get a healthy dose of togetherness, but I also managed to learn that Rosina's belongings had been cleared and her family was free to pick them up at their convenience.

And yes, her cell phone was one of the items.

"Now come here, babe," Hunter said, "and let me fall asleep with you in my arms. Shut those big, beautiful eyes."

Life doesn't get any better than that.

Thirty-one

❦

Daylight savings time is always a huge personal adjustment for me in the fall. For the last few months of the year it will be dark enough to need indoor lighting at four thirty every afternoon. By five the sun (if it even bothers to shine at all) drops over the horizon and long, cold nights descend on us. Then by the time I finally adjust to the short days, February arrives with its "ray" of hope for future warmth, enough anyway to keep me going just a little longer.

Many Wisconsinites have seasonal affective disorder and need artificial sun treatments to cope, but as a grocery store owner with early opening hours, I'm relieved that I don't have those wintertime mood swings.

So by the time Ben woke me from my nap with a nose nuzzle, indicating that he could use a pit stop, daylight had already disappeared. He nudged me again. Why always me? Isn't he Hunter's companion and partner? Why does Ben come to me every time he needs to go outside? Probably because I actually tune in to his needs in a way a man doesn't. I rubbed the sleep out of my eyes, rose, pulled on my robe, turned on a few lights, and let Ben outside to go about his business.

A little later Hunter came out of the bedroom fully dressed and looking like he was ready to conquer the world. It's amazing how a nap can refresh a person. He pulled on his leather jacket. "I have to check in with the department," he said. "I'm taking the Harley."

"It's freezing outside," I had to mention, even though I know my guy will ride his bike in weather much colder than this. He shrugged.

"Take good care of Ben, okay?" Hunter said after giving me a passionate kiss and grabbing his helmet.

"Don't I always?"

"Mostly he takes care of you."

Which was sort of true. Ben has saved my butt more than once in the past. I trust him almost as much as my man. First because of his size. The beast is seriously intimidating. Second because he's smart, intuitive, ultra brave, and loyal to a fault.

Hunter went out, and Ben came back in. He plopped down in the entryway and washed his paws. I called Greg and asked him to pick up his aunt's things. If it was convenient. I asked nicely but was ready to get firm and insist, if necessary, but it wasn't. Greg agreed to stop by afterward. I lured him with a promise to share new information with him when he arrived.

I wasn't one bit worried about being alone with Greg. Because I wasn't. Tonight Ben would watch my back instead of Hunter's.

Doing a little calculating, I guesstimated how long Hunter would be gone—an hour for the round trip into Waukesha, at least another hour inside the cop shop, then probably a stop at Stu's Bar and Grill. (Hunter wasn't a drinker but he sure liked the socializing part of bellying up to the bar.)

Not that I was sneaking around behind his back or anything. Okay, maybe a little. I justify my secrets by believing that Hunter has some of his own. Nothing that would harm our relationship, of course, that was a given, but we didn't have to share every single little detail. A little mystery was sort of spicy.

Should I call Patti and find out if she'd been successful in her heist?

No, I decided. If she was in the middle of a burglary and had forgotten to turn off her phone, that would not be a good thing. Maybe in an hour or so she'd contact me.

I'd barely had time to ditch the robe and pull on jeans and a sweatshirt before Ben let out a soft-spoken throaty warning that indicated someone was outside my house. Sure enough, seconds later the back door buzzer rang. Ben stood up, alert, prepared for anything.

Greg Mason was at the door right on schedule.

I went through the necessary motions of introducing Ben to Greg. Only then did my protector stand down from orange alert. What an amazing canine! And to think I would have been scared to death of Ben in the past. These days he's one of my best friends.

"Dad's business made it through the weekend without taking a financial hit," Greg said when we were seated at the kitchen table sampling a little of some of last year's honey wine. This batch of mead had turned out really well, with a hint of cinnamon, cloves, ginger, and cranberry juice, squeezed from northern Wisconsin cranberries. "But we don't know what next weekend will bring."

"The community is behind Al," I told him with a bunch of confidence I didn't feel. After Lori's gang had gone out to the farm, and I'd overhead them casting blame all over the place, who knew what my customers would come up with in the end. "And tourists from Milwaukee and Waukesha will continue to visit just like always. How is Joan taking all this?"

"She's upset and doesn't know what to think."

"Is she standing by your dad?"

"I guess. She's still going to help with the business."

That was a good thing. Al didn't need his girlfriend bailing on him at a time like this. His arrest had really affected Joan. The poor woman; first, a widow, then involved with a man accused of murder. Hopefully, Al would be a free man very soon.

With that, I moved on to the business at hand. "Did you pick up your aunt's things?"

"Yes. I have Aunt Claudene's cell phone." Greg dug it out of a pocket and placed it on the table under his palm.

"Let me see it," I said, trying to play it cool, but hearing the excitement in my voice.

"Why?"

I glanced over at Ben, who had his head down between his paws, but his eyes were alert.

What should I tell Greg? Why not start with the truth and see where it leads?

No way was I starting at the very beginning of this tale and relating every single tiny detail, though. It would take all night, and I didn't have all night. So I kept on topic. Just the store part when I'd first met them.

"It's probably nothing," I added. "But I'd really like to trace that call your aunt made at the store."

"It *is* a loose end," Greg agreed. "But didn't the cops already think of pursuing the origin of that call?"

"I'm not sure they thought anything of it," I said, sure that the police would have looked at her phone calls at some point. "I didn't consider it myself until today, and totally forgot to mention it to anybody before now. And the police were more concerned with the witches who were present, not the one who was a no-show."

Why would they? The women out at the farm had supplied the whole town with plenty of suspicious characters to focus on.

Greg picked up the phone and powered it up. I had to scoot my chair around to his side to get a view, and that was only a limited one. Guys! Always have to be in control of every little thing. Sure he was the surviving nephew, but yours truly was the investigator.

Part of me wanted to grab the thing right out of his hands. The other part of me practiced patience. *Ooohhhmmmm.* After all, this was a suspect sitting at my kitchen table, for a meeting that wouldn't have taken place if not for the protective presence of Ben.

Then while I was mentally reciting my mantra, Greg's expression changed. He frowned in puzzlement. "That's odd," he said.

"What? What? Let me see." I reached out my grabby little fingers. Ben sat up, his ears erect, paying attention to every move we made.

Surprisingly Greg handed the phone over. Then he waited for my reaction.

Which didn't take too long.

Because right away I could see that all the data on the phone had been erased.

Wiped clean.

Gone for good.

"Who would do that?" he said, more to himself than to me. Next he looked me right in the eye. I looked right back.

That was a good question. Who *would* do that?

"There would still be phone records," I suggested.

"Which neither of us can access."

"True." Hunter could check into it for me, but he'd want a full story before deciding whether to help or not, and just because he had the power to invade people's privacy didn't mean he abused it. Plus, anytime he wielded that power, he had to file a report with his supervisor, who was a certified battle-ax.

"So it's a dead end," Greg said.

"Yes," I agreed. "It is."

And with that I walked him to the door and bid him good night.

And really hoped that Greg Mason hadn't been the one who'd deleted all the history from that phone. But who else had the opportunity?

A private eye can't let every little setback bring her down. We still had the victim's computer to explore. If Rosina had been in contact through social media or e-mail, we'd follow the clues and crack that nut. Or rather Patti would. She was a techno whiz.

She had better come through.

Thirty-two

❦

Hunter called about an hour later. He was *not* a happy camper.

"We have Patti Dwyre in custody," he told me in a ticked-off voice. "And you'll never guess whose name keeps spilling from her lips? I'll give you a clue. It's not the name of her attorney."

"What happened?" I asked, fully aware by Hunter's transparent guessing game that my partner had thrown me under the bus. It wouldn't be the first time. And now that we were once again in cahoots, it probably wouldn't be the last time, either. How had this happened?

"Milwaukee issued an APB for her car about an hour ago," he said. "One of our officers on patrol spotted the vehicle heading west in Waukesha County about four miles from Moraine, and he busted her. He actually had to run her off the road into a culvert to get her to stop."

I gave myself an internal high five for not being in her passenger seat. "So what did she do this time?"

"Broke into an apartment, but you already know that, don't you? The downstairs neighbor called nine-one-one while Patti was inside, then attempted to chase her down the street on foot when she took off before a squad could respond. The neighbor isn't much of a runner. Patti got away, but not before the neighbor took down her license plate number."

"I can't believe that woman," I said, sounding incredulous as I should.

"Quite a coincidence that this neighbor turns out to be Lucinda Lighthouse. Anything familiar about that name? Oh, and the apartment in question was recently occupied by our murder victim."

"Uh, yes, that *is* strange."

Hunter actually snorted as though he didn't believe a word. Go figure. "Patti's calling out your name."

"She didn't admit to the charges, did she?" Confessing to a crime wasn't P. P. Patti's style, but I was buying time, racking my brain for a way out. Any little wormhole would do.

"No," he answered, "but she's whining that you should come down and get her."

Hang on, that was all he had? No big finger-pointing by Patti? Yes! "Um," I said, thinking fast.

But my heart sank. The wiped-clean cell phone had been a bust, now this. Hunter must surely have confiscated the laptop. Our last hope, my final lead, flushed away down the proverbial drain.

Hunter went on. "We didn't find anything that didn't belong to her inside the vehicle when we stopped her, although Lucinda claims the deceased's laptop was taken. Do I need to send a Milwaukee officer inside the flat to check?"

"Why are you asking me? What does Patti say about these charges?"

"Denies them, of course."

"So it's her word against Lucinda's. What if Lucinda took it?"

"Lighthouse has her own believability issues. I ran a background check on her. The Wisconsin bar has had numerous complaints against her. Apparently integrity isn't her strong suit."

"Well, there you go. Case closed. One nut after another." Whew, this was what Hunter in front of the bathroom mirror might call a close shave.

I was beginning to suspect that the cops had nada, and Hunter confirmed that by saying, "I'm going to have to let Dwyre loose on society, as much as that pains me. You wouldn't believe what she's wearing around her neck, either—a crucifix the size of her head. She says she's been born again."

I almost burst out laughing at the reminder of her latest fashion wear. I'd forgotten completely.

He went on, "And if you were involved in her recent shenanigans, you're asking for trouble."

"I found trouble the day I hooked up with you, Wallace."

"Sass will get you in even deeper."

"Let's discuss this further."

"First, I better go break the good news to Dwyre."

"Please don't say I have to come and get her? She has her own car. Besides, *we*"—I thought the plural "we" was a nice touch, implying he and I were on the same team against the crazy neighbor—"we can't believe a thing that comes out of her mouth." My big mouth just kept going on its own, so the next statement that it produced was involuntary. "Trust me," I said. "I'm not involved."

Now why had I gone and said that, when he hadn't asked for any further explanation? Out of habit? Have I deceived him so many times that it's now second nature? Would our relationship survive me? And worse, was I subconsciously sabotaging us in some kind of twisted way? Did I need a shrink?

I called Holly, who's the next best thing.

"I'm sort of busy right now," she interrupted my lament to say. "I'll deal with your issues after the wedding."

"Is that Story?" I heard Mom ask.

Then they had a conversation while I waited. "Yes, she wants relationship advice," I heard my sister say.

Mom: "I can give her a piece of my mind."

Holly: "Not necessary, Mom."

Mom: "Didn't I advise her against dating Hunter Wallace, let alone living with him?"

Holly: "You did, Mom. But he's . . ."

Mom: "Don't tell me how nice he is these days. Remember I had the misfortune of dealing with him as a teenager. A wolf in sheep's clothing is nice, too, until he eats you."

I decided to intercede with a few harsh words of my own. "I see Mom's back to her old self," I said to Holly.

"I heard that!" Mom shouted.

A belated thought occurred to me. "Holly, am I on speakerphone?"

"You sure are," Mom answered for her.

Grams piped up, "Come over to the house, Story sweetie, and let's take some pre-wedding photos for my album."

No way was I walking into that lioness's den.

"I'm too busy. Tell Mom to take a chill pill," I offered. "By this time Tuesday she'll be a married woman, if she doesn't go over the edge and blow it."

"I heard that."

I hung up and thought about poor Tom and what he thought he was getting in my mother and what he might actually find himself stuck with instead.

Been there, done that when I married a two-timing jerk who happened to be a skilled actor.

And just because I've known Hunter since we were kids wasn't enough of a reason to let my guard down. What you see isn't always what you get. People put on their best faces at the beginning of a new relationship, and some of them can maintain that illusion for a long time. Sometimes you think you're getting the real deal when all along you had a cheap copy.

Thirty-three

Patti's fatigue jacket was streaked with dirt and grass stains when I slipped into her car after she pulled up at the curb outside my house.

"Geez, what happened to you?" I asked.

"That witch chased me on foot. Lucky for me, she wasn't very fast. She tried to cast a spell on me though, and might have killed me if I hadn't been on my game and remembered my crucifix, which I made sure she got a good look at. And you didn't think faith would work against evil. Now you'll have to believe there's a higher power."

"I never said I didn't believe." I just didn't believe in Patti, who as far as I knew had never invoked the name of any higher power until the witches arrived in Moraine. "Besides, what makes you think her hex didn't work?" Patti turned on an overhead light and peered at herself in the rearview mirror before turning to me. "Do I look like I'm under one of her spells?"

"Did she say any abracadabra stuff out loud?"

"I was pretty busy defending myself with the cross and running at the same time with that other witch's laptop." Patti fingered the cross around her neck.

"Then how do you know she was casting a spell?"

"When I got in my car, she was standing behind me and she had her arm stuck out toward me and she was mumbling something."

"Did you see a wand?"

Patti shook her head and said, "Well, did she zap me?"

I studied Patti's beady little eyes, then shook my head. "No, you look the same crazy as usual."

With that reassurance, Patti flipped off the light, pulled away from the curb, and did a U-turn. Then she turned right on Main, where everything was closed for the night except Stu's, where (judging by all the cars outside) quite a few customers were hanging on to the very last of the weekend. Hunter's bike wasn't outside the bar, meaning work had slowed his progress (thanks to Patti), so time wasn't running out for me yet.

"Okay, let me get this straight," I said, trying to recap all the twists and turns of the story Patti had related by phone as she drove from the jail to pick me up. "The gist is—you nabbed the computer, Lucinda chased you, you managed to toss the computer in a bush without her seeing you do it, then you got away, but you snuck back for the computer, thinking 'mission accomplished.'"

"Right."

"Then when you thought you were safe and were almost home, out of nowhere flashing lights and a siren went off behind you. You attempted to outrun a Waukesha sheriff's deputy, but he ran you off the road."

"Right. Or almost right. I wasn't really trying to outrun him, just buying some time while I prepared to chuck the evidence out the window."

"How is that even possible while steering?" I attempted to figure out the logistics of doing that but gave up.

"You'd manage, too, if you were about to get arrested with stolen goods."

"We'll be lucky if her computer is all in one piece after the abuse you subjected it to."

Now Patti slowed down near a farmer's field. "It's somewhere along here. And quit worrying. I wasn't going very fast when I threw it. Besides, I wrapped it in a blanket before I tossed it. I'm not a complete idiot, you know."

Maybe not a complete one, but a partial one for sure. "Are you telling me the cop didn't see what you did?"

"That cop looked about twelve years old and was too full of himself to see past his own shiny badge. You'd think he was our police chief's over-bloated relative, that's how self-important he was."

I shook my head in amazement. Why did Patti get all the breaks? If it had been me, I wouldn't have escaped from the witch let alone snuck out of criminal charges. Not only had Patti bamboozled a very crafty witch, she'd also gone on to dupe the police. Then she said, "Over there. That's it."

I couldn't see a thing in the dark (was the woman nocturnal?), but Patti pulled into a ditch, stopped the car, killed the lights, and said, "Over to your left. Go get it, and make it quick before someone comes driving along and spots us."

"Why aren't you getting it yourself? You're the one who threw it."

"Because I'm driving the getaway car. Hurry!"

I ended up tripping over the bundle and fell to my knees. Wouldn't you know Patti just happened to have wrapped the thing in a black blanket, too? I got up, snatched up the blanket and its content, and ran for the car. Out of my peripheral vision I spotted headlights coming from the opposite direction.

Patti's car window slid down.

"Throw it in!" she yelled, an uncharacteristic trace of panic in her voice.

Apparently I take orders without question when under

perceived distress, because I did just that. Pitched it through the window, blanket and computer tumbling onto the seat.

My hand was on the door handle when the car started moving forward. "No time!" Patti was still yelling. My brain registered what she was doing while my legs tried to keep up. In spite of my effort to leverage myself through the window, she left me there in the ditch, eating her dust, roaring away in the dark without any lights.

What on earth had just happened? Had I just been used and tossed aside? Had her whole scheme been designed to pump me for information then abandon me? Leave me out in the cold (literally)? It was frickin' freezing out here!

I glanced down the road in the opposite direction, saw brake lights go on from the vehicle that had passed us, then the car turned around and came at me. I prepared to stick out my thumb to hitch a ride. Ha, I'd teach Patti to treat me this way. Wait until I get my hands on her. And I'd turn state's evidence against her for breaking and entering, too.

Suddenly, the approaching car turned on its lights and siren. Oh geez. Please don't be . . . Johnny Jay.

"Fischer," he said as he pulled alongside me, looking puzzled for a change. "Where's your vehicle?"

"What vehicle, Johnny?"

Now he had on his standard mean face, the one I knew how to handle. "It's Police Chief Jay to you."

Did we have to go through this same spiel every single time?

"And don't play dumb with me."

"I'm not playing." That didn't come out quite right. Although if I told anybody what had just happened, they might label me with a big "dumb" stamp on my forehead.

I blinked and looked at my surroundings as though just now realizing I was in a strange setting, and I set my facial expression to major confused. "How did I get here? Last I remember I was watching television. Either I have amnesia or I've been sleepwalking. I do that sometimes."

The police chief got out, slammed his door hard, and stalked over to me. We went nose to nose. "So you're out in the middle of nowhere and expect me to believe that hogwash? That's the trouble with you, Fischer. You're the town's biggest liar. Now, what was going on and who was driving that car?"

At least Patti hadn't driven off with my phone. So instead of arguing with him, I called Hunter.

"Where are you?" I wanted to know.

"Finishing up some paperwork. Why?"

"The chief is harassing me for no reason again."

"What did you do this time?"

"Nothing. But I need a ride home. He has me trapped out in the middle of nowhere and I'm scared."

Johnny rolled his eyeballs. "Give me that thing." He grabbed it out of my hand. "Wallace, is that you? Figures . . . She's up to something . . . No, I don't have cause . . . No, but . . . I don't do favors for you Wallace, you should know that by now . . . Well if something happens to her out here, why should it be my responsibility? . . . Fine!"

He ended the call and handed back the phone.

"Wallace seems to think I have a duty to make sure you get safely back to Moraine."

I grinned. It was true. I happened to be a taxpayer and had rights.

"So get in the backseat and shut up. And this isn't a cab service. You'll walk from the southern edge of Main."

"If something bad happens, I'll have your badge."

The chief snorted and did exactly as he'd threatened—he dumped me on the outskirts of town, then turned around and headed for the police station.

I hadn't dressed for an outdoor stroll, so by the time I arrived home I was shivering from the cold, brisk hike, cursing the chief, saving a few choice words for P. P. Patti, who had once again left me high and dry. At the same time, though, once I'd calmed down, I realized that if I'd been in her shoes, behind the wheel, and I'd seen Johnny Jay bearing down on us, I'd have done exactly the same thing.

The only difference would have been that Patti would've somehow plastered herself against the rear bumper, maybe crawled onto the hood and hung on for dear life. She'd have made sure she got away, too.

Instead of standing there, dazed and confused like you-know-who.

To every person out there, for every time I've unkindly and thoughtlessly declared, "Well, she sure isn't the sharpest knife in the drawer," I apologize profusely.

Facts are facts, no matter how brutal. I sure wasn't as sharp as I liked to think, either.

I didn't have to be a magic practitioner or own a crystal ball to forecast the immediate future. Once I made it back to Willow Street, I found Patti waiting for me in my living room, sitting calmly on my sofa. She'd also had the nerve to help herself to my microwave popcorn, which she'd slathered with way too much butter and salt. "You borrowed a lightbulb from me last week," she said in her defense.

I made a mental note to never ask to borrow a single item from her ever again.

"Want some?" she said, offering me the greasy bag.

I ignored her generosity with my popcorn. "So you spotted the chief driving toward us?"

"And I had to act fast. Aren't you going to congratulate me for once again using my fine mind to get out of a jam?"

"You might have let me get into the car before taking off."

"My survival instincts kicked in. It's automatic. Nothing I could have done differently. Besides, you look like you handled yourself just fine."

"You didn't even consider coming back for me?"

"You're a survivor just like me. Why should I hold your hand? You don't hold mine when I need *you*. And if you want, I can delve into our past and dredge up bunches of examples." There was the P. P. Patti whine.

The black blanket was at her feet. I picked it up and carefully unwrapped it to find that our prize (the laptop) was also covered in a black pillowcase. I kept unwrapping, hopeful that when I opened it, it wouldn't be damaged beyond repair.

It wasn't. The screen was all in one piece and actually lit up when I powered on the machine.

We were back in business.

Which brings me to the matter of our current investigative techniques—Patti's and mine versus, for example, Hunter's. Or even Johnny Jay's. Or my mother's, or a professional private eye's for that matter, which my mother sort of is based on how many times she's caught me in one act or another. Patti and I need to work on finesse if we are going to continue to handle this highly sensitive situation. We have to make more of an effort to become:

- adroit instead of clumsy

- skillful rather than inept

- clever instead of practically brain dead

- elusive versus incarcerated

But I couldn't verbalize any of this because after brief consideration I decided that I was perfectly normal and on the good side of all those finesse moves. It was Patti who had to make more of an effort.

Besides, after blowing her own cover with Lucinda and the Waukesha sheriff's department, and almost ruining our chances of discovering evidence with the police chief, here the woman sat, free as a bird and wily as a fox, if not wise as an owl.

"Hunter could come home any time." I thought I should mention it, for both of our sakes.

So we hustled over to her house with me toting the laptop and Patti handling the bag of popcorn. We plopped down on her sofa.

Patti wiped her buttery fingers on a napkin, then took the computer from me. Hacking is more her thing than mine. I mostly use computers to record inventory at The Wild Clover or to search for new flip-flops online.

"It's password protected," Patti said, chewing her lip in concentration. "But don't worry. I'll figure it out eventually."

"How soon?" I asked, not liking the sound of *eventually*.

"It's already late. Come back in the morning."

There wasn't another choice. The laptop was going to be slow in giving up its secrets.

Back at home I got ready for bed, tucked my mojo bag under my pillow (because I really, really want my secret wish to come true), and made up a mental list of questions that needed answers, without bothering to determine whether they were important to the case. Since their relevance was a big, fat unknown, I decided to assume everything could be a critical component. My short list:

- Who had Rosina been speaking to on the phone? I needed the name of the witch who canceled at the last minute. I felt certain it was a missing piece of the puzzle.

- Why had Rosina's personal information been erased from her phone and by whom? Had Greg tampered with it on his way over to my house?

- Who had Rosina gone to meet in the corn maze that night? Find that out, and we'd have our killer. With any luck it was NOT Al. With all the people out at the farm, someone must have seen something. Note to self—ask Hunter about that.

My list seemed to be in ascending order of importance. Rosina's phone history had to be a big clue since someone went to such lengths to protect it. And the clandestine meeting in the corn maze had to have been with the person who stabbed her to death. It remained to be seen whether the missing number thirteen had any relevance.

So I had three questions and decided that tomorrow I'd stay positive and start knocking them off, one by one.

I must have dozed off because the next thing I knew, Hunter was sliding into bed beside me and wrapping his strong arms around me in a spooning bear hug. I snuggled in, and we talked quietly about our day. To be on the safe side, since I didn't want to accidently blab certain parts of the day's events, I mostly encouraged him to talk about himself, which isn't a hard thing for a woman to get a man to do. Then I told him how Greg Mason had come by with his aunt's personal effects, and we'd discovered that her phone had been tampered with, and all her personal information was gone. Hunter surprised me by replying, "I have the phone company printout for that phone number. You treat me right, and I'll let you have a peek at it in the morning."

Well, well, well. But first:

"Mom and Tom are getting married Tuesday, so Grams doesn't have time to invite everybody in town."

"Uh . . . that doesn't give me time to ask off from work."

"It's going to be short and sweet—a few vows, a little reception. Besides, that's not true. You can come and go as you please."

"You think so, do you?"

"You're not getting out of this."

"Does that mean I get to see you in your bridesmaid dress?"

I groaned at the image of that puce monstrosity. "On second thought . . ."

Eventually we got around to Al Mason, and an opportunity presented itself for me to ask if anybody had seen anyone near the corn maze.

Hunter's answer was a negative, either no one had or they weren't admitting to it during interrogations. Even Al, the number one suspect, denied being there.

So if my man with all his resources hadn't been able to solve that one, I doubted that Patti and I could.

We'd have to find another way.

Thirty-four

Monday morning arrived chilly but with a promise of warmer afternoon temperatures, and tomorrow's forecast predicted more of the same, which would be perfect for Mom's wedding.

Since we were working on an accelerated schedule, first thing I did Monday morning was pick a handful of withered rosebuds from the bushes along the side of my house. I took them with me to my honey house, which is a small, shedlike building where I store my beekeeping supplies and conduct honey experiments. There, I concocted my own sort of magic love potion—the bride's honey for Mom and Tom to share before their vows. Honey, rosebuds, cinnamon, and cloves. Now it needed twenty-four hours to meld, so I'd just be getting it under the wire in time for the wedding.

The wedding. I couldn't believe my mother would be walking down the aisle tomorrow.

What exactly had I volunteered to do anyway? After

pondering for a few minutes without coming up with an exact answer, I went back inside and called Holly.

"You're my assistant," she reminded me. "I have a list for you to take care of today."

Hunter came into the kitchen and sat down across from me.

"I'm sort of busy today," I told her. Back when I'd raised my hand and waved it around, I hadn't been right in the middle of a murder case. I'd been bored, which I certainly wasn't at the moment. Besides, gopher hadn't been what I had in mind. "Very busy, in fact."

My sister gave an enormous sigh of frustration for my benefit. "You made a huge squawk about me being the wedding planner and you not getting to help, and now in the final hours you're way too busy? I don't think so."

"Fine, fine, just give me time to open the store."

"Carrie Ann is opening. I checked. *You* need to drive your truck into Waukesha and pick up some outdoor heaters I've rented. Mom insists on doing this outdoors, so I rented several propane patio heaters." Then my sister chuckled. "In any other cold-weather state we'd be called crazy to have a wedding outside in October in these temps, but here we sunbathe if it's fifty degrees outside."

Which was true, but I still was stalling. "I'll have to find someone to cover for me."

"Stanley and one of the twins are working today. I checked on that, too."

"Um." She'd effectively blocked all my moves as though we were on a mat wrestling it out.

"No more excuses." Holly gave me the address for the pickup.

"Can't they deliver?" I asked.

Holly hung up.

"Family issues?" Hunter asked, why, I don't know, because I always have family issues.

"Nothing I can't handle."

Then he produced the promised phone log.

"That was fast," I said, pretty amazed.

"I contacted the office and had it sent as an e-mail attachment. Anything for you, sweet thing. But you're wasting your time on this. Shouldn't you be focusing on your mother's wedding?"

"Holly has it covered." I scanned the list and found what I was looking for. A date and time that matched my first meeting with the witches. Looked like a call was again placed from that number to Rosina's phone several hours later.

"That's the call our victim made from The Wild Clover," I said, sounding just like a television cop about to expose the killer.

Hunter leaned across the table to see where my finger was marking the spot.

"It might not mean a thing," I said. "But I'm sorry I didn't mention it earlier so you could have followed up. Can you find out who that number belongs to?" I asked.

"Of course I can." Hunter smiled. "And I plan to do just that."

"Keep me in your inner circle," I told him.

Then Hunter and Ben, the daring duo, headed out to protect our citizens by fighting crime. I pulled on a fleece, tucked my mojo bag in a pocket, and walked over to Patti's house. She didn't answer my rings. The house was locked up tight. No sign of her presence, which was really annoying.

Next I walked to the store.

"Your sister dropped off this to-do list for you as soon as I opened," Carrie Ann told me, handing it over. Holly had been out and about that early? Wow. She was taking her position seriously. "There's more on the back of the paper," Carrie Ann added.

"I can't possibly do everything on this list in one day! What is she thinking?"

"Why don't I take a few of these chores and knock them off? Some of them are just calling and confirming. By the way, Milly called a few minutes ago to say she's right on schedule with the catering, so you can cross that one off. See? Easy peasy."

"I love you, Carrie Ann!"

Just then, Joan Goodaller came in, and she mentioned that Greg had asked her to stay at the farm for a few days rather than return to her own house.

Carrie Ann chuckled. "That's because you are holding the place together," she said, "and he's taking advantage of that fact."

"I enjoy the farm, and all the animals, and the visitors. I'm considering taking him up on his offer. It makes me feel closer to Al." Joan's face scrunched up as though she were about to cry, but she took a deep breath.

"You've done so much already," I told her. "And there is a distinct possibility that Al will be back home very soon. I'm working on an angle."

That had slipped out unintended. Blast my blabbing. So I had to tell my cousin and Joan all about the suspicious phone call between Rosina and an unknown caller. "I have the number and will know the name of the MIA witch before noon. And," I bragged, "that piece of information is only one of many that I'm tracking down."

Carrie Ann returned to check out customers. Joan pulled me aside.

"I've given some thought to that night," she said, "and I'm convinced one of the campers had as much opportunity as Al."

"My thought exactly."

"But the evidence is stacked against him."

"It could have been planted."

Joan seemed surprised that I was taking Al's side when so many of the locals were waiting for charges to be filed. "We're on the same page, then. I wish you the best of luck," she said. "And don't overlook the tent partner. She'd been through the corn maze over and over."

Tabitha? "That's curious. Why would she do that?"

Joan shrugged. "Who knows, but there might be a motive we're overlooking."

Hmm. That was something new to ponder, when I had time. "I have to run an errand. My mother is getting married tomorrow," I said.

"So I've heard. Can I help in any way?"

"Geez, Joan, you have enough on your plate."

"Really, it'll take my mind off my troubles. We found a college kid to work the stand, and the corn maze has been finished. I'd really like to help out."

This woman was like the energizer bunny. "Ask Carrie Ann then. She has a list. And thank you, thank you, thank you!"

When I went out back, Patti was waiting for me in my truck with the stolen goods on her lap.

"You should lock your truck," she advised me. "You don't want just *anybody* having access to it."

Tell me about it.

"Did you crack Rosina's security code?" I slid into the driver's seat and started the engine.

"I sure did, but it took all night. I'm exhausted."

I glanced over. Patti looked perfectly normal in spite of the lack of a good night's sleep, and I envied her that gift. If I missed my beauty sleep, not only did I turn mean and cranky, but my body showed it.

"Where are we going?" Patti wanted to know as we pulled away from the store.

"To pick up something for the wedding. Tell me what you found on Rosina's computer."

"I don't know why I'm doing all the work on this case," Patti whined. "All day and all night, while all you think about is the next party."

"It's my mother's wedding, Patti, lighten up. Besides,

I'm working on something related to the case right this minute."

"Oh, sure."

"Really. I'm serious. In an hour or so I'll have the name of the witch who backed out of the ritual."

"Maybe I already have that."

"You do?" Great! This was good news. Especially if that was only the tip of the iceberg.

"I said *maybe*," Patti said with a hint or two of dodging the issue in her whiny little voice.

"So you don't have a name."

"It's complicated."

For the rest of the trip into Waukesha, Patti gave me a dissertation on the nuances of computer breaking and entering, the moral issues involved (Patti's pro open-source everything, so she wasn't too bothered), and the extremely complex process of mining for information.

"Will you please just get to the point?" I finally demanded, as my destination came into view and I still didn't know anything new.

"She had one very close online friend, and the two of them exchanged e-mails after meeting on a social networking website and hitting it off. But I don't have a real name yet. This friend went by a user name, or at least that's what I assume, because nobody's real name could be . . ."

Here, Patti paused, and booted up the computer.

Talk about frustrating! "What? What the heck is her name?"

"Nemesis," Patti said. "She called herself Nemesis. Listen to this, 'Thanks for inviting me along, but I won't be able to take you up on your offer for a ride. I'll have to join you out there. Directions, please.' And a reply from Rosina, 'Can't wait to finally meet you.' And then she gives the directions out to our street."

"What about a real name?"

"Nothing in any of these e-mails," Patti said. "But this

Nemesis person is definitely the one who opted out of the evil dance with the devil."

I slowed to check an address, then pulled into a parking lot.

"I'll wait here," Patti announced, already turning her attention back to the laptop.

After filling out paperwork and paying the deposit (which my rich sister hadn't bothered to mention), we waited for the heaters to be loaded into the truck bed. I used the time to do an Internet search with my phone while Patti did her computer thing.

"Nemesis," I repeated the name. "As in 'enemy.' Like Lori and me; she's my nemesis. Does that mean Nemesis was Rosina's enemy?"

"Or everybody's enemy?" Patti added.

"That doesn't make sense."

Several sites with references to Nemesis popped up on my phone screen.

"Wow," I said after reading for a minute.

"What?" Patti wanted to know.

"Nemesis was a legend in Greek mythology. She was the goddess of revenge, punishing mortals."

"An avenger. She sounds almost as scary as those witches," Patti pointed out. "If you believed in goddesses, that is."

I glanced up. "So you don't believe in gods and goddesses," I said, "but witches exist?"

"Isn't that obvious?"

I went back to the screen. "And get this. Nemesis was also called Adrasteia."

"Which means?"

"One from whom there is no escape."

Patti and I stared at each other.

"We might be onto our killer," I muttered.

Patti nodded.

"You keep digging through data," I told her.

On the way to Holly's house with the heaters secured with ropes in the bed of my truck and Patti bent to her task, I called Hunter.

"Any luck with that phone number?" I asked him.

"Hold on a minute while I check," he said.

Patti had to pause to put in her two cents. "That's Hunter Wallace on the other end, isn't it?" When I didn't answer she made the assumption (not much of a leap) and proceeded to give me grief. "How many times do I have to remind you that we don't need his assistance? You lean on him too much, and pretty soon, if you aren't careful, you won't have a single thought in your head that isn't planted there by him."

"He's a cop with inside information," I informed her. "He's my most trustworthy contact. And it's absolutely ridiculous that he's going to control my mind. Geez."

"Is that Patti Dwyre's voice I hear?" This came from the other end of the phone. Hunter had come back quicker than I'd expected.

"The radio," I lied, then added a bit of truth to ease my guilty conscience, at the same time raising a finger to my lips as a cue to my yakking passenger. "I'm in the truck delivering patio heaters to Holly's house for the big event tomorrow. Did you get that name?"

"Have a little patience, Story. But don't get your hopes up. Al Mason's been a Moraine fixture for his whole life. I've known him as long as I can remember, and this is as shocking to me as it is to you, but you can't change the facts by substituting wishful thinking. We have some very damaging evidence against him."

"Just so you know, Holly has a list a mile long for me," I told him. "These errands will take all day and all night." I didn't mention that I had help in the form of Carrie Ann and Joan. Their contributions would free me for a little investigative work, and now I could accomplish that without having to explain myself or my whereabouts to Hunter. "So don't expect me home when you get there."

"No problem. Ben and I are training a K-9 rookie tonight."

"A new police dog?"

"He's not the rookie; it's his human partner who needs the training."

"Ben will whip him into shape. Don't forget the wedding is tomorrow."

"I'm looking forward to you in that dress."

I heard another voice in the background and muffled communication between another person and Hunter. Then he came back.

"This is so weird," he said.

"What's weird?"

"Those particular calls to the victim's phone. This doesn't make any sense. Are you sure you have the day and time correct? I bet that's what happened, you calculated wrong. Because this can't possibly be right."

I almost said that I was absolutely positive, which I was, but something made me hold back. "I don't *think* I made a mistake, but I guess it's possible. Why? What's the name?"

"It isn't a name exactly. It's a location."

What a letdown. No name again? I seemed to be encountering one roadblock after another.

Then Hunter told me where the calls had originated, and that certainly was a big, fat surprise, one I had *not* seen coming.

He said, "Those two calls came from a gas station pay phone, the one just south of the police station."

I felt a shiver, and it wasn't from the cool fall weather, either. Whoever had been on the other end of the line was right down the road at the time. What the heck was going on?

After blubbering about maybe being mistaken after all, and him advising me to focus on my family event and leave detective work to the detective, I hung up and shared the grim news with Patti.

"Any Tom, Dick, or Harry could have used that pay phone," Patti said, sounding as disappointed as I felt.

"Which, I can't help thinking, is exactly why our mystery caller went there."

If she wanted to remain anonymous, she'd certainly done a bang-up job.

Thirty-five

We arrived to a flurry of activity at Holly's lakeside mansion. Workers were assembling a large white canopy tent. Tables and stacks of chairs were off to the side, a florist's truck was parked in the driveway, and Holly, clipboard clutched against her chest, was consulting with Milly.

Grams had her point-and-shoot out and was busy immortalizing the pre-wedding scene while Mom sat at one of my sister's wrought-iron patio tables, deep in conversation with someone. At first I couldn't tell who, because her back was to me, but then I realized the visitor was Iris Whelan.

Both she and Mom were dressed in somber attire rather than in pre-wedding glitter. So was Grams, now that I noticed.

"Why the funeral apparel?" I asked Grams.

"We're on our way to a memorial service for Claudene Mason," my grandmother answered.

"I didn't hear a thing about a service."

"It's not like Al was going to do anything for her, so Iris

put together a small group of us to have our own little ceremony, to send her off properly."

"I didn't get an invitation."

"Me, either," Patti said, although why in the world
should she? Patti hadn't known Rosina at all. Okay, so I had
barely known her myself, but at least we'd actually spoken.

"This is for a select few," Grams informed us. "Your
mother says you aren't invited."

Which was fine by me. Except what if they started telling stories about the deceased woman and mentioned
something significant, a gem from the past that might shed
some light on her murder?

"Where is it going to be?" I wanted to know.

Mom overheard us with her bionic ears and gave everybody an order. "Don't tell her where we are meeting. Story,
you aren't invited." Then to Iris, "She's a bit of an event
crasher."

"That doesn't surprise me one iota," Iris agreed.

"I am not," I said in my defense.

"Yes, she certainly is," Patti, the eternal brownnoser,
said to my mother.

"Don't worry," Grams whispered to me. "I'll give you a
rundown if anything exciting comes up."

Grams's dog Dinky, looking as scruffy as ever, ran up to
me. I picked her up and we shared hugs and kisses. Then
she squirmed, and I put her back down before she could pee
on me (an old habit of hers) and sidled over to Holly and
Milly where I had a better chance of being appreciated.

"What do you think of this menu?" Holly said, handing
me a sheet of paper. "After the date was moved, we thought
we better scale back. Mom has decided to have the ceremony at one in the afternoon, with champagne and a few
hors d'oeuvres following."

"And a red velvet wedding cake for dessert," Mom
yelled over.

The choices sounded yummy:

- shrimp cocktail

- assorted seasonal fruit with an amaretto cream dipping sauce

- Italian wedding soup

- pear and gorgonzola crostini

- spanakopita

"How about a Wisconsin cheese fondue? I have some baby Swiss at the store that will be perfect," I suggested, which both Holly and Milly thought sounded great.

"You'd think we were feeding an army," Mom called out.

Grams winked at me, giving me a heads-up that she had a conspiracy in motion. Mom didn't stand a chance when Grams put her mind to something. If she wanted to invite the entire aging population of Moraine, she was going to do just that. My grandmother doesn't exert her influence often, but when she does, it's amazing how powerful she can be.

Then Grams said to Mom, "We better skedaddle to the memorial. I'll drive."

"Helen says your driving isn't so good," Iris said to Grams, referring to my mother's experienced observation, one she shares with anybody who will listen.

"She's a good driver," I lied. "I drive with Grams all the time."

While Grams and Mom fluttered around getting ready, I took a moment to question Iris.

"Did you ever hear Claudene refer to somebody called Nemesis?" I asked her.

"Who has a name like that?"

"It doesn't ring a bell then?"

"Not a one."

"Did Claudene have any enemies that you knew of?"

Iris thought about that. "There was one person who had it in for her."

I wasn't about to get my hopes up, since every time so far had been a big disappointment. But I couldn't help feeling a small rush of anticipation. I held my breath.

"Her dead boyfriend's family," Iris went on. "They were the reason Claudene was a suspect in the first place. And even after Claudene was cleared of any wrongdoing, they wouldn't stop accusing and threatening her, the mother in particular."

"Maybe that was the reason Claudene changed her name to Rosina."

"She *did* move away right after that."

"This Buddy Marciniak. I tried to find him using old Milwaukee city directories online, but Buddy must have been a nickname. Do you remember his real name or his mother's first name?"

Iris shook her head. "Buddy was all she called him." Then her eyes widened. "Oh, wait, the mother's name started with an *E*."

"That should be easy," I said. "I mean really? How many female names are there that start with an *E*?"

As it turned out, there were a ton.

"Elma?" I asked. "Elizabeth? Ellen? Eve? Esmeralda? Estelle? Emma? Eunice?"

Iris shook her head at every single one, until I ran out of steam.

Then she snapped her fingers. "Eleanor!" she exclaimed. By now Grams and Mom were in the Caddy. Mom leaned over Grams and laid on the horn.

Iris said to me, "You Fischers are all alike. Man crazy and impatient." Then she scooted away, calling over her shoulder, "Her name was definitely Eleanor."

I felt like I'd won the lottery.

For the first time I had a name: Eleanor Marciniak.

Thirty-six

Best of all, there was an Eleanor Marciniak in the current online white pages. It had to be the same woman. On the way back to the store, with Patti riding shotgun and working the computer, I called the phone number. After four or five rings I got voice mail, and a woman's voice asked me to leave a message.

So I did.

"My name is Story Fischer and my mother was a Marciniak," I said. Patti's head swung up and around at my fib. "I'm researching my family history, and hope you can shed some light on my past. If you would please call me, I'd really appreciate it."

When I disconnected, Patti said, expressing awe, "There's hope for you after all."

"Something was odd," I muttered.

"What was?"

"That voice seemed familiar in some way."

"Like you know her?"

I shook my head. The moment had passed. "Here's what might have happened," I said, working up another of the zillion scenarios that have gone through my head since the murder. "The dead guy's family blamed his girlfriend for his death. The mother could have known that Rosina was a witch, and never stopped believing that Rosina had killed him."

Patti, always loving to throw a crimp in things, said, "So instead of just murdering her in her sleep one dark night, Eleanor follows her all the way out here from Milwaukee, sneaks into the middle of an entire coven, and stabs her to death?"

"It sounded better in my head, before you had to go and verbalize it."

"One of the witches did it," Patti insisted, staring at the computer screen. "And none of them could be the mother because Rosina would have recognized her. Even that new neighbor of ours could have had plenty of time to run down to the gas station and make those calls. If only I could find proof in all this data."

"Let me finish my theory," I said, working on my own argument. "Eleanor found out that Claudene had changed her name to Rosina."

"That's public record," Patti added, sort of listening.

"So she tracked her down. Eleanor became Nemesis online to get close to Rosina. But all the time she was pretending to be a friend, she was actually plotting her revenge. Oh my gosh!"

Was I excited or what? "And Nemesis was the number thirteen who cancelled," I continued. Finally, a small bit of light was shining where none had been before. Unfortunately, we didn't have a single shred of evidence. I have to give Patti credit, because she was giving me a little benefit before the doubt.

"You're right about one thing," she said. "If we go with your cockamamy plot, Eleanor couldn't actually show up because Rosina would recognize her."

I didn't let her calling my plot cockamamy slow me down. "But she *would* know exactly where her victim would be camping. So . . . so . . . she popped into the gas station on her way out here to make an untraceable call to say she couldn't make it. Then later she made a second call to arrange their meeting, maybe claiming whatever had caused her to cancel had been resolved and she still wanted to come out. Then she snuck around in the dark, helped herself to the coven's knife, and met up with Rosina in the corn maze. She could have scoped out the camp ahead of time, deciding the corn maze was the best place to commit murder. Why not? It's closed up after dark, no lights, so nobody was going to come strolling along and interfere with her plan."

"That still doesn't explain the pentacle in Al's house," Patti had to go and say. What a spoilsport!

"A minor detail," I said, before remembering what Hunter had said about not substituting wishful thinking for actual facts.

Patti shook her head in my direction. "It's a reasonable theory, but one of many. If Al didn't do it, my bet is still on a witch, probably that new neighbor of ours. In fact, the more I think about it, the more likely it becomes. Those two witches could have been fighting to the death for power."

By now we were in the back parking lot of The Wild Clover. Neither of us made a move to get out of the truck.

"It's sad," I said, "that you make that sort of statement simply because you don't understand them."

"Everybody in town thinks the whole group is guilty of controlling Al with some kind of hex and making him do it. It isn't just me. But they are all wrong. Al didn't kill Rosina. One of the witches did."

"The locals used to blame you for everything, too, when you were new in town. That's what they do. They look for an outsider to take the rap, and if they have to blame the witches for Al's actions, they will. You notice nobody around here suspects Greg. That's because he's from these parts."

"What did they blame me for?"

"Never mind." I had more than twenty examples in mind and at least half of them were true. "That was a long time ago."

"*You're* looking for an outsider to take the rap," Patti pointed out.

"But my suspect has a perfect motive."

"So does that new neighbor. So does every last one of them."

"Oh yeah? And what would their collective motive be?"

"Power and control. People like that don't have feelings like you and me."

"People like what, Patti? See, there you go again. Making ridiculous assumptions based on outdated perceptions. The real truth is that you're afraid of what you don't understand."

"At least my suspects are real."

"And mine is imaginary? I just heard my suspect's voice on the phone. What about that?"

"Yours wouldn't have had access to Al's house to plant evidence."

We were both getting worked up. Me, because I had a new angle to explore, one that absolved the coven members as well as Al and Greg Mason. I really wanted Al back on the farm doing what he does so well. And I'd met the group of women and hoped they'd work out their differences without curses or murders. It would be so simple if the killer were an unknown, someone who hadn't been inside my store and inside my life.

Patti was getting all ticked off for a different reason. She desperately wanted Dy out of our neighborhood. As far as she was concerned, getting rid of Dyanna meant the rest of the witches would disappear for good, too. "We have to clear Al," she said.

"At least we agree on something."

"You're really going to pursue the vengeful mother theory?"

"You're really going after Dyanna Crane?"

"We're at an impasse."

"Obviously." But how to work around the deadlock? "Can't we work on both, eliminate one or the other?" There. That was me compromising like a good friend.

"No way, Fischer." Uh-oh, Patti has never called me by my last name. That was more Johnny Jay's style. Then she said, "You're either with me or against me."

She stared into my eyes and must have seen my answer, because she was out of the truck before I could blink.

"Don't you dare take off with that computer!" I called after her, realizing belatedly that it had already slipped through my fingers along with my temperamental partner.

Before I went into the store, I called Hunter.

"Hope your day is going better than mine," he said right away.

"Now what?"

"Let's not discuss it."

"Then you shouldn't have brought it up."

"Well, aren't you testy."

"Just tell me."

The gist was that it was Hunter's job to prove beyond a reasonable doubt that Al Mason had murdered his sister. He probably had enough, but Hunter is a perfectionist when it comes to his career. He doesn't like to make mistakes, and he's climbed the professional ladder to land the position of detective because he's good at what he does. That perfectionist part is important when you're dabbling with people's lives.

"Ben picked up a scent out at the farm. We were doing another routine search and he found something."

"Something new, you mean? Something he didn't find

before?" That wasn't like Hunter's K-9 partner. If evidence was there, Ben always found it.

"This was inside the barnyard. At the back, in a pile of manure. Whatever was buried there, though, is gone now."

I didn't think this was such a big deal, but this was my man and I had to support him. "If only Ben could talk," I said.

"Wouldn't that solve a whole lot of problems? Anyway, he could have missed it the first time, because of where it was buried. Ben is the best tracker on the force, but animal manure is just too much for even the best."

"What do you think he's trying to tell you in dog language?"

"I'm pretty sure he's telling me that whatever was there had the victim's blood on it. Probably an item of clothing, since we already have the murder weapon. I've been wondering how the perp managed to stay blood free."

Okay, maybe this was a big deal. I connected a few dots. "You know, somebody let the animals loose the other day. I'd assumed it was an accident, that somebody didn't close the gate properly. But what if the killer needed to create a diversion in order to have the opportunity to remove some incriminating evidence?"

"I don't know, Story. Possibly. This complication wouldn't even have surfaced if it had been left where it was. Somewhere in the unearthing, a new, fresh scent clued in Ben."

"What does Greg say?"

"He claims he doesn't have any idea. In fact, he actually challenged Ben's training. Greg accused me of planting false evidence against his father." Hunter sighed. "Sometimes I hate this job."

"Because now you have a little bit of doubt as to Al's guilt?"

"Nothing conclusive, nothing that changes what we

already have on him. But I don't like it. How is your day going? Cheer me up with some local color."

So I shared the wedding menu and the ongoing contest of wills between Mom and Grams.

"Your grandmother will win," he said with a chuckle. "How many chairs did you see? That will give us the answer."

How many had there been? That's the difference between a detective like Hunter and an amateur like me. He would have known the answer. Me? All I could say is, "We'll find out tomorrow, won't we?"

As I approached the back door, my step was lighter and my spirit had improved.

Hunter didn't have to say any more than he had to get my hopes back up. Because if someone had really created a diversion so they could remove a bloody piece of evidence, it couldn't have been Al.

He was already in jail the day his barnyard pets ran free.

So who had let the animals loose?

Thirty-seven

❦

Gosh, The Wild Clover was busy for a Monday. Sometimes there's no rhyme or reason to the ebbs and flows in the service business. Luckily, Carrie Ann has a sixth sense when it comes to staffing and rarely gets it wrong. The twins were restocking the shelves from the weekend rush, and my cousin and Stanley were working the checkout line.

I pitched in and was rewarded with small talk, which has been a bit lacking since the store has grown. Not that I'm complaining. I may miss the socializing, but I never want to go back to stocking shelves. Arranging a pretty display for visual effect is one thing; it's quite another to struggle with heavy boxes filled with melons or large canned goods.

As Monday afternoon wore on, everybody and his uncle passed through our doors, many of them mentioning tomorrow afternoon's wedding. Even Lori wandered through complaining that she didn't have her invitation yet. I didn't mention that invitations wouldn't have been sent through normal channels, that Grams would have given word-of-mouth invites to a certain circle of her friends. Plus, she's no fool. She knows better than to put the two of us at the same event.

"What's the blushing bride going to wear?" someone asked.

"Off white?" someone guessed. "Ivory?"

"Pure white, I'm thinking."

"That's for new brides."

"In this day and age you can wear whatever you want. Red, blue, the sky is the limit."

"Let us in on the secret, Story."

I gave them a Mona Lisa smile to imply that Mom's wardrobe secret was safe with me, when in actuality I hadn't even seen Mom's dress. It could be black for all I knew.

"Since Story isn't telling, we'll just have to wait and see tomorrow."

It seemed that Grams hadn't left out a single one of her peers.

Milly came in.

"Which one of my family members gave you a head count?" I wanted to know. "Grams or Mom?"

"Your mother gave it to me," Milly said before flashing a sly smile. "But your grandmother amended it."

"And Holly is aware of any last-minute surprises for seating and all?"

Milly beamed, having so much fun. "Everybody who needs to know knows. I'm all set except for a few items that I'm getting here now, like that cheese for the fondue."

The wedding caterer disappeared down one of the aisles.

Holly rushed in in a panic over forgotten this and that. "How's the list coming?" she asked me, sounding frazzled.

"Don't worry about a thing," I said, suddenly worried

because Carrie Ann had been so busy I'd completely forgotten to ask if she'd had time to work on it at all.

Johnny Jay came in and strutted up and down the aisles like a peacock. I had the pleasure of checking out his purchases. Nothing special. Enriched white bread, whole milk, peanut butter.

"How's the sting operation coming?" I asked him. "Catch your smut thief yet?"

"These things take time," he said, all-important. Then he gave me one of his menacing glares. "Fischer, it was probably a mistake to discuss official business in front of you. A serious lapse of judgment on my part. You haven't been blabbing it around town, have you?"

"Of course not. If someone is stealing from the library, they need to pay for their actions," I said, meaning what I said. Emily, the library director, is a good friend, and doesn't deserve to be ripped off. Neither does the town. Our taxes help support the library. Still . . . "I just don't think it's the kind of crime that needs police involvement and security cameras."

I could have added that the chief and town chairman must be bored to smithereens to have even concocted this scheme. Once again, I thought of Lori Spandle and how much she was disrespecting her husband by carousing around town, chasing after construction workers. If anyone deserved to get caught doing something lascivious, it wasn't some kid sneaking erotica out of the library. It was Lori.

A little later Greg stopped by to pick up the box of leftover produce I always send over on Mondays for the farm animals, all stuff that would just get thrown out otherwise.

"How is the investigation going?" he asked in a low voice. "Have you made any headway on clearing my dad?"

"Not yet," I said, "but I'm working on a few ideas. I can't say more quite yet."

Greg nodded and left toting the food box.

Had I spread myself too thin? I hadn't been effective as

a wedding planner's assistant *or* as a private investigator. I hadn't even been a good live-in girlfriend, and was lucky that Hunter had been preoccupied with the case himself. Patti was ticked at me, so I wouldn't win the good-neighbor award, either. Once the wedding was over and the case solved to everyone's satisfaction, life would return to normal.

I'd totally forgotten about my other to-do list helper in all the commotion, until I found time to visit the back room and discovered Joan Goodaller as she was finishing up a phone call at my desk.

"There you go," she said, handing over Holly's list for the wedding with every single item crossed off.

"You have to be the most efficient woman I've ever met," I told her, overjoyed. Gleeful, really. She'd saved me from certain damaging criticism from the matriarch in our family.

Then I realized this volunteer should be invited to Mom's wedding. "Please come to the wedding tomorrow," I thankfully remembered to say. "The family appreciates everything you've done."

"I'd love to," she said. "Count me in. If Al gets out, can he come, too?" Joan gave me a weak smile, though I could see in her eyes that she wasn't hopeful that would happen.

"But of course," I told her. "He's welcome as well."

"But on a more serious note," she went on to say, "Greg tells me you're working hard to free his father."

"I have a few loose ends to explore. Keep your fingers crossed that they work out."

"I've crossed my toes, too," she said before breezing out the door, leaving me alone to realize how exhausted I was both mentally and physically.

I plopped down in my office chair, folded my arms over the desk, and rested my head on them. Where to go from here regarding the murder? Nowhere, that's where. Since Hunter had a new sliver of doubt about Al Mason's guilt, he would dig (no pun intended) through the b.s. (as in manure), and, just to help him along, I'd bring him up to speed on today's findings. Especially Nemesis. Excluding, of course, any mention of Patti.

How could one individual be so high maintenance in the friendship department?

Still, while I realized that I complained pretty much nonstop about Patti, geez, she sure does make life entertaining. Maybe it was time to stop running away from her and her escapades and embrace her for who she is and what she brings to my life.

I lifted my head from my crossed arms, thinking I must be really tired, slaphappy, even, to be thinking of a long-term relationship with the person whose main contribution to our friendship is conflict and frustration.

I stood up, yawned, and wandered out the back door into the parking lot. While there, I noticed Stanley Peck standing in the cemetery at one of the markers, head bowed. When was the last time I'd walked its worn paths?

It had been a while. When I was a little kid we used to play hide and seek among the markers. Looking back, that wasn't very respectful, but kids don't know any better.

Stanley looked up and spotted me, so I waved and walked over to where he stood.

"Thought I'd stop and pay my respects before heading home," he said. "My great grandmother and grandfather are buried right here."

"I remember you saying something about that." I read the inscriptions etched into the stones. "They died the same year?"

He nodded. "Grandpa went first. After that, my grandmother didn't have the will to live. But they were both in their nineties and had lived full lives. We all should live so long."

After a few moments of respectful silence, Stanley said, "Well, I'm off. Have a nice evening."

He headed toward Main Street as I rubbed my weary

eyes. Another day almost done. And not much to show for it, except pretty decent sales.

Some of my ancestors were buried in this cemetery, too. Not Fischers from my father's side, but Morgans from Grams's maternal line. They were buried in the oldest part of this small church cemetery, and I wandered over to give them a nod.

Which I did, reading the inscriptions, imagining daily life way back when.

After that, I walked along, reading names on other gravestones, recognizing many names of families still living in the community. Then my eyes swept across another one. Why, I don't know. The inscription was faded, the letters worn down with age.

I came to a sudden halt.

And read it again.

The first name, which had been carved on the gravestone, was as common as could be. *Jacob.* A nice biblical name. The surname is what threw me, because it wasn't common at all. In fact, I'd only met one person with that particular last name, and she wasn't even from Moraine.

I read it again. *Goodaller.*

Jacob Goodaller.

Joan Goodaller.

What were the odds?

Thirty-eight

All kinds of bells went off. Literal ones, too. When I converted the old Lutheran church into The Wild Clover, I'd left the bell tower intact. The community had missed hearing the bell rung and requested that it be brought back to life, so I had the automatic controller repaired and set to ring twice each day—once at noon, and again at five in the afternoon. The five-o'clock bell sounded now.

As I stood staring at the inscription on the headstone, all kinds of thoughts went through my muddled mind.

One random piece of trivia came through. What was another name for a bell tower? A belfry. What did it mean to have bats in the belfry? Insanity. It was insane what my mind was coming up with.

I glanced upward, half expecting a whole colony of bats to take to the air.

The other bells going off weren't dinner bells or jingle bells.

They were internal warning bells.

Hell's bells.

Sweet, grandmotherly Joan, always on the periphery of every little crisis, pitching in wherever she was needed, quickly becoming part of our community. Widow Joan, dating divorced Al Mason. My customers and I thought they were a good match.

Part of me reasoned that the names were just a big coincidence and that if I asked Joan about it she would have an acceptable explanation. Maybe that's why she wanted to be part of our community, because she'd had ancestors living in Moraine long ago. In fact, she might even say she'd been named after one of them.

That was reasonable, right?

Yet, she'd never mentioned a local connection, and we'd had quite a few chats together. Remembering back, some of our topics had even included local history. Wouldn't that have come up then? She'd have had a perfect opportunity to share that connection. She could have said, "My great grandfather is buried in the cemetery right next to your store and his name was Jacob Goodaller."

That would have been a perfectly normal response.

If it had been true. Which intuition told me it wasn't. Had she been walking through this very cemetery while considering a move to Moraine? Had the name on the gravestone caught her attention? And later, she'd remembered it when she'd chosen an alias, moved to town, and . . . what? Why would she do that? And another glitch in my theory—Joan had never mentioned children, especially not a dead son. Wouldn't that have come up?

It wasn't much of a leap for me to wonder if "Joan Goodaller" could possibly be Eleanor Marciniak, the woman with a vendetta against Claudene Mason. After a few brief calculations, I deduced that she was the right age to be Buddy Marciniak's mother. Eleanor Marciniak, who had been instrumental in the inquiry into her son's death.

Perhaps she was also known as Nemesis. And/or witch number thirteen.

That was a whole lot of aliases for one woman to have. One innocent woman, at least. Was I crazy to even be thinking this? Perhaps I was barking up the wrong tree (as Grams would put it in her endearing way). This had to be a coincidence, right?

I rushed back inside the store, relieved that my sister had finished up and taken off. I did an online search for Joan Goodaller and refined it by adding the keywords Milwaukee and Waukesha County. Geography didn't matter, because when I expanded the search out from Wisconsin, the only name even close was Jane Goodall, famous for her life's work studying chimps.

Carrie Ann was checking out a customer when I pounded up to her. My heart raced when I noticed it was Officer Sally Maylor, off duty and out of her cop uniform. Both of them turned and stared at me.

"What?" I asked, working at breathing normally.

"You look spooked," Carrie Ann said.

Really? I looked that bad? "No, I'm perfectly fine. Um, Sally, can Al have visitors yet?"

Sally shook her head. "Not yet. Why? You want to visit Al?"

I considered sharing my crazy hypothesis with Sally, but it was complicated and would take a lot of time to explain, and she'd get Johnny Jay involved, and what if I was wrong?

I went the evasive route. "I'm helping with his animals and have a few questions about feeding them."

"Can't you ask Greg or Joan?"

"Um, it's okay, I'll manage." Now what? I needed to ask Al one quick question.

And with that thought, something magical happened.

Sally said, "I can get you two on the phone, but you'll only get a minute."

I grinned. "Can you do it now?"

Sally popped her cell phone from its case on her belt, dialed, explained the reason for her call, waited while the call made its way through the proper channels, then handed the phone over to me.

"Carrie Ann," I said as I took it, "why don't you help Sally pick out a jar of honey from the display." Then to Sally, "It's on the house."

"Why thank you," Sally said, and the two wandered off, leaving Al and me to talk in private.

"I only have a minute," I told Al, "and I need to know one thing. And I don't have time to explain why I'm asking. Not right now, anyway, but I promise I will as soon as we get you out of there."

I heard a rush of air as Al exhaled. "I thought you all abandoned me. I haven't talked to a single soul since they let me have that one call to Greg. He asked you for help, right?"

"Yes, that's why I'm calling."

Sally had her jar of honey and was turning back my way. So I took a leap and said, "What was Joan's son's name?"

I could have asked if she had any children and if so, was one a boy, and then if so, what was his name, but I didn't have time for twenty questions.

There was a pause on the other end of the line. Sally reached out for the phone. I raised a finger in the air to let her know I needed a second longer.

Al started to say, "Joan wanted that kept a secret. I don't know how you found out or why you're asking, but—"

"Al?" I interrupted, with a little pleading in my voice, which wasn't faked at all, and with growing excitement, too, because he'd already started to confirm my sneaky suspicion.

"Time's up," Sally said, ready to take the phone away. "Don't get me in trouble."

"Robert," Al said.

"Gotta go." Sally reached out and took the phone from

my hand. I'd lost the opportunity to ask if her son went by a nickname and if it happened to be Buddy.

But I had confirmed she'd had a son. Joan could very well have been the vengeful mother. She could be Nemesis.

Had she been hunting for the woman whom she felt was responsible for her son's death? Had she ingratiated herself with Al and then lay waiting in the weeds for the opportune moment?

Had the murderer been in our midst the entire time?

Thirty-nine

It was all speculation, of course. Circumstantial. Intuition. A hunch. Instinct. I couldn't go to Hunter and tell him, "I just have a feeling that she is our killer," because then he would lecture me on gathering evidence versus making up stuff.

What did I have to support my hypothesis? Let's see:

- someone with the unlikely name of Nemesis who had befriended the murder victim online and who turned out to be the MIA thirteenth witch

- two unidentified calls from the gas station to the murder victim's phone

- the discovery of a grieving mother, who had blamed the woman her son had been dating for his death

- a gentle, aging widow who had exhibited a kind and generous heart and just happened to have the same surname as a dead man in the cemetery

What now?

I called Greg. "Are you out at the farm?" I asked him.

"Yes, why? Did you find something?"

"I'm not sure."

"Why don't you come over? We'll talk about what you have so far."

"Yes. It might help to get another opinion. Is Joan there?"

"She went home for the night. Tomorrow she'll make arrangements to stay out here for a few days."

With the comforting news that Joan wouldn't be around, we disconnected, and I went back inside the store where Trent and Brent were holding down the fort to let them know I was leaving for the night. "I'm driving out to Al's farm," I told them, feeling that I needed to tell someone where I'd be.

I hopped in my truck and took off, wondering why I was so fixated on a sweet little grandmotherly woman like Joan. Did she even have the physical strength to stab someone to death?

Doubt set in. What about the witches, who were perfect candidates?

Lucinda gave me the creeps. Suddenly I remembered something she'd said to the coven the night Hunter found the pentacle inside Al's house. The witches had expressed concern about cops arriving at the campsite. Lucinda had reassured them. How could she have known the search would end with the house? Of course, then I also had to ask myself how Aurora had perceived my distress when Johnny Jay had me trapped at the police station. And hadn't I added Greg to the list of suspects, and here I was going to be alone with him out at the farm? But recently, I'd been relying on my intuition, and it was telling me that a boy born and bred in Moraine would never harm his own aunt. Nor would he frame his dad for her murder.

I had to trust my gut.

When I pulled into the long driveway and parked, I was still playing "what-if?"

A single light was on inside Al's house, and after knocking several times without an answering greeting, I tried the door. It swung open.

I followed the light source through the living room into the kitchen, calling Greg's name, a little annoyed with him, since he knew I was on my way. Then annoyance turned to concern and then horror.

Because Greg was on the floor on his back, blood pooling under him.

Oh! My! God!

I crouched down and tried to rouse him. He was breathing but didn't respond. I had to call nine-one-one and get help!

As I rose to check my pockets for my phone, I felt a presence in the room. Joan Goodaller had been standing off to the side, watching.

Then my eyes locked on the handgun she was pointing at me.

"I apologize for not returning your phone call," she said, "but your cover story was pretty silly. Family history! I thought you were smarter than that."

"You did this? You shot Greg? Why? What has he ever done to you?"

Joan shook her head, seemingly in distress. "The boy would have been perfectly fine if you hadn't insisted on interfering. I was outside, ready to leave for my home, when I remembered I'd left my house keys inside. That's when Greg told me you were coming over with important information. And that's the moment when I knew the gig was finally up."

"He's going to die if we don't help him."

"You've been such a busybody and now you've involved this innocent boy. Look what you've done."

What *I've* done?

"Please toss your phone this way," she ordered, and all the sweetness had evaporated. "We won't be making any phone calls."

"But I don't understand," I said, understanding perfectly.

"Sure you do. It's no surprise to you how easy it is to find out anything you want to. Claudene could run, but she couldn't hide. She killed Buddy, but no one would believe me. I came out here to bide my time, not realizing that she and Al were estranged. Then Greg let something slip. He'd been in contact with Claudene. It didn't take much prompting to have him arrange for her to visit. It was all working out perfectly. If only you'd stayed out of it. Now toss me the phone."

What choice did I have? I tossed it, but instead of taking her eyes away to catch it, which I'd hoped for, she let it fall beside her. I kept her talking.

"You were Nemesis, too," I said. "And you made those calls from the gas station, one to cancel as number thirteen, and the other to suggest a meeting place later after the ritual."

"Nemesis, yes. How else could I have gained that horrible murdering woman's trust? And after our wonderful virtual friendship she was more than enthusiastic to finally meet me. I really surprised her!"

The gun in her hand scared me silly.

"Wait! Don't shoot me just yet," I pleaded, realizing that she could pull the trigger any second. "First tell me, why did you set up Al? One of the witches would be a more obvious choice."

"If that leader hadn't been so alert, you mean. I couldn't get near their camp after they went on high alert, let alone get one of their prints on the pentacle."

"How in the world did you get Al's fingerprints?"

Joan gave me a sly grin. "Ever since he sprained his ankle, he's been self-medicating, doping himself into oblivion. It was easy, actually. He never even budged when I cupped the pentacle in his hand."

While we'd been having this friendly little conversation, I'd been thinking about how Eleanor must've surprised Greg when she'd shot him up close, and judging by his position, she'd fired into his back. Not nice and grandmotherly at all.

Unless I wanted to end up in the same mess, I had to make a move.

At least I was wearing sturdy shoes instead of flip-flops. And I was a fast runner. That is, if I got the chance to run.

I considered my limited choices. I could continue to stand here like a sitting duck and take a bullet, but that wasn't my favorite option. I thought about jumping Joan. I had the advantage of youth, but she had the deadly weapon, so I rejected that choice and went with the only other possibility.

I bolted for the living room, heading for the front door.

A shot rang out. Then another.

Had she hit me? Nothing hurt. I was still on my feet, so maybe not.

Then I was out in the yard, with her closer behind me than I'd anticipated.

No time to get to my truck. She'd shoot me before I got the door open.

I ran for the corn maze.

And disappeared inside.

Forty

❦

I hadn't been inside Al's corn maze for several years—not that it would've helped, since Al changes the design annually. Besides, a maze is a maze, confusing as heck, and as fast as I had been able to make a run for it, that ability was offset because I have absolutely zero directional aptitude.

Another frightening realization was that my pursuer not only had the huge advantage of holding a gun, which was scary enough, but she'd been the one to actually design this maze. She knew the twists and turns and which paths led to dead ends and which pointed to the way out.

Hoping to throw her off, I decided not to follow labyrinths or look for corridors leading to exits.

I'd simply focus on a direction and force my way through the stalks until I arrived outside the maze. Let's see. That way? Or that way?

The sound of crackling, treading, something, came from behind me. I cut through a corn wall, only to discover that thrashing and hacking my way through had one serious disadvantage:

I was creating enough noise to warn Joan of my location.

A shot rang out, too close. I swear it zinged right past my head, stirring up a few strands of hair.

That certainly was incentive for me to get moving faster.

Except it was so dark.

But that's okay, I reassured myself. *It's dark for her, too. And she's older. Her eyesight has to be worse than mine, right?* I changed my mind and decided to stay within the maze's paths, placing my left hand on the left wall. I'd follow every left turn. At some point it would lead me out. Or so I hoped.

Every minute or two, I stopped and listened. The first few times, I didn't hear anything unusual. Maybe she'd given up, decided to run for it instead.

Then I heard something, a disturbance of dried corn husk, faint like a light breeze.

Eleanor was still hunting me.

My hand on the left wall led me into a dead end.

I crouched and listened as hard as I could.

She was moving, and not very far away.

My breathing was ragged and labored from fear more than exertion. I cupped a hand over my mouth and nose, squeezed my eyes shut, and forced myself to stop and think.

What did I know about guns? Hunter had taken me shooting. I had terrible aim. Hunter, though, was a real professional; he could place his shot dead center in the target. Eleanor hadn't looked confident like that. She'd held the weapon more like I had. Amateurish. And she'd missed when she'd shot at me in the house.

I opened my eyes.

Okay, stay calm, because she can't shoot straight.

And another thing. Didn't handguns only carry six

bullets? How many had she fired? At least one at Greg, two at me when I ran, another inside the maze. She couldn't have more than two shots left.

Okay, she's almost out of bullets. Plus she's a very bad shot unless she's right on top of her target.

So don't let her get on top of you!

Then, out of the darkness, a small flashlight popped on, its glow shining through one of the cornstalk walls. She was headed directly toward my hiding place. I wanted to slink lower and cover my eyes, but then I'd be a motionless target, an easy kill. This would be a dead end in more ways than one.

The only way out was back toward the woman with the weapon.

I forced myself to jump up and started zigzagging toward the light, making all kinds of racket.

Eleanor fired.

Instinctively I hit the ground.

Number five.

I was up again, moving, first left then right.

The light swept up, blinding me momentarily. I dove again. She didn't pull the trigger this time, saving her last bullet. Joan had been counting, too.

She was really close, not five yards away, coming steadily forward, when the light suddenly went out.

I didn't waste time trying to run away. Instead, I rushed the spot where she'd last been standing in the glow of the flashlight.

And connected with her body. We went down. For a moment I was on top, straddling her. Then she bucked up, wrenching away.

The gun went off, deafeningly loud.

I waited for the impact of the bullet, for a searing pain, for something.

Instead, Eleanor slumped back, no fight left in her.

That's what I thought at first. That she'd given up.

But she had gone so limp.

I fumbled for her flashlight, found it on the ground a few feet away, and turned it on. The beam found her.

Eleanor must have turned the weapon on herself.

I stood there for a moment, shocked and panicked. Shocked that someone like the Joan I had come to know and befriend could do the things she had done. Panicked because time must be running out for Greg and I didn't have any idea how to get out of here and get the help he needed.

I heard a sob and realized it came from me.

I had to make the effort.

What direction had I come from? Where in the maze was I? The middle? Farthest from the house? Where?

Should I continue along the left wall? Or the right? Or lurch along randomly?

My mind threatened to go numb.

Later, I told it. *Get moving.*

Then when I was just about to give up on ever getting out, I heard a new sound. The call of the wild. Well, maybe not exactly that. But close enough.

It was Ben.

Howling.

Hunter must be here.

I started shouting their names and running in the direction of Ben's call.

Another howl, then a yip.

I started to cry.

Then suddenly I felt Ben brushing against my side, taking a nip at my pant leg as if to say, follow me. I grabbed his harness and held on for dear life.

I finally stumbled out of the corn maze and into Hunter's arms. "The twins told me where you were," he said. "I hadn't expected to find this scene, though."

"Greg," I gasped.

"It's okay, sweet thing," he said. "An ambulance is on the way. He's still breathing. Are you okay?"

Was he joking?

I'd never been so okay in my life.

Forty-one

❦

Mom was determined to have an orderly, structured, traditional wedding, which wasn't a big surprise since that's totally Mom.

The bride and groom came down the grassy aisle, which was bordered with ropes of flowering black-eyed Susan vines. She wore an ivory satin lace knee-length sheath with a cropped, three-quarter length jacket, the epitome of refined and elegant.

At least someone was.

Because she was framed by her two daughters in our puke . . . I mean puce-colored bridesmaid dresses. Hunter still wore the same amused smirk on his face that he'd had earlier when I appeared in our living room wearing the thing.

Grams fluttered around wearing a dusty pink mother-of-the-bride dress and taking pictures with her point-and-shoot, getting in the way of the professional photographer whom my sister, the wedding planner, had hired. But he didn't seem to mind.

The most surprising thing to me was that the service was attended by exactly the guests whom Mom had put down on her invitation list. No more, no less.

Right before the minister went into the kissing-the-bride part of the ceremony, I even got to offer up the bride's honey on a little silver tray with two tiny spoons and fresh rose petals scattered on it. Mom and Tom each sampled a taste, and I said a little bit about their union being sweet as this honey. Then they were kissing, we were clapping, and the music started up.

Only the music wasn't coming from the three musicians who had agreed to play certain traditional songs at the beginning and end of the service, starting, of course, with "Here Comes the Bride."

Now, at the end of the ceremony, instead of the "Wedding March," I heard the beginning of "Walk Like a Man" by the Four Seasons. What the heck . . . ? We all stopped to consider the source, since the three musicians were putting away their instruments.

I was pretty sure Mom didn't have a thing to do with the disc jockey who had apparently been setting up where none of us noticed, because the stage was hidden under a big white canopy tent that we just assumed was the reception area. Party helpers were now drawing back and tying the canvas walls, exposing the long tables inside that had been filled with all kinds of serving dishes, all colors, all shapes, and more tables than we should need, each decorated with Carrie Ann's roses floating in crystal bowls and more rose petals scattered everywhere.

"It's a potluck," Grams whispered to me after she took a picture of Mom's surprised face. Then she shouted out to Holly, "Tell the guests to come out of hiding."

As it turns out, the entire senior citizen community had been hiding behind one of the outbuildings. And we hadn't suspected a thing!

When Mom saw what was happening, when it finally

sunk in, which seemed like forever but really was less than a minute or two, she started crying.

We all stood around, staring at her, not sure what to say or do. Somebody must have stopped the DJ, because even the music died.

Tom put a protective arm around his new bride and muttered something inaudible from my position. Then Mom shook her head and said loudly enough for all to hear, "I'm so, so happy. Thank you all for coming."

And she smiled, a big beaming one that was so bright it competed with the sunshine from above.

Hunh? Those were tears of joy? After all the bickering that had gone on between Grams and Mom?

"It's like when someone has a birthday," Grams explained to me later while we were chowing down on the wedding cake. Milly had made the best red velvet cake I'd ever tasted. "If the birthday girl tells you not to go to any trouble, not to do anything, no party, no frills . . ."—here my grandmother took a bite of cake and washed it down with a sip of a lemon drop honey martini, which had been another of my contributions (although in my opinion, cake and martinis do *not* go together, even if honey is one of the ingredients). Grams continued, "Your mother protested too much. That meant she really wanted all the extra fuss."

We glanced over at Mom. "Look how happy she is," I commented. "You were right, Grams."

Grams nodded. "Yup," she said, "we finally got her married off."

And with that, we high-fived each other.

A little later, I paused to reflect on my family. The mojo bag had delivered on my wish. I'd briefly considered using it to bring down Lori Spandle, but I couldn't waste a

perfectly good wish on that woman. Instead I had wished
for those close to me to stay healthy, because as Grams
always says, you don't have anything if you don't have your
health. In retrospect, that wish might have saved my life
inside the corn maze, because I guess *I* qualify as someone
close to me.

"Can I have this dance?" Hunter asked, reaching for my
hand.

I smiled and melted into his arms. We danced the night
away.

Forty-two

Several other events worth mentioning happened later in the week.

The first was that Hunter and his team found all kinds of evidence inside a rented storage unit to support Eleanor Marciniak's claim to infamy. They found:

- pictures of Buddy and Rosina in happier times
- bloody clothes with traces of manure
- a computer with a whole lot of incriminating data
- a journal of all her twisted thoughts and actions

More than enough evidence to put her away forever.

Because Eleanor didn't die that night in the corn maze. Her self-inflicted wound damaged her mind, not her body. Hunter says she will probably live out her life in a nursing home.

Greg is on the mend, both mentally and physically, and Al has been exonerated. Greg intends to stay on in Moraine and become a real active partner in Country Delight. His father is delighted.

On the other hand, Dyanna Crane moved back to Milwaukee. My small town wasn't exactly welcoming, and she felt the vibes. Some things just aren't worth fighting for, and this was a battle she decided she could do without. Lucinda and Dy managed to resolve their differences, and the entire coven, led by Lucinda, arrived on moving day and pitched in to help her while the recovering Greg supervised from the sidelines.

That means the house next door is vacant again, and Lori Spandle has been hovering like the mosquito she has become. I'm through giving her my blood, though, and that's final. Which brings me to the rule of threes. Iris and Grams are absolutely right on in that regard. And I have examples to prove their point. With Rosina gone, Dy and Lucinda made their peace with each other. And way back when, Iris and Rosina became lifelong friends after Mom left the threesome. Even among my friends, the chemistry changes when three of us are together. Like when Holly, Patti, and I get together, it isn't the same as when Holly and I hang out. And Patti really lets loose when it's just the two of us. I want to explore these dynamics more.

I've also learned a thing or two about human behavior and pack mentalities. I thought I was an open-minded woman until the witches came to town. It took me a long time to look beyond the coven for a suspect, and even then Joan fooled me with her sweet, grandmotherly demeanor. She definitely made me aware of the concept of a wolf in sheep's clothing.

At least with Patti and Johnny Jay and Lori Spandle, what you see is what you get. Warts and all.

Speaking of those last two, about a week after Mom's wedding, Patti, Aurora, and I were all sitting on a bench outside The Wild Clover. (Yes, Patti and I are "buddies" again, and I'm not even hiding it from Hunter. He'll get used to it eventually.) The leaves were swirling through the air, landing at our feet, all reds and yellows and oranges, as we watched Grams attempt to drive away from the curb in the Fleetwood without taking out any other cars or signage posts.

Patti had some kind of electronic device on her lap and she fiddled with the dials. All I heard was static.

Then voices.

Patti beamed.

"That's Johnny Jay's voice," I said. "Where is he?"

"The police station," she replied.

"You bugged the police station!!??"

"Relax, this is a tape recording."

That wasn't an actual denial. She *had* bugged Johnny Jay's office.

"Just shush and listen," she said.

"Does this have anything to do with the library sting?"

"Shhhh," she said.

We heard Grant Spandle's voice next. "Is that who I think it is? Is that my wife?"

"That's her," Johnny Jay said, and I realized that the men were watching the library recording. "Practically having sex right there in the romance stacks."

"You did this on purpose, Jay," Grant said, sounding like he was gasping for air. "To make a mockery of my marriage."

"Spandle, you can't blame me for your personal problems. How was I supposed to know she'd pick that spot right where we hid the surveillance camera?"

"I'm going to kill her."

"You can't say that in front of a police officer. What the hell are you thinking? Spandle, where are you going? I mean it, stay away from the library. Spandle?"

Patti turned off the recording and we sat for a few minutes, silently savoring the moment.

Aurora, who had been sitting quietly through the recording, said to me, "Sometimes you have to be careful what you wish for."

Which stunned me, because I'd never mentioned my mojo bag to Aurora, or my fleeting thoughts of wishing that Lori would get caught in the act, but Aurora's comment implied she knew. Or did she? The woman was a big mystery.

The mojo bag was still tucked in my pocket. It had worked so well in the corn maze, I figured I should continue to carry it.

Aurora was giving me a satisfied smile.

"I thought I only had one wish," I told her.

She shook her head. "One wish, two, who knows." Then she casually glanced at the exact same pocket where I carried the mojo bag. Had Tabitha told her? That was the only reasonable explanation.

"Now I feel responsible," I said. And I did feel bad. If I hadn't considered wishing for Lori to get caught in exactly this way, would it still have happened? Sure, she deserved it, but had I played a part? And what about Grant's feelings? Shame on me!

Aurora kept on smiling, reminding me of Mona Lisa, all knowing. "Don't feel too sorry for her husband," she said. "He's playing the same games as his wife."

"Really?"

"Really."

Just then Grant's car flew past going about a hundred miles an hour.

"I thought you said that was a recording we were listening to," I said to Patti.

"So I lied. Come on, let's go check out a few books from the library."

"I'll see you later," Aurora said.

"You aren't coming?" I asked.

"The rule of threes," she said, turning toward Willow Street and her home.

With that, Patti and I headed for the library.

To watch Lori Spandle get her just deserts.

The Wild Clover
🐝 Newsletter 🐝

Notes from the beeyard:

• No matter how cold the weather gets outside, inside a beehive the workers have to maintain a temperature of over ninety degrees.

• They do this by shivering, vibrating their flight muscles to raise their body temperatures.

• So they need lots of honey stored up in their combs for energy.

• Take care of that queen bee, worker bees, and see you in the spring!

Crescent Cakes

1 cup ground almonds
1¼ cups flour
½ cup confectioner's sugar plus extra
3 drops almond extract
½ cup butter, softened
1 egg yolk

Combine almonds, flour, sugar, and extract until thoroughly mixed. Add butter and egg yolk until well blended. Chill for one hour. Preheat oven to 350 degrees. Pinch off pieces of dough and shape into crescents. Place on greased sheets and bake for about 20 minutes, watching carefully the last few minutes. Roll in more confectioner's sugar after baking.

Makes 1 dozen

Bride's Honey

Infuse the following ingredients over a very low heat for 10 minutes, then let the flavors meld for twenty-four hours before serving in a small bowl with tiny spoons.

1 pound honey
1 teaspoon dried ground rosebuds
1 teaspoon cinnamon
¼ teaspoon cloves
¼ teaspoon nutmeg

Lemon Drop Honey Martini

2 ounces vodka
1 ounce honey simple sugar (4 parts honey to 1 part hot water)
Juice of one lemon
Honeycomb
Sugar for rimming
Lemon wedges
Wooden honey sticks

Rim a martini glass with sugar. Place a piece of fresh honeycomb on the bottom of the glass. Mix vodka, lemon, and simple sugar in shaker with ice cubes. Shake and pour into glass. Garnish with a lemon wedge and a wooden honey stick.

About the Author

Hannah Reed lives on a high ridge in southern Wisconsin in a community much like the one she writes about. She is busy writing the next book in the Queen Bee Mysteries. Visit Hannah and explore Story's world at queenbeemystery.com.

Searching for the perfect mystery?

Looking for a place to get the latest clues and connect with fellow fans?

"Like" The Crime Scene on Facebook!

- Participate in author chats
- Enter book giveaways
- Learn about the latest releases
- Get book recommendations and more!

facebook.com/TheCrimeSceneBooks

Obsidian

M884G1011